Will lifted Katy's bare foot in the palm of his hand.

The feeling shot straight up her leg and she sucked in a breath, surprised that his touch should have such an effect on her. He tenderly fit her foot into her shoe, then set her foot back down again. His fingertips traced over her ankle for a brief moment, sending shivers up her calf.

"How clumsy of me to lose my shoe," Katy said softly.

"My fault. I was rushing again. Do forgive me?" Will asked, still kneeling before her.

"Of course. But do you always rush?" she asked.

He stood and crooked his arm for her, his green eyes locking with her own. "No. I quite like to take my time."

His words sent a quiver through her, but she tried to shake off the weird intimacy that had sprung up between them.

Will wasn't what she was looking for.

His cousin Trevor was. He was a viscount!

Have Glass Slippers, Will Travel

Lisa Cach

POCKET BOOKS
New York   London   Toronto   Sydney

This book is a work of fiction. Names, characters, places and incidents are products of the author's imagination or are used fictitiously. Any resemblance to actual events or locales or persons, living or dead, is entirely coincidental.

An *Original* Publication of POCKET BOOKS

POCKET BOOKS, a division of Simon & Schuster, Inc.
1230 Avenue of the Americas, New York, NY 10020

Copyright © 2005 by Lisa Cach

All rights reserved, including the right to reproduce this book or portions thereof in any form whatsoever. For information address Pocket Books, 1230 Avenue of the Americas, New York, NY 10020

ISBN-13: 978-0-7434-7089-6
ISBN-10:   0-7434-7089-3

First Pocket Books printing September 2005

10 9 8 7 6 5 4 3 2 1

POCKET and colophon are registered trademarks of Simon & Schuster, Inc.

Front cover illustration by Ben Perini
Front cover design by Anna Dorfman

Manufactured in the United States of America

For information regarding special discounts for bulk purchases, please contact Simon & Schuster Special Sales at 1-800-456-6798 or business@simonandschuster.com

To Clark,
who made my own fairy tale come true

The iron tongue of midnight hath tolled twelve;
Lovers, to bed; 'tis almost fairy time.

—William Shakespeare,
A Midsummer Night's Dream

Acknowledgments

Special thanks to Jim and Diane Hunter of Hunter's Greens for the information on organic farming, to Karla Thomas for insight into the life of a Seattle technical writer, and to Val Phillips for proofreading the manuscript from an Englishwoman's point of view and answering myriad questions along the way.

Have Glass Slippers, Will Travel

Chapter 1

Katy Orville clicked off the television as *The Oprah Winfrey Show* ended and the local news came on. She lay for a moment, red curly hair hanging over the end of the couch, and listened to her roommate Rebecca's fingers clicking on her computer keyboard at the desk in the corner. Rebecca Treinen faced into the shadowy nook with slumped shoulders, as if being punished for bad behavior.

"What would Oprah do?" Katy asked aloud.

Rebecca gave no response. The clicking of the keyboard continued, echoed by the taps of raindrops on the windowpanes.

Katy shortened her question. "W.W.O.D.?"

"Hmm?" Rebecca finally said, still facing the monitor.

Katy could see an edge of the screen and knew her roommate was doing her online banking. Rebecca's straight brown hair was a curtain of disinterest in W.W.O.D., and hid her face from Katy's view.

Katy popped another couple of M&M's into her mouth. "What Would Oprah Do? If she were us."

"Isn't that supposed to be 'What Would Jesus Do?' " Rebecca asked, hand now motionless on the mouse, her back stiff. The banking news was undoubtedly bad.

Katy sat up, then frowned as she saw the way her pale thighs spread against the cushion. She tugged down the cuffs of her shorts, trying to hide her thighs from her sight. "Maybe Oprah is a modern-day messenger from God."

Rebecca spun around in her desk chair, her Pantene-polished shield of hair swinging to the side, interest engaged at last. Or maybe it was to avoid further perusal of her bank statement. "That's *it*. We're canceling the cable. We can't afford it, and it's rotting your brain."

"Certainly she's a *child* of God, as are we all," Katy said with deliberate, wide-eyed naïveté, as she rolled closed the bag of M&M's. She shoved it into the small drawer in the coffee table, hoping she'd forget it was there. "Oprah says that God is love. Oprah herself is a pure embodiment of love. Therefore, Oprah could be considered an incarnation of God."

Rebecca's brows lowered into a straight line. "Your logic is flawed. Oprah is hardly a pure embodiment of love, nor is she the only source of that emotion. Even if God could be defined as nothing other than love, the argument fails."

Katy waved away the protest. "Logic, shmogic. I am a follower of Oprah and demand respect for my religion."

Rebecca raised a brow, then turned back to her monitor. "Maybe you should pray to Oprah to find us jobs."

"Maybe I will."

Katy plopped back against the cushions, temporarily defeated, and propped her feet on the coffee table to consider new approaches to the battle plan of life, with or without Oprah's divine influence.

She was a technical writer, Rebecca a software engineer, and a month ago both had been laid off from their jobs at WxyTech Industries. "Wixy" was circling the drain of bankruptcy, sending its employees down the tubes ahead of it like dead bugs in a tub.

It was a situation with haunting tones of Katy's past. Once upon a time, welfare and food stamps had been humiliating necessities for her family. Every time her mother had used them, Katy had vowed that she herself would never be dependent on them as an adult.

No matter how self-sufficient Katy became, though, she had never been able to shake the fear that the wolf of poverty was prowling around her door. The loss of her job brought back all the old feelings; she could almost hear that wolf snuffling at the crack under her apartment door.

The only way she could block the wolf from her mind was to watch TV and eat M&M's. They kept her from thinking too much. A psychologist might say she was in denial, refusing to face reality.

So be it. She'd had a lifetime of reality.

She needed to get a new job, but the thought of going back to the cubicle, of returning to the land of Dilbert, gave her about as much delight as contemplating another Seattle winter: her mind filled with visions of gray drizzle, and a superstitious dread that the light would never return to the world. Although lucrative, technical writing was as mind-numbing as reading an owner's manual.

She'd once been glad to sell her soul to the devil of boredom in exchange for financial security. But the devil, damn his polyester hide, had proven himself a cheap cheat when it came to exchanging jobs for souls, for here she was, unemployed. When it came to pinching and stretching, she was tops: by living frugally and in a bad part of town, she'd managed to pay off both her car and her student loans, and sock away close to $5,000 in rainy-day funds. But she could still hear that wolf.

She really didn't know what she wanted to do now; all she knew was that she wanted to pursue a *passion*, like Oprah advised. And live comfortably, without fear of poverty. Maybe even have enough money that she could someday buy a house of her own, with a window seat where she could sit and read, and a yard where she could put a fountain and goldfish.

Oprah would know how to get all that. Oprah wouldn't be sitting on the couch like a slug on a rotten potato, waiting for the salt shaker of life to come shrivel her into a gray ball of mucus. Oprah would get out there and . . . and . . .

W.W.O.D.?

It was time to summon the goddess. To go directly to the oracle. She would burn a bag of potato chips at the Altar of Love. She would visit oprah.com.

"Can I use your computer when you're done?"

"I'm done now," Rebecca said, clicking out of the banking site and heading for the kitchen.

Katy waited until Rebecca was out of sight of the monitor, then started to type in the URL to Oprah's site.

Rebecca suddenly emerged from the kitchen. "I'm going to run down to the grocery store. Need anything?"

"No, don't think so," Katy said, spinning around in the desk chair to put herself between the monitor and Rebecca. Not that looking at Oprah's site was shameful, like browsing porn sites. She grinned blankly as Rebecca put on her shoes and got her coat.

"What?" Rebecca asked.

"Nothing!" Katy turned back to the screen.

"Whatever, weirdy girl. Be back in a bit."

"Bye!"

Rebecca made a noise, and then Katy heard the door open and shut. She relaxed, and focused on the screen in front of her.

Oprah's site had links to a newsletter, message boards, "O Groups," and on and on. Even a link to "Oprah's Angel Network."

Ha! Oprah *was* a goddess. She had her own angels!

Katy wandered through the site, a veritable bible of the Oprah way of life, and eventually stumbled on a section for "Discovering Your Passion."

Seek and ye shall find!

Katy glanced at the clock. Rebecca would be back soon. She clicked on "Print" for a page of instructions for creating a Life Map, an exercise that promised to help you "discover what you want for yourself and your life."

The printer finished just as Katy heard a key in the door. She shut down the computer, gathered up her papers, and slunk toward her room like a teenage boy with a copy of *Penthouse*. Some things you just couldn't let other people see you doing.

It was 2:30 A.M. by the time she finished, sitting cross-legged on the floor of her room. The Life Map was a collage of images and words taken from magazines and catalogs: anything that had felt "right" to her, she'd obediently torn out and glued onto a massive sheet of taped-together printer paper.

Among the images were a castle; a silver-haired

man in tweed selling cologne; nearly nude males posing in Jockey underwear; a Jaguar sports car; a particularly luscious-looking roast duck in cherry glaze; Rapunzel Barbie; half a dozen British actors in period costume, including several pictures of that delicious Ioan Gruffudd, who played Horatio Hornblower in the A&E movies; an iguana; and an abundance of flowers.

Among the words were *twenty-four* (her age), *sexy* (she wished she were), *chocolate* (self-explanatory), and *"I can't believe"* (the rest of the phrase had been "it's not butter").

She rubbed her bleary, stinging eyes, and looked over at the picture of Oprah she'd torn from an old *People* and tacked to the wall. There was a candle burning in a glass votive beneath it, turning the photo into an impromptu shrine.

"So what does it all mean?" she asked the photo.

Oprah said nothing, silently resplendent in the vanilla ball gown she'd worn to the Emmys to accept a humanitarian award. One hand was raised as if bestowing blessings on the world.

Katy scratched herself through a hole in the armpit of her Wonder Woman sleepshirt. She didn't know what this collage was supposed to have taught her about herself.

She looked at all the pictures—at the castles, the handsome men, the beautiful clothes, the beautiful food—and an unexpected sadness crept into her heart. She had none of these things. Her life looked nothing like her Life Map.

The collage was all a fantasy—a fantasy in which she had the breasts of a Victoria's Secret model and could attract Jaguar-driving men who ate roast duck. In her fantasy, she wasn't a flat-chested, bird-boned, frizzy-haired geek.

She sniffed back self-pitying tears.

She had been born at the very hour that Lady Diana's wedding was being broadcast around the world. As Diana had been reciting Prince Charles's stuffy string of names, Katy had come screaming into the delivery room. She used to think that meant she was destined for a fabulously romantic future of her own.

Ha-ha. The joke was on her.

Katy wiped her nose with the back of her hand, then looked again at the photo of Oprah, disappointed. Oprah's diamond earrings sparkled, her smile warm and friendly. The oracle was unperturbed.

"Easy for you," Katy said to the photo. "Barbie's bust has nothing on yours. What are you, a double D?"

She blew out the candle and stood up. Time for bed. It had been a stupid idea, anyway.

Katy dreamt.

She was walking down a hallway, toward a doorway through which light softly glowed. She came through the doorway into a dining room, its walls painted in a buttery gold harlequin pattern, an elaborate gold chandelier over the center of a long, dark wooden table. Candles were burning everywhere, just like in the scene from *Great Expectations* where Pip meets the disappointed elderly bride, Miss Havisham.

Or like any of those "filmed at home" segments on *Oprah,* where every guest seemed to live in a house filled with lit candles. Did Oprah have any idea how expensive that would be for the average woman?

At the head of the table sat Oprah, in her vanilla ball gown. To her right stood Ioan Gruffudd. He was wearing a black, tailed formal jacket and a pair of white Jockey briefs, and nothing else. Katy tried not to look at his cotton-covered crotch, although she wanted to. Very much.

Oprah gestured to the seat at the opposite end of the table. When Katy hesitated, Ioan came down and pulled the chair out. She sat, sneaking a glance at his bare chest. His dark brown eyes met hers and he smiled.

She blushed, and looked away.

"Can I offer you something to eat? To drink?" Oprah asked.

"No, thank you," Katy said, returning her attention to her hostess. Katy sat very straight, her buttocks on the edge of the seat. This was Oprah. This was The Goddess.

"Are you sure? It's no trouble. I have a chef. Ioan can fetch you something. Macaroni and cheese, perhaps? Mashed potatoes?"

Ioan nodded.

"I can't eat when I'm nervous," Katy said.

Butterflies were flapping up a tempest in the teapot of her stomach.

"Try to relax. You're here because I want to help you."

"Oh?"

Oprah smiled. "O. Yes."

Ioan handed Oprah a large cylinder of paper, which she unrolled on the table. She took a tiny pair of reading glasses out of a silver tube and put them on.

Katy recognized her Life Map and cringed. "It's not very good."

Oprah looked at her over the glasses. "This is you, Katy Orville. There is no right or wrong. You are not being graded."

"But . . . There's Barbie."

"Hmm, yes." Oprah sounded concerned. "I see."

Katy fidgeted while Oprah examined the collage, the narrow spectacles halfway down her nose, her head moving up, then slowly down again as her gaze moved over the paper.

Ioan stood with his hands behind his back, his gaze focused on some point in the distance. Katy was grateful. She didn't want him to notice the pictures of himself in her collage or the models in Jockey shorts. How embarrassing.

After a few minutes, Oprah took the glasses off her nose, folded them, and met Katy's gaze.

"Well?" Katy asked, unable to bear the suspense.

"It's clear enough."

"It is?"

"You want the fairy tale," Oprah said. "You want the castle and the prince. Gowns and banquets, and a gilded chariot. Or Jaguar, in this case."

"But it's silly to want that. I'm a grown woman, not a little girl," Katy said.

"You're judging yourself."

She flushed with shame. The Goddess had her there.

"Do you always say no to yourself?" Oprah asked.

"No . . . but—"

"But?" Oprah cut in. " 'No, but'?"

"But aren't you against rescue fantasies?" Katy rushed out, heart thumping at her temerity. How dare she argue with Oprah? "I'm not supposed to want Prince Charming to come sweep me away from my life. I have savings, I get my tires rotated, I even fixed the toilet when the handle got jiggly. I thought this is what I was supposed to be: self-sufficient."

"What of your spirit, Katy? Don't you feel something missing inside? There is an empty space where the joy should be. It's where you're dumping all those M&M's."

"I just really like M&M's," she mumbled.

Oprah gave her a steady, challenging look. "I used to say that about potato chips."

Katy fidgeted. She really didn't want to give up the M&M's. "Won't a new job fix any empty spaces?"

"Only if you remember your spirit when you seek it. No more selling your soul to the devil." Oprah tapped her bottom lip with her folded glasses, thinking. "Is it that you can't believe you can have a better life? Do you think you're not worthy of that? That somehow you fall short?"

Katy felt her mouth turn down unhappily, and she shrugged, afraid her voice would crack if she spoke. She was of average looks, with an average mind, so why should her life be anything but average? There was nothing special about her. There was nothing unique.

Oprah nodded, and pointed to the words *"I can't believe"* in the collage. "You can't believe that you can have those things of which you dream in your quietest, most private moments. That is what holds you back. You've got to believe in yourself, and go after your passion! With everything you've got."

"Even if it's British men in castles?"

"Even if."

"But—"

Oprah gave her a sharp frown.

Katy pressed her lips shut.

Oprah released the Life Map, and it rolled itself back into a cylinder. Ioan picked it up, then pulled Oprah's chair back as she stood and gave Katy a serious look. "Live your best life, Katy Orville."

She swept out of the room, Ioan trailing behind.

Katy sat in confusion, then something brushed her ankle. She bent down to look under the table.

A giant iguana stared back at her out the corner of its cold reptilian eye, its mouth open, about to take a bite out of her leg.

She shrieked and jerked awake.

Heart thumping, she stared into the darkness, then glanced at her digital clock. Four A.M.

For a moment she could almost believe that Oprah really *was* a goddess, and had paid her a visit.

She rolled onto her side, snuggling into her comforter and pillow. Oprah's words repeated in her head. *Go after your passion. With everything you've got! . . . Live your best life, Katy Orville!*

What passion? To marry a nobleman and live in a castle? But that was silly. It wasn't realistic. It was childish. The stuff of fairy tales. Oprah would never advise pinning one's happiness on finding a prince to take away all your troubles.

Then again, wasn't it every woman's secret fantasy, which she'd never really grown out of? And weren't they all too ashamed to admit it? She wanted a real Prince Charming.

I can't believe.

But maybe, alone at four o'clock in the morning, she could let herself. She had enough money saved for a trip to England. She could buy some nice secondhand clothes, find a cheap bed-and-breakfast in London, and spend a month there looking for a wife-hunting lord with an estate. Someone with centuries' worth of money behind him and a burning readiness for marriage.

No uncommitted, impoverished losers for her. It was Prince Charming or bust. She just had to believe.

Chapter 2

Kent, England

"Hey! You! What are you doing there?" Will's Irish setter Sadie ran off ahead of him, barking madly at the intruders, her tail wagging in delight at having someone to scold.

Will Eland stumped through the garden in his muddy Wellingtons, catching up to Sadie and to the middle-aged couple who were each holding a fistful of his rare, expensive, frilled blue tulips.

"We're just gathering a bit of spring flowers," the woman said, her mouth pursing in disapproval as Will approached in his dirty work clothes. Sadie was sniffing at the woman's leg, and the woman tried to knee the dog away.

"You can't just walk into someone's garden and start picking their flowers," Will said.

"The park's open to the public, isn't it?" the man asked, belligerent lower lip stuck out.

"The public pathways of the woodland and park do *not* extend into my garden! You can't wander in here and pick my flowers."

"Well, they're picked now," the woman said. "You should put up signs if you don't want people to take them, being on the edge of the park and all. It's easy to get confused."

Will ground his teeth. They had to know that they were standing in his private garden: they were less than fifty feet from his home, and it wasn't like a moated manor house was easy to overlook, no matter how decrepit.

"Five quid."

"Eh?" the man said.

"Five quid, if you want to keep my tulips."

"Bloody hell, we're not paying five quid for a bunch of tulips that should be free for the taking! Look at them. Their color's all wrong!" The man threw his flowers to the ground and grabbed his wife's arm. "Come on, Gladys."

Gladys *eep*ed and dropped her flowers, stumbling off after her husband.

Will bent down and tenderly gathered up the flowers that were supposed to have been part of an ethereal bed of blue blossoms and silvery white foliage.

"Couldn't you have scared them off?" he asked Sadie. "Growled, or bared a tooth? Chomped an arse?"

Sadie met his gaze with jaws open in a happy pant, tongue lolling, then shook the damp of the fields off her glossy red coat as if shrugging.

"If you can't do that, then at least run ahead and put the kettle on."

Sadie ignored his demand, taking her place by his side as they walked around the front of the house. Will paused on the bridge over the moat to search out sign of the koi who lived in the green water, then continued into the central courtyard and then to the service entrance, picking up the post from its box on the way.

He shucked his boots and coat in the mudroom, then put the kettle on in the kitchen that had last seen refurbishment in the 1950s. He padded in stocking feet through dark hallways to the unused drawing room. He found a vase in one of the crowded old cabinets and blew dust off it. A look at the bottom revealed a confusion of Chinese characters. It was a mystery to him whether the thing was worth a penny or £1,000. Either way, it would do for the tulips.

Back in the kitchen, he went through the post and found the usual assortment of advertising circulars, the electric bill, an estimate for roof repairs, and a letter finalizing an agreement to repair an extensive stretch of dry rot. He'd do large portions of the work himself, but even so, he'd be eating canned beans for a month to be able to afford the professionals' repairs.

Last but unfortunately not least, there was a thick,

creamy white envelope addressed to His Grace William Richard Eland, Duke of Marreton. It could only be an invitation.

His stomach sank.

He sipped his mug of tea and pulled over the new roofing estimate, finding its horrors less than those contained in the creamy white envelope.

With the cup drained and the rest of the mail read, even the circulars, there was no avoiding the envelope. Will picked it up, his work-roughened fingertips dirty against the pristine surface. He wedged a finger under the flap and tore it open.

When he read the enclosed wedding invitation, he blew out a heavy breath. Cousin Marjorie, on his mother's side, was getting married. They'd been friends as children. She'd be hurt if he wasn't there.

Bugger. He'd have to go.

The wedding was in London, which meant he'd have to put on a suit, scrub the dirt out from under his nails, and pretend to be civilized. He had an innate abhorrence of socializing with masses of relatives and acquaintances, of driving the crowded streets of London, of dealing with the stumbling streams of tourists with white trainers on their feet. He'd rather have his teeth drilled than endure inane small talk. And then there was the dancing to pop tunes.

He shuddered. Adults in formal wear ought to know better than to try to gyrate like eighteen-year-old MTV stars.

Maybe he could just send Marjorie a nice present and a note explaining that he couldn't leave the farm at such a crucial time. *Best wishes, anyway! Congratulations!*

The idea was gaining appeal when the phone rang. He picked up. "Hello?"

"William! Why don't you ever return the calls left on your answering service?"

He winced. "Hello, Aunt Agatha." He loved his aunt, but God save her, she could be a controlling creature.

"I assume you've received an invitation for Marjorie's wedding? You'll stay with me and your uncle here in Chelsea, of course," she went on, not waiting for an answer. "And I expect you to stay at least a week. None of this zipping in for one night, then disappearing. Your aunt Louise has been looking forward to seeing you, not to mention several of your cousins, including Trevor."

Marjorie and Trevor—the rotter—were the children of Aunt Louise. Louise, Aunt Agatha, and his mother had been sisters.

He sighed.

"Do I take it by that wordless exhalation that I can expect to see you on my doorstep in three weeks' time?" his aunt asked.

"I'll be at the wedding."

"I'm having a room made up for you."

He didn't say anything.

"William!"

"Yes, I'll stay with you." It would save the expense of a hotel, after all. And his uncle Harold was good company: they'd spent many a silent hour in the same room, each engrossed in his own thoughts, the quiet broken only by the rustle of a turning newspaper page.

"Good. Phyllis Dawby's daughter, Helena, is back in London, and I want you to spend some time with her."

Will clenched his jaw and prayed for patience. He tried to remind himself that his aunt always meant the best for him, no matter how contrary that might be to his own wishes.

"You spend too much time stuck away on that farm," Aunt Agatha went on. "You need a woman to keep you civilized. There are times I almost wonder if you've forgotten how to hold a conversation. Still, you should be able to attract a presentable young lady . . ."

Will opened a well-thumbed seed catalog that was sitting on the counter and perused it while his aunt talked. He would let her have her say, murmur vaguely positive noises at appropriate times, and then do as he pleased, as he always did.

His parents had died in a small airplane crash in Greece when he was eighteen. Aunt Agatha had taken him under her formidable wing, treating him like the child she had never had.

Five years later, his father's older brother had died, leaving Will heir to the dukedom and lands, as well as the severely dilapidated manor house.

He had been twenty-three then, and had decided it was a grand age for abandoning his stultifying city job and pursuing his secret dream: organic farming. Against his aunt's wishes, he had abandoned London for the country, poured the small financial inheritance from his uncle and all his own money into greenhouses and farming equipment, and set to work learning everything he could about making green things grow. That was nearly five years ago, and he had not once regretted the decision.

Aunt Agatha claimed it was an eccentricity that he must have inherited from his father's side. *Her* people indulged in a bit of pottering about the rose gardens, but were not so dotty as to make it their life's work.

The lands and estate were a mere nub of what they had been in grander times, his ancestors having shown a particular talent for dying young, thus opening the estate again and again to the assault of inheritance taxes.

As relatively small as the remaining estate was, Will loved it, and intended to spend the rest of his days slowly restoring Marreton House to its former glory.

"Do get your hair cut, William, won't you? If you must be a farmer, at least look a *gentleman* farmer. A wedding is an excellent place to meet eligible young ladies. You're not going to unearth one in a furrow, you know. You must go out and *look* for one if you hope to wed . . ."

Did he wish to wed? He had grown quite comfortable in his bachelor life, rambling around the house and park with Sadie.

Then again, so had his uncle grown comfortable as a bachelor, and had spent his later years inhabiting only the kitchen, sleeping on a cot in the corner, and eating his meals out of tins. After he'd died in hospital, Will had had to burn the nastily neglected bedclothes. No loving wife would have allowed such a decay in lifestyle.

He caught a glimpse of himself in the window over the sink, the faint reflection showing dark, ragged hair and a pullover with a frayed neck.

Sodding hell. Maybe his aunt was right, at least about the haircut. He looked like a hedgehog mauled by a hound with a salivary disorder.

"So I'll see you the day of the wedding," she said.

"Yes. Give my best to Uncle Harold."

They said their good-byes, and Will rang off. He looked again at his ruffian reflection in the glass, then turned and looked round at the antiquated kitchen: the spots where the linoleum had worn through, the stained paper on the walls, and Sadie sleeping on her dog-dirty bed. The rest of the house was little better, and the whole east wing was about to be torn open for dry-rot repairs.

Why even think about finding a wife? He barely had the money to feed himself and his dog; he certainly hadn't the means to support a wife and children. There were some misguided girls with family money who might consent to wed him for the chance to be a duchess, but the idea was revolting on two scores: he didn't want a shallow woman who cared about things like titles, and his masculine pride would never allow him to marry for money. He would support his wife and children with the sweat of his own brow, which was the way things were supposed to be. He was not going to be an aristocratic dinosaur, living a life meant for a frivolous fop of the eighteenth century, powder on his cheeks and carmine on his lips. He was a *man*, for God's sake.

Much as he loved Marreton House, he could see that any woman with a bit of sense would take one look at it and run back to central heating and reliable plumbing while she still had her ring finger unshackled by gold. One whole section of the house hadn't even been wired for electricity. A wealthy woman might throw a bag of money at it, but he insisted on restoring the house himself. It was his home, damn it.

Marriage would just have to wait until he was financially secure and had made his house into a nest where a woman could be happy.

And when he eventually did catch a wife? What would he do with her? Besides the obvious, and *that* surely couldn't fill more than two or three hours out of a day. He couldn't imagine a young, intelligent, attractive woman enjoying life here. If she were from London, she'd miss her friends and her career and be bored to death. And he'd yet to meet any eligible single women out here in the country. Most seemed to flee their rural roots, returning only when married with children of their own.

The thought sent a painful twinge through his

heart. After a long moment, he recognized the twinge as loneliness. There was no woman to whom he could tell his innermost thoughts, and there was no woman who would let him into her own secret world, held private from all others. There was no woman who came to him for tenderness and shelter in the night, or who wanted him to be the father of her children.

Wasn't that the reason for having a house to begin with? To lure a mate and then rear children?

He got down on the floor beside Sadie and bent his head down to hers, meeting her forehead to forehead, his eyes closed.

Someday he wanted to come in from outside and find a warm, pink-cheeked woman in his kitchen, who would let him wrap his arms around her waist and nuzzle her neck with kisses, and who would laugh and talk and bring something utterly new to his day that he could never have on his own.

He didn't want to end up living on a cot in the corner and eating his meals from tins. He didn't want his only physical affection to be from a dog. He didn't want to be trapped alone inside his own heart.

Sodding, bloody hell. This is what he got for talking to his aunt.

Chapter 3

London, three weeks later

Katy dragged her suitcase out of Paddington Station, where she'd just disembarked from the Heathrow Express. Cars zipped by on wet pavement, their tires making sticky tape-peeling sounds. The sky was gray, the buildings white-painted wood and cream stone and somehow wonderfully *English*, with their Grecian-inspired door surrounds and sash windows. A sunburst of delight exploded within her. *Yes!* This is what she had come to England for! *Englishness!*

And there was an English taxi up ahead—black and old-fashioned, exactly like in the movies. She hurried up to it, yanked open the rear door, and started to climb inside. "Titania's Bower!" she called gaily to the driver, naming her bed-and-breakfast.

A gasp stopped her with one foot inside the cab, and she found herself face-to-face with the older woman ensconced in the plush gray interior. The woman had the well-coifed frosted hair and quietly rich clothing of old money, and a deeply affronted look on her pale, taut face.

"Sorry! Sorry! I didn't know this cab was taken!" Katy squealed, backing out.

"This is *not* a cab," the woman snapped.

"*Oh, fudge,*" Katy exclaimed under her breath. "Sorry! Sorry! My mistake!" She slammed the door, then took a better look at the car as a hot sweat of embarrassment dampened her body. What was it, a Rolls-Royce? A Bentley?

The car pulled out into traffic. Katy could see the silhouette of the woman's motionless head, neck undoubtedly stiff with affront.

Ten minutes in London and she'd been an idiot already. She remembered the disheartening conversation she'd had with Rebecca after revealing her Marry a Prince plan.

"*Are you crazy?*" Rebecca asked. "*You're going to make a fool out of yourself.*"

"*Maybe. But if I fail miserably and end up back here, back in a cubicle, at least I'll have had an adventure to console me.*"

"*They're going to laugh at you.*" Rebecca laid her hand on Katy's arm, an unusual gesture of affection and concern from this woman who hated to be touched. "*You're going to get hurt if you do this. The*

*type of guy you're going after, the life that sort must
lead—it will be another world, and they'll treat you
like dog doo on their shoes, and try to scrape you off
on the curb."*

Katy was feeling a bit like dog doo right now.

She crept down the block and around the corner,
looking for a cab. There was a taxi rank up ahead
and a minute later she was happily ensconced in
the bare, functional backseat of the cab, relieved to
have the driver in charge of getting her to her B&B
in Mayfair. She needn't risk humiliating herself
again for at least ten minutes.

The taxi wound through streets lined with more
of the Grecian-looking buildings, then came out on
a busy road filled with black cabs and red double-
decker buses. A park ran along one side of the
street, divided from the sidewalk by black wrought-
iron fencing. It really *was* all so English. It was like
discovering that the kingdom in a fairy tale was real.

"What park is that?" Katy asked the driver, shouting to be heard through the small opening in the
glass partition.

"Kensington Gardens and Hyde Park," he said,
and his accent made her smile. They turned off the
main street, and as the cab crawled slowly down the
street he asked, "What was the name of your B&B
again, miss?"

"Titania's Bower." She'd told him it was on South
Audley Street when she'd gotten into the cab, and
he had nodded as if he were well acquainted with it.
She'd read in her guidebook that London cabbies

knew every street, lane, and alley in the city, and every building to be found along them. They were the best in the world, with no address unknown, nor the most efficient route to reach it.

"You, er . . . wouldn't happen to know the number of the building, would you?"

"Two and a half," she said. "You mean you don't know where it is?"

He made a noise as if to dispute such a wrongheaded idea, and turned the cab around, retracing his route up the street. A few minutes later he pulled the cab off the road into a deep square of open pavement in front of a parking garage. "Here it is, then. Just as I thought."

His eyes met hers briefly in the rearview mirror, as if checking that she would buy this story.

Katy squinted out the window. Immediately in front of her was the parking garage. A beautiful old building on their right bore a brass plaque proclaiming itself the Embassy of Qatar. The two buildings stood side by side. "Here?"

"The embassy is number two, the car park is number three."

"But where . . . ?"

The driver got out and unloaded her luggage from the trunk, so she got out, too, walking to where the front of the garage nearly met the side of the embassy. There was a narrow alley in between. Deep in the shadows of the alleyway was a small cement stoop leading into the building behind the embassy.

"It's there?" she asked doubtfully, pointing.

"Yes, of course!" he said, although the look on his face showed a suspicious amount of relief. He named the fare and she paid it, digging into the small supply of British pounds she'd obtained at the airport. "Cheers!" he said, and then was gone.

She dragged her suitcase down the alley to the steps. A small sign hung above her head, the painted words reading TITANIA'S BOWER B&B. According to her research on the Internet, Titania's Bower had once been a nobleman's town house, which was part of what drew her to it. That and the name. *A Midsummer Night's Dream* was Katy's favorite Shakespeare play.

Titania's Bower had also been by far the cheapest lodging Katy could find in Mayfair, the district where it seemed every rich historical character in fiction had owned a house. She was going to stay in style, in the neighborhood of aristocrats.

And parking garages.

The half-glass door was locked, so she rang the bell. A minute later, a hunch-shouldered woman wearing a purple sweater and short gray buzz-cut hair let her in, then scurried like a bad-tempered ogre behind the reception desk, muttering under her breath.

Katy pulled her suitcase inside and took a look around. There were hints of former glory in the high ceiling and wide staircase, but the gold and brown patterned carpet and 1970s flowery wallpaper hid any hints of elegance. An unpleasant musty smell subtly permeated the air.

"I have a reservation. Katy Orville," she said.

The woman put on a pair of spectacles and turned to a computer screen. It was the only modern item visible, but its green screen and yellowed plastic casing declared even it an antique. "Orville, Orville," the woman muttered, scrolling down the screen. "No, no . . ."

Had her reservation been lost? She had nowhere to stay, she'd have to go looking for lodging in this unfamiliar city . . .

"Here you are. I have you on the fourth floor."

"Great!"

The landlady frowned at her. "It was the only room open. There are renovations going on elsewhere."

"Okay. No problem."

The woman blinked at her, and put a paper card and leaking pen on the countertop. Katy filled out the card, making an ink blot test of it in the process. The woman took it back when she was finished and looked it over.

"You're from Washington, the capital."

"No, the state. On the west coast. Seattle. You know, Microsoft. Bill Gates." Katy smiled.

The woman frowned, as if she'd never heard of Microsoft. "My name is Millicent. Millicent Suntory," she said abruptly, still frowning.

"Uhh . . . It's a pleasure to meet you, Ms. Suntory."

"Millie. You're leaving June twenty-fourth?"

"That's what my plane ticket says," Katy said

lightly, and winced as it came out sounding flippant. She was finding this odd exchange very uncomfortable. The woman had an odd manner for someone in the hospitality industry; it was as if she rarely interacted with her fellow humans.

"You'll be here for the summer solstice, then." Millie nodded as if this were good.

"Er . . . yes. I guess so." When was the solstice? Who knew these things anymore?

Katy looked the woman over a little more carefully, noting the strangely shaped silver medallion hanging from a black cord around her neck. Maybe she was Wiccan and practiced some sort of primitive pagan rites.

"This is your first time in England, isn't it?" Millie asked, a bit of sparkle coming into her eyes.

"Yes." Was it so obvious?

"You'll be wanting to see the Tower, then. The Victoria and Albert Museum is quite nice, and some people make a fuss over that oversized ferris wheel, the London Eye, but you really shouldn't miss the Tower of London."

"It's on my list of places to go," Katy lied. Her list of places was mostly nightclubs and expensive shops—places she might run into young lordlings. "So, breakfast is included in the room rate?"

"Seven thirty to eight thirty, downstairs."

Good heavens, who got up that early on vacation?

The woman slid a room key to her. "Front door is kept locked, but someone is always at the desk. Just ring. There's a library and a music room with a telly on the first floor. And remember."

"Yes?"

"Don't forget to see the Tower while you're here."

"I won't." Enough already! Katy glanced around. "Elevator?"

"No lift."

"Oh. Okay. I'll see you tomorrow morning then."

Millie blinked and flashed her small teeth in a smile.

Katy dragged her suitcase over to the stairs and took a deep breath. Good gracious. Fourth floor.

Several sweaty, heavy-breathing minutes later, she reached the landing that was marked ROOMS 401–405. She could have sworn she'd gone up more flights of stairs than she should have to reach the fourth floor, but maybe it just felt that way because of her luggage, and because the stairs had grown progressively narrower and darker the higher she'd climbed. She'd had trouble banging the suitcase round the final tight bends.

She pushed through the swinging fire door at the landing and into a dark hallway. She fumbled at the wall and found the light switch, a buttoned piece of black Bakelite equipment probably dating from the 1930s. Dim sconces clicked on, revealing dull brown walls and a water-stained, rumpled strip of carpet. The musty smell was stronger, and a darting shadow caught her eye along the floor.

Was that a mouse? Or . . . a *rat*?

Whatever it was, it disappeared through a crack

in the wall. Katy kept an eye on the crack as she trundled her bag down the hall to her room. No wonder there were renovations going on; the place looked like a tenement.

After several tries she got the key to turn in the lock, and when the door opened she could only stare in dismay. The tiny room held a narrow single bed that sagged in the middle, a straight-backed chair, a radiator, and a sink with fly-specked mirror. A sash window looked out over the hoods of cars in the open-sided garage across the alley.

If she had been hoping to be Cinderella, she was certainly starting out in the right accommodations. All she needed now were three wicked stepsisters to torture her, a prince who didn't know who she really was, and a fairy godmother to make it all end well.

Fat chance.

Chapter 4

The next morning

$\mathcal{W}$ill shifted gears and accelerated out of the turn, his 1964 Ford Econoline van rattling with ecstasy at the unaccustomed speed. The narrow, empty road ahead was a tunnel of leafy green, inviting Will to roar down it like a knight on a quest, faithful hound at his side. Sadie sat on the passenger seat, nose stuck out the crack in the window, a canine safety harness fastening her in place.

This was the only way Will could bear to drive to London: sticking to the B roads and avoiding the bleak motorways. He would happily double his travel time if it meant a drive he stood a chance of enjoying. Never mind that it meant he was risking being late to the wedding.

Never mind, too, that he hadn't gotten around to getting a haircut, or that he'd discovered late last night that his suits from his days in the city no longer fit—all the work on the farm had broadened his shoulders. He tried not to think of how Aunt Agatha was going to react to what he was wearing when he appeared at the church.

"I look all right, don't I, Sadie? It *is* formal wear, after all."

Sadie's eyes flicked to him, then she turned her attention back to the crack in the window as if tactfully declaring, "No comment."

Will fiddled with the ancient AM radio, flipping through religious music and pointless chatter until he landed on the overture to Rossini's *William Tell* opera. The music alternately boomed and faded out of the semiworking speaker, but the galloping theme was well suited for a run through the countryside. He bobbed his head along to the music, leaning forward, the wheel in his hands becoming a horse's reins. Like the rest of the televised world, he couldn't hear the theme without thinking of *The Lone Ranger*.

Did the Lone Ranger have a girlfriend? He couldn't remember. Will could imagine himself in a mask, though, banging through the front door of a cabin in the American West, and having *her*, the woman who was meant to be his, turn round with a gasp. She'd be in one of those tight, long dresses with a high neck, her hair twisted up, her expression all surprised innocence.

The look in her eyes, though, would beg for experience. She'd fall into his arms, and he'd sweep her up and carry her toward the quilt-covered bed in the corner. "Will, Will, take me," she'd say, her soft lips—

A deer leapt out of the greenery and froze in the middle of the road.

Will jerked the wheel hard, sending the van scraping along a thick hedgerow. The van jounced over unseen lumps and bumps, and Sadie yelped as she was jerked up against her harness. The van slowed to a stop.

Will sat frozen for a long moment, gripping the wheel in white hands. William Tell continued to thunder intermittently from the speakers. He reached forward and turned it off, his hand starting to shake. In the quiet he could hear the motor still running and shut it down, too.

Sodding hell.

Will's heart thumped painfully, as if suddenly restarting after a long pause, and a cold sweat broke over his skin. With weak muscles, he released his safety belt and opened the door into the branches pushing up against the side of the van. He struggled through them, cursing as they tore at his clothes and skin, and stumbled at last out into the road.

The deer was nowhere to be seen.

He took a deep shaky breath and tried to pretend his legs weren't made out of jelly. He went back down the road to where he thought he'd seen the deer, but there was no break in the hedgerow; no place where deer or man could fight their way through. Sleeping Beauty's castle could have been on the other side of that wall of greenery, and no one would ever know it.

He shook his head. It was not a good start to the day, and he hated to think what else could be in store for him.

Katy stepped out of Titania's Bower, her belly full of cornflakes and her heart full of determination. She was going to St. Paul's, where Lady Di had gotten married, a pilgrimage to where the mother of all fairy tale weddings had been held, on the very day of Katy's birth. She hoped it would bring her good luck. A blessing for her endeavors.

She felt like she needed it. Last night she'd dreamt of a wedding in a ballroom hung with crystal chandeliers and of a giant cake wheeled in by Millie. The landlady had worn a purple robe, a chef's hat, and had had a silver pentagram dangling round her neck. She'd crackled and whispered to Katy that she'd put poison in the frosting.

It had been a disturbing dream, sadly lacking Oprah's comforting presence. Or maybe the dream was a message from Oprah—although if so, its meaning was as unclear as the meaning of the iguana in her Life Map.

Katy made her way to the nearest Underground station, and figured out the route to St. Paul's Cathedral. She bought a ticket and followed the other passengers down through the gerbil maze of stairs and white-tiled, echoing corridors. Gusts of warm air and distant rumbles spoke of the trains passing below.

Once on the train, she saw her reflection in the windows opposite, pale-faced and shadow-eyed. A horrible thought suddenly struck her: Did she— might she—look more goofily dowdy than aristocratic?

She wore a yellow skirt suit she'd found at Goodwill and a large brooch of a bee on one shoulder, its stripes picked out in yellow and brown rhinestones. Shoes and handbag were faux alligator: eight dollars for the set, Value Village. She'd used the clothes of Queen Elizabeth as her guide, on the theory that no one dressed more aristocratically than the queen.

Her bee sparkled encouragingly on her shoulder. Katy relaxed and lifted her chin. She thought she looked quite proper, especially with her hair done up in a tight French twist.

A few stops later she was at her station. She followed the signs pointing the way to the cathedral, but once in front of it she was distracted by a tourist information center across the street. The lure of free maps and brochures was too powerful to resist.

She went to the crosswalk. The signal was against her, but a quick look showed no cars coming, and she dashed out into the street.

Tires squealed, and Katy's heart stopped in her chest. She turned in what felt like slow motion to see an old white van bearing down on her, sunlight glinting off the broad front windshield, bits of greenery stuck in the grillwork like spinach stuck in oversized teeth. She tried to move her legs but they seemed to know there was no time left, so she stood still, dumb and frozen.

The van swerved, then screeched to a stop with its front fender making a gentle, anticlimactic crunch against the crosswalk pole. Katy found herself staring in the open driver's window at a wild-eyed, unkempt man with hands clenched tight to the steering wheel. He slowly turned his head and stared at her.

She stared back, too stunned to think, and then after a few froglike croaks, found her voice. "Oh, jeez, I'm sorry!" she said, stepping toward him. "I must have looked the wrong way; I didn't see you coming. I'm so sorry! Are you all right?"

"Hi ho, Silver," he said in a deep, richly accented voice, still staring at her.

Huh? Was it some sort of joke about her American accent? He must be in shock over their near miss. She was, that was for sure—she was starting to shake.

Whiskers shadowed the man's strong, square jaw, and his dark brown hair stuck out every which way. Maybe he was crazy. The thought scared her.

"I think you may have dinged your fender. I'm so sorry. Can I pay for repairs?"

He made some sort of guttural response, then broke his stare and looked over to the passenger seat, where a beautiful Irish setter was wide-eyed and panting, ears flat to its head.

"I'm so sorry!" Katy said again. "Is your dog okay?" The dog met Katy's eyes, and its long ears perked. Katy barely restrained herself from reaching across the man to pet it.

The man muttered something that sounded like "She's getting used to it." Then he checked his rearview mirror, stuck his head out the window, and backed his '60s-vintage van more neatly against the side of the road.

Katy found a safe spot on the sidewalk to wait, feeling ill. She hoped he wasn't a bad-tempered man, or one of the sort who would try to get all he could from her. The lettering on the side of the van said ELAND'S ORGANIC GREENS, and she hoped he wasn't the kind of fanatic who was kinder to vegetables and animals than to people. She'd met a few like that in Seattle.

At least he had a nice dog. That meant something, didn't it?

The man got out and came around the front of the van, and her mouth dropped open. He was wearing a *kilt*. An honest-to-God kilt, with a short black jacket, white ruffle-fronted shirt, sporran, and cream kneesocks. He wore strange black shoes whose laces crisscrossed around his ankles.

He was big, too—maybe six two, with broad shoulders that looked far too well developed for the tight little jacket. He looked ready to burst out of his entire ensemble, actually, like the Incredible

Hulk. His face was flushed red, and she hoped it was with the stress of the near miss and not anger.

She could see the headlines now: "American Tourist Pummeled to Death by Lunatic Scotsman in Dented Vegetable Van."

He stopped a couple feet from her, frowning. "Are you hurt?" he asked brusquely.

"No, I'm fine, just embarrassed," she squeaked. "I'm really, really sorry. That was stupid of me—I should have waited for the walk signal. I'm so sorry about your van."

He blinked, black eyebrows rising, and turned to his vehicle as if surprised it was there. She timidly stepped forward to join him in examination of the fender, bending down to look at the new indentation.

He squatted down and brushed his long, strong fingers over the spot, his fingertips etched with fine dark lines, the dirt of his work embedded more deeply than soap could remove. The backs of his hands looked roughened by weather, and she was sure his palms would be callused.

He glanced at her, bent close like she was, and she saw that his eyes were a remarkable deep, dark green, fringed by black lashes. She stared, having never seen eyes quite that color, or so beautiful.

He stood so quickly that she narrowly missed getting her head bumped. "It's nothing," he said, and thumped the front of the van as if it were a sturdy old horse. "Just one more mark of character."

"Are you sure?" she asked, straightening, surprised by this apparent bonhomie from the muscular giant.

His eyebrows lowered sternly as if admonishing her for her apology. "It was my fault, not yours. I was in a hurry. I should be the one apologizing, for giving you such a scare."

She squirmed under his gaze. "Ah. Mm. No, really, not necessary. Are you late for something? Am I holding you up?"

Again a look of startlement. "Bloody hell!" he swore, making her jump. His lips parted as if he wished to say something, but then his face flooded again with red. "Damn! I have to go."

"Oh, all right, then. Bye. And thanks!" She backed away.

He looked at her intently, a strange desperation in his eyes, and then went round to the driver's side of his van, hopping in without another word. She thought she saw him look back at her for a moment with a sort of manic confusion as he pulled away from the curb.

She waved feebly as he drove off.

Well. How altogether strange. What a peculiar encounter. What a peculiar man. And he hadn't sounded Scottish, despite the clothes.

He hadn't been bad-looking, though, especially with those amazing eyes and broad shoulders. Clean him up a bit, and . . .

And he'd still be a lunatic in a vegetable van. *Get a grip, Katy.* She'd seen plenty of that type, convinced the government was trying to mutate them into zombies by genetically altering their green beans.

Still, he'd been attractive in a rough, unkempt, masculine way, and much nicer than he needed to be, considering she'd made him drive into a pole.

She was extra careful as she crossed back to the cathedral. She bought a ticket and wandered through the vaulted, echoing spaces, avoiding the roving bands of tourists with their droning guides.

The cathedral was too big to take in with mere human eyes, and she had a moment's longing for the compact view offered by a television camera. It wasn't quite the same without wedding music and a bride in a dress with a yards-long white train, either. She felt dissociated from the inanimate grandeur around her. Or maybe she was still feeling shaken by the near miss.

She climbed the broad spiral staircase up to the Whispering Gallery inside the dome, and looked down over the railing to the space below. Where had that non-Scotsman been going to in such a hurry on a Saturday? She could think of nothing that made sense, given his attire and his vegetables.

She sat on the curved bench that hugged the wall. The merest whisper of sound was supposed to carry across the perfect acoustics of the dome, thus giving the gallery its name.

She'd heard that Scotsmen wore nothing under their kilts, and wondered if he had been nude under his plaid. Were men circumcised in Britain like most were in the U.S.?

"Penis," she whispered.

A moment later a teen girl across the dome gave an astonished look round. Katy forced her face to innocence, and as soon as the girl looked away, dashed to the nearest doorway to give way to hysterical giggles. As she gasped for air, it struck her that the giggles were a delayed reaction to the near miss in the road.

There was another set of stairs spiraling upward yet again, and still giggling helplessly, she decided to climb them. She eventually came out on a narrow parapet at the top of the dome, with a view of the Thames laid out before her.

The city looked made up of gray Lego bricks, uninspiring despite a brilliant blue sky streaked with white clouds overhead. Bright sunlight did nothing to enliven the dull brown water of the Thames. The polished metal of the pedestrian Millennium Bridge glared white, adding nothing to the romantic view she'd hoped to see. The rebuilt Globe Theatre across the river was the only hint of the London that lived in her dreams.

A pair of teenagers, talking in a Slavic-sounding language, bumped by her. It struck her suddenly that the guy in the kilt had been the only "real" person she'd spoken with since arriving in England. Everyone else had been someone she was paying for a service—the waitress in a restaurant last night, the landlady, the cabbie, the ticket seller in the cathedral. She was on the other side of an invisible wall that separated visitors from the real life of Londoners.

She chewed her lower lip, wondering how she was going to break past that.

She went round the parapet, squeezing past more foreign students, and looked left up the river. She could just pick out the narrow towers topped with small black domes that marked the Tower of London.

Visiting the Tower hadn't been in her plan—she'd intended to haunt the shops of Savile Row after seeing the cathedral, in hopes of spotting a young lordling—but she was still feeling too shaken by the near miss in the road to take up her hunt in earnest.

A couple of Henry VIII's wives had lost their heads at the Tower of London, so marrying a king clearly hadn't turned out to be as good a choice as it had at first seemed. Refusing to consider the implications that had for her dream of marrying nobility, she dug out her guidebook and plotted her route to the Tower.

Chapter 5

Will pounded his hand on the steering wheel, cursing himself for an idiot. Why hadn't he asked her her name? Why hadn't he untied his tongue long enough to ask her to dinner?

He groaned with regret. He could have spared five minutes for the first woman in several years who'd aroused his interest.

What was it about her that had caught at his attention? Maybe it was the weird similarities between her and the woman he had idly imagined while driving earlier this morning, Rossini thumping through his brain and heart. It was a strange coincidence that he'd nearly run down that imaginary woman's incarnation today, just as he'd nearly run down that deer.

He wasn't one to believe in omens, in portents

and fate, but it felt as if he'd just been given a slap in the face to insure he paid attention. And what had he done? Run off, too shocked to take advantage of the opportunity.

All this when just a few weeks ago he'd been whinging about being lonely.

His unknown lady had the pale skin and dark red hair of a beauty in a pre-Raphaelite painting, her hair coming loose round her sweet oval face. She dressed as if she were from another time, another place.

And she *was* from another place: her accent said the United States. *Just like he'd imagined.* What was she doing here? She didn't look like a tourist. Was she here for work? To visit friends?

He should turn round, go back and look for her. This time he'd force himself to behave like a human who knew how to interact with his fellow apes instead of like a grunting caveman.

He glanced at the small clock taped to the dashboard, over the place where the original had long since ceased its movement. *Blast!* No time. He had to find a place to park and get to the wedding.

He was probably making too much of all this anyway. So he'd almost run over a deer and an American. Where was the significance? The adrenaline of the near misses was fogging his thinking. He'd forget about her by nightfall.

Street parking was free on Saturday afternoons, and consequently near impossible to find. An eternity of searching eventually yielded up a place a ten-minute walk from his destination—maybe half that time, if he ran.

He hoped his pinched feet would be able to stand it. He felt like a boiled haggis, ready to burst out of his casing, and the cascade of ruffles down his front made him feel a fool. His outfit had belonged to his uncle, discovered in the back of an old wardrobe. Although a bit too small, it was suitable attire for a wedding and fit better than any of his own suits.

What had *she* thought of him, dressed like this? He leaned over to look at his reflection in the rearview mirror and grimaced. Driving with an open window had left half his head in a wild stir of hair. He'd forgotten to shave, too. He looked like a refugee from *Braveheart*.

Well, there was nothing to be done about it. He ran his fingers through his hair, poured some water from a canteen into a dish for Sadie, decided not to lock the van since the windows were open anyway, and set off at a run.

He was halfway there when he remembered he hadn't had time to buy antiperspirant, either.

Katy people-watched as she stood in line outside the Tower, waiting to buy her ticket, shifting her weight to relieve the pain in her feet. Alligator pumps were not good for walking round a city.

There were lots of young people in jeans and backpacks in line; older, soft-in-the-middle people in cotton knit shirts and tennis shoes; and frazzled couples somewhere in between, riding herd on their jumping, bouncing, chattering children.

Then something different caught her eye. Outside the line, a foursome of well-dressed, slender people went by. The women wore pastel sheaths with matching short jackets and enormous hats. The men were in formal wear.

Katy shifted to see round the people in front of her, craning her neck to watch the foursome as they showed white cards to the guard at the entrance and were let through. What on earth was going on? There must be some sort of event inside.

Her heart fluttered. She wasn't dressed much differently from those people, except for the hats. Might she be able to slip into their midst?

No, she'd be found out in a heartbeat. Wouldn't she? Maybe if she kept quiet, and just smiled and nodded . . . And if questioned she could always plead ignorance, or a search for the ladies' room. Unless of course this was a royal event, and the queen was here, in which case she'd get arrested and dragged off to jail for trying to sneak in.

No. She couldn't dare try it.

Could she?

She'd wanted a chance to break through the wall between tourist and real Londoner. Maybe this was it. Maybe she had been guided here.

Oprah wouldn't be afraid of a few Englishwomen in hats.

She bought her ticket and made her way through the gate of the Middle Tower, walking underneath the royal symbol of rearing lion and unicorn. There was another well-dressed woman up ahead, this one in dark purple with a hat surrounded by glossy green-black feathers. Katy followed her.

They went through another tower, down a stone-paved lane between high walls, through a third tower, and then climbed a slope and stairs into the open center of the Tower of London. Katy blinked in surprise at the trees and the swathes of green lawn. To her left were a quaint row of attached houses. It could have been anywhere, if not for the red-coated guardsman with his tall bearskin hat on duty in front of one of the houses.

The feather-hatted lady and a few other men and women were all heading toward a small church in the corner.

It must be a wedding!

Katy shadowed the woman, then slowed her steps as they neared two Beefeaters at the entrance through a chain barrier. They were checking invitations. Katy hung back, assessing her courage.

The Beefeaters were silver-haired men in elaborate navy blue and red uniforms, their hats looking like round gift boxes atop their heads. They seemed genial enough, and there was another one nearby leading a tour with a certain dramatic flourish. They might be the sort to take pity on a girl who'd misplaced her invitation.

She chewed her lip. The church looked like too small a place to blend in amongst strangers. But who ever knew everyone at a wedding?

"You!" a deep male voice declared loudly. A shadow fell over her, and she sensed someone looming near her.

She turned to look and sucked in a breath. "You!" It was the crazy vegetable man. "What are you doing here?"

"The wedding. Like you." He dug an invitation out of a pocket inside his jacket as if to prove his point.

"*You're* going to the wedding?" she said stupidly.

His answer was a grin. He took a step toward the guards, then paused and cocked his elbow for her to take.

She gingerly put her hand into the crook of his arm. Who was she to refuse?

One guard briefly examined the vegetable man's invitation while the other smiled at Katy. She smiled back. They'd assumed she was the nutcase's girlfriend.

"Are you one of Marjorie's friends?" the nut asked as they moved forward.

"I haven't met Marjorie," she said truthfully. Marjorie must be the bride. She thought quickly, determined not to trip herself up in lies. "And I don't actually know the groom. My parents . . . couldn't be here today."

"So they sent you?"

"I really don't know anyone at all."

He smiled even wider, his teeth strong, white, and straight. "William Eland." He dropped his arm and held out his hand to her. "Please call me Will."

"Katy Orville," she said, and shook it. His hand

was as callused—and as strong—as it looked. But also gentle, as if he were aware how his big paw swamped her bird-boned little fingers.

"I am pleased to meet you a second time," he said with a little bow, "and especially under such fortuitous, happy circumstances."

She chewed her lip, unsure how to respond to this archaic formality. "Err, yes."

They slipped in the door just before it was closed by the ushers, and Will led her along the back of the church, finding a place for them at the end of a row. The music changed, and everyone stood as the bride made her entrance.

As the ceremony continued, Katy surreptitiously gawked at the guests and at her companion. There was a faint smell of mothballs and some sort of herb to his clothes, and she was getting a whiff of body odor off him, too, as if he'd been exercising. It wasn't unpleasant, but was unexpected in a place where cologne was the odor de rigueur. The fine hairs along his forehead were plastered down with drying sweat.

He seemed . . . earthy. Raw. Like he should be off in the woods wrestling bears instead of sitting in a chapel amidst a bunch of women in hats. He caught her looking, and she swiftly turned her eyes to an examination of the details of the simple chapel.

"Have you been here before?" he whispered in his low, absurdly attractive English voice.

She shook her head.

"There were over fifteen hundred bodies buried

under this floor. Most of them were executed on
Tower Hill, just up that way," he whispered, tilting
his head to the left.

"That's *horrible*." She frowned, looking around.
There wasn't much square footage. "How did they
all fit?"

A guffaw of laughter burst out of him, quickly
hidden under a coughing fit. Heads turned, and
Katy slid down in her seat, trying to make herself
invisible. He had a very loud laugh.

The ceremony finished, the couple made a smiling
exit, and then everyone slowly filed out. Will stood
silent beside her, also watching the other people
leave.

A few of them noticed him and raised amused
eyebrows a fraction of an inch. One or two looked
mildly censorious. Katy wondered how he fit into
this rarefied realm, and what they'd think of her by
extension.

Will hung back, waiting until everyone else had left
the chapel before gesturing to Katy that they, too,
should go. They trailed out after the others, Will
hoping, vainly, that the lot would have disappeared
by the time he emerged with her. He was certain
that she'd be lured away by those more sociable
than he, and he would lose this stunning second
chance to speak with her.

He'd done a double take when he saw her waiting outside the chapel, not believing that it was her.
What were the chances?

As luck would now have it, some of his family and acquaintances *had* drifted away from the chapel, toward the entrance to the Tower, but a few still lingered, chatting inanities.

Even worse, his cousin Trevor was still there, and spotted him. Slender and polished to a glaring sheen, Trevor lifted a hand in a wave and sauntered over to join them. Will felt the fires of possessiveness come alight within, and barely resisted the temptation to shove Katy behind his back for protection. He did not mistake the smirk on Trevor's finely formed lips for good humor.

"Will, I thought that was you when I heard that great burst of laughter in the back of the church," Trevor said, holding out his hand to be shaken. "Trying to give Marjorie something special to remember on her wedding day, were you?"

"Trevor," Will said flatly, ignoring the hand held out to him.

Trevor dropped his hand and put it on his hip, as if that were what he'd intended all along. He looked Will over. "God's sake, man, why the Rob Roy impression?"

Will's only audible response was a low grumbling noise from deep in his chest. He had a brief, happy vision of punching Trevor on the side of the head and seeing him collapse like a wet noodle.

Trevor turned his attention to Katy, lips stretching like earthworms into a slimy smile, although such a comparison was an insult to good worms everywhere.

"Are you going to introduce me to your beautiful companion?" he asked Will, and then in an exaggerated aside to Katy: "Our Will needs the occasional prompting, don't you find? Such a dear brute of a man. He brings all the charms of the country with him whenever he visits."

A thwack to the side of Trevor's head would be too gentle. Bring him an ax and he'd revive the use of the block at the center of Tower Green, then chop the bounder into bite-sized chunks for the ravens to devour.

"Ms. Orville, may I introduce to you my cousin, Trevor Mangold. Viscount Stanley, as I'm sure he'll find a way to slip into the conversation soon enough. Trevor, Ms. Katy Orville. She's a guest from Douglas's side of things."

Trevor's face had taken on an angry undertone during this speech, but he quickly mastered his features. "Marjorie's new husband's name is David, not Douglas. Do try to get it right, Will, when you meet him." He turned to Katy, taking her hand in his and lifting it, kissing the air just above its back. "It is an honor to meet you, Ms. Orville."

Katy blushed, her eyelids falling. "It's a pleasure to meet you, too, Lord Mangle."

Will snorted, a laugh choking out.

Katy's eyes flew open, and she gazed, appalled, at Trevor. "Oh! I'm so sorry, did I address you incorrectly? I don't know how to do titles. I'm American," she offered sheepishly.

"Yes, I can tell by your lovely accent," Trevor

said, managing to keep his smile in place. "And please ignore my cousin. No one pays any attention *at all* to titles any more, and I would be delighted if you would call me by my Christian name."

Katy smiled, and mocked wiping sweat off her brow. "Phew! That's a relief. Please call me Katy."

" 'Phew,' indeed," Trevor said, and cocked out his arm, offering it for her hand. "Would you—"

"Ms. Orville, do you need a lift to the reception?" Will interrupted. Damned if he'd let that poisonous snake Trevor snatch her away from him.

"I suppose I do—"

"Then allow me," Trevor said, placing her hand on his elbow and casting a sly look of victory at Will.

Will grabbed Katy's free hand and forcibly pulled her away from Trevor, making her stumble after him as he dragged her across the cobbled square toward the steps. The technique lacked Trevor's finesse, but got the job done. He saw her throw a look of helpless apology back over her shoulder at his cousin.

Trevor himself looked as if someone had just pulled a plate of cake out his hand. Then he forced a laugh and waved, as if he had intended to share the cake all along, and wasn't plotting bloody vengeance. "I'll see you there," he called after Katy. "Don't let Will scare you. He's mostly harmless, really. And don't let him sell you any vegetables!"

Will muttered foully under his breath, but then Katy stumbled. He felt her grab him for balance, and quickly wrapped his arm around her waist, holding her up. She was pressed tightly to his side, her body plastered against his.

"Oof," she said, and looked up at him with wide, startled eyes. They were beautiful eyes, the color of the sea off Cornwall on a summer day.

"Are you all right?" he asked gruffly.

"Yes, fine."

He softened his voice, not wanting his loathing of Trevor to intrude between them. "You're sure?"

"Uh, yeah. You can let go of me now." She gave him a look that told him he'd passed considerate concern and was moving on toward nutty.

He reluctantly let her loose.

She swayed, trying to keep balanced without putting one foot fully on the ground. "My shoe came off," she said, turning to look for it.

"I'll get it." He fetched it, then knelt down in front of her. "You can use my shoulders for balance, if you wish."

He awaited the touch of her hands on his shoulders, and was caught by the absurd sensation that he was kneeling before a queen, awaiting the dubbing that would proclaim him her knight.

Katy stared at the bent head before her, wondering at the queer sense that this was a moment beyond what it seemed. She felt . . . revered. And as if laying her hands on his shoulders would somehow mean accepting more than an offer of help with her shoe.

Feeling thoroughly off balance, she obeyed, laying her hands lightly on his shoulders. One hand landed near his collar, his longish hair brushing the tops of her fingers, and she found herself staring at the tender little bare space behind his ear. She edged her thumb over and touched it.

He went stiff under her hands and glanced up at her. She put a wide-eyed look of innocence on her face, not quite understanding herself why she had done it.

He lifted her bare foot in the palm of his hand, cupping the sensitive underside of her arch in gentle warmth. The feeling shot straight up her leg and she sucked in a breath, surprised that his touch should have such an effect on her. He tenderly fit her foot into her shoe, then set her foot back down again. His fingertips traced over her ankle for a brief moment, sending shivers up her calf.

"How clumsy of me," she said softly.

"My fault. I was rushing again. Do forgive me," he said, still kneeling before her.

"Of course. But do you always rush?" she asked, and it came out sounding as if it had more meanings than she'd intended.

He stood and again crooked his arm for her, his green eyes locking with her own. "No. I quite like to take my time."

His words sent a quiver through her.

She took his arm, and tried to shake off the weird intimacy that seemed to have sprung up between them.

Will wasn't what she was looking for. Trevor was.

Trevor . . . now *there* was an interesting young man, she tried to tell herself, forcing her thoughts onto him. He was a viscount!

What *was* a viscount, anyway? Were their wives viscountesses? No, that sounded silly. She'd done a brief study of British titles on the Internet before she left the States, but at the moment it was all blending together.

Trevor's features were model regular, his eyes a deep warm brown, and his hair a sandy red that had been bleached by the sun. His skin was tan, and he had the look of a well-polished man of leisure. She could easily imagine him riding polo ponies, skiing in the Alps, or racing speedboats off the coast of Monaco.

He was so slick and polished, so classically pretty-boy handsome, he made her uneasy. He was the type of guy that normally would look right past her, not even acknowledging her existence. She'd always hated that type of man, classifying them as jerks while secretly knowing that some of her dislike was because she wished that such a smoothie would for once see her as prey fit to pursue instead of chasing after ski bunnies and bikini models all the time.

He was, in short, the type of guy a geeky girl like her might sigh over in the movies, verbally disembowel amongst friends, and know she hadn't a hope of getting if she was foolish enough to try. Plant a title on him, and he looked exactly like what she'd come here to find. In his wedding finery, he looked like he could have stepped straight from a BBC historical drama.

Will, on the other hand, looked like he might be an English version of the sort of wacky Green Party voter she'd left back in Seattle. He didn't look like he had the proverbial pair of pennies to rub together, either. He looked downright impoverished, with that shaggy hair and ancient van. Say what one wished about love conquering all, it wasn't going to do squat about debt or poverty. And it wasn't going to make her Lady Katy.

She firmly tried to shove Will into the "friend" pigeonhole, ignoring the sexy tartan and mussed hair. He was not a marital prospect, like Trevor.

She wouldn't have to try to impress him, or hide her ignorance. She wouldn't have to make an effort to be charming or appear refined. She could be herself, and let that forge a comfortable little chasm between them. She'd gotten the feeling that he might be a little interested in her, and everyone knew that being completely yourself was the best way to chase off a potential suitor. Why else did people act so disappointed after getting married, if not from discovering what their spouses were really like?

"So, how did I mess up Trevor's title?" she asked, as they left the walkway around the Tower and began the hike to wherever his van was parked. Maybe Trevor would find her more appealing for being temporarily out of reach. Whatever small interest he had in her might have died during the ride to the reception if she'd failed to be witty and clever.

"He's properly addressed as 'Lord Stanley,' " Will explained. "But that wasn't why I laughed. His surname is Mangold, not Mangle."

"Mangled?"

"Man-gold."

"Still sounds like Mangled." She shrugged. "Guess it'll just be 'Trevor.' " She chewed her lip and frowned, mentally trying out 'Katy Mangled.' It sounded like a cat had misbehaved in one's closet, visiting destruction on a favorite blouse.

"So would his wife be 'Lady Stanley'?" she asked.

"Some unfortunate woman will eventually bear that title, yes."

The viscount was single. Very good! "I think having a title would be wonderful, no matter how little attention people might pay to them nowadays. It still makes a person sound rather special."

"It's better to actually be special than just to sound like one is."

Well, harrumph! "How do you know the bride?" she asked, changing the topic.

"She's my cousin. Trevor's sister."

"I take it you like her better than you like him? I noticed a tiny bit of tension."

"He's a first-class cad, is Trevor," he growled. "My apologies for introducing him to you."

She murmured a vaguely *pshaw* sort of sound.

"Did you come to London just for the wedding?" he asked after a pause, sounding as if it had taken great effort to come up with this conversational salvo.

"It's a vacation of sorts. I've always wanted to visit England, but never had the time."

"If it's England you want to see, then you can't spend all your time in London. You need to go out into the countryside."

"I'd be too terrified to try to drive on the left side of the road. Look what happened when I tried to cross a street!"

"I'll drive you," he said.

"Oh, I couldn't ask that of you." Damn it, how was she going to get out of this? She couldn't let him soak up all her time when there were lordlings to hunt.

"I could take you tomorrow."

"I've hardly seen anything of London yet. What is that famous quotation? 'When a man is tired of London, he is tired of life'?"

"It's a noisy sewer."

"Oh, don't be a killjoy. *I'd* like to see it, sewer or not," she said.

"You're a city girl, then?" he asked, a bit mournfully.

"No one from the Pacific Northwest is really a city person. We're outdoorsy. It's just that I didn't come here to see fields and cows."

"The Pacific Northwest?"

"Mm. I'm from Seattle. You know, Bill Gates, Microsoft. Lots of fir trees and volcanoes, Puget Sound, killer whales, Dungeness crab."

"Ah," he said, without sounding like her explanation had clarified things much. "It sounds a lovely place."

"But it's all so new compared to London. I love that the buildings are still standing from hundreds and hundreds of years ago—and knowing that Romans once lived here. And castles! How many castles do we have in Seattle? None!"

"You like castles."

"Of course. Doesn't every girl want to be a lady in a castle, waiting for her knightly husband to come home from the wars, clad in shining armor, his enemy's head on a pike?"

"God's sake, I hope not!"

They got to his van, and she reached for the door handle.

"The passenger side is over here," he said, opening the other door.

"Oops." She scampered round to it and waited while he greeted his dog and unfastened the leash that had ensured it wouldn't escape out one of the open windows. He brushed dog hair off the passenger seat and then stood back. She slid into place where she'd normally find a steering wheel, and was immediately fawned upon by the Irish setter.

"Who's a good puppy?" Katy cooed, playing with the dog's ears and rubbing its head. "Who sat so patiently all day? What a pretty dog you are."

"Her name's Sadie," Will said, getting behind the wheel. His kilt slid up his leg, revealing a well-muscled thigh. *Was* he wearing underwear? It took an effort to tear her gaze away.

"Sadie, place," Will ordered.

Sadie gave Katy's hand an extra lick, then obediently lay down on a big dog cushion behind the front seats, panting happily.

Katy flapped her feet on the dirty floor, amused by the absence of pedals on the left side. "This is going to be wild," she said, grinning at Will.

"Er, yes."

He slammed his door, then opened it and slammed it shut three more times before it closed properly. The sound echoed in the bare interior of the van. There was no carpeting and the seats were cracked vinyl, glossy with age and use. Katy found the ancient lap belt and strapped herself in, not at all certain that she wouldn't tumble right out her own door if he took a corner too fast.

The van was filled with the same strong herbal scent she'd detected on Will. She peered into the shadowed depths behind her. Jury-rigged shelves were partially filled with cardboard boxes.

"Where's that smell coming from?" she asked.

"The lavender?" He reached back behind them and snagged one of the boxes, then opened it for her to see. A wreath of lavender in the shape of a heart lay nestled within on a bed of tissue paper.

"Oh, how pretty!"

"Some of the young girls in my neighborhood make them from my lavender plants. They make sachets and things, too, to sell in local shops.

They've been pestering me to show samples up here in London, where they think they can get a better price." He shrugged, putting the lid back on the box. "The girls and I split the profits."

"They sound like quite the little entrepreneurs." And he sounded desperate for cash, if he was taking half the profits from little girls.

"You have no idea." He put the box back on the shelf, then grabbed a sheaf of printouts on the shelf.

"What are those?" Katy asked, reaching for the sheaf.

"Just some advertisements the girls made up, playing around on the computer. Not worth looking at, really."

Katy took them before he could stop her and thumbed through the color printouts. They were advertisements for the hearts, made by "The Duke of Lavender." The girls had apparently spent many long hours with Photoshop and graphics programs to produce them, including a great quantity of rainbow-colored hearts. " 'The Duke of Lavender'?" Katy asked.

Will pulled out into traffic, his cheeks coloring. "They thought it would sound more sophisticated than 'Eland's Organic Lavender,' especially to tourists."

"Very smart," Katy said, and tried to keep a straight face, but a gurgle of laughter snuck out.

Will gave her a dark look.

"No, really, it's a great idea," Katy said. "Americans

are suckers for that type of thing. It'd be even better if they put in a coat of arms."

"I'll tell them," he muttered.

"Hey, how exactly do you address a duke, anyway?"

He seemed to hunch down into his shoulders. "Why?"

"Just curious, in case I ever meet one."

He grumbled under his breath, then said, " 'Your Grace,' but 'sir' is fine after that, although he'd probably just want you to call him by name. 'Your Grace' can also refer to an archbishop, of course."

She laughed. "You could be the *Archbishop* of Lavender instead! I love it! Maybe you could wear one of those tall hats."

"Yes, well . . ."

"Oh, I'm sorry," she said in sudden panic. "You aren't religious, are you? Have I put my foot in my mouth?"

"No, no worries, I'm not sensitive on the topic of archbishops. It was the 'duke' bit—"

She reached over and laid her hand on his leg. It was meant to be reassuring, but it seemed to shock him into silence. "I can see why you'd be embarrassed, especially after you gave Trevor such a hard time about his title. Here you are pretending to have one to better sell dried flowers!"

He looked on the verge of answering, then shook his head and sighed.

"I might have been taken in by those lavender ads myself, if I hadn't met you," she said. "I'd have imagined your fictional duke to be a silver-haired man in tweed, standing amidst the formal garden at one of his country houses, delicately sniffing a sprig of lavender."

"Silver haired?" he complained.

"Very dignified." Her gaze slid over to Will's bare knees. No dignified duke here. No archbishop, either. She giggled.

And then slapped her hands on the dashboard in sudden fright as they turned a corner and headed down the left side of the street. A moment later she realized that the left side was the correct side and sat back, trying to be calm. "What else do you grow, besides lavender?" she asked to distract herself from the sense of impending traffic doom.

"Salad greens, mostly. I grow them in greenhouses through the winter and spring. People are willing to pay much more for fresh greens at that time of year, especially upscale restaurants."

"And the greens are all organic?"

"People pay more for that, too."

"So you don't farm that way for philosophical reasons?"

He shrugged, eyes intent on the traffic as he changed lanes. He didn't look too comfortable driving on these streets. "I enjoy composting. Worm farming. Plowing under a good cover crop. I like to watch living dirt at work—there's a whole world, an entire cycle of life and death, to be found in a fistful of good soil."

"Really."

He glanced at her. "Really. It's nothing like farming with chemicals."

She flagged his attention back to the road, her own eyes wide as a truck squeezed down the narrow street toward them. Somehow they missed each other, but waiting at the end of the street was an intersection with streets going off in five or six different directions, traffic lights, and pedestrian islands strewn through it willy-nilly. She gripped the edge of her seat, nails biting into the vinyl. The van swayed and swerved, and something fell off a shelf in back.

"Do you grow anything else?" she asked tightly.

"Flowers for cutting, in the summer. I grow those outside, not in the greenhouses."

"Can you actually support yourself doing that?" she asked.

He laughed. "No." He wove through the maze, the clunky van picking out an escape route like a clever rabbit darting through its warren. "As a farming operation, I'm just managing to break even. Most of what I make goes right back into the greenhouses."

"Oh. Can I ask, how old are you?"

"Twenty-eight," he said.

"I'm twenty-four. I wish I could be as excited about my career as you are about yours. I've spent a few years dinking around in a software company, but it's nowhere near a passion."

"No?"

She looked out the window at the passing buildings. "No. I haven't found a calling or a passion." After a moment of quiet she looked back at him, smiling wryly. "It's not what a modern woman with a good education is supposed to say, is it? I'm supposed to be energetically pursuing a fabulous, groundbreaking career, or at the very least doing refugee work in Africa. I should be making something of myself."

"Should you?"

"Shouldn't I?"

He looked at her, his brows knotted in confusion. "Why are you asking me? The last way you'll ever please yourself is by caring about the opinions of others."

"But I have to care. We're social creatures. We die if we're ostracized."

His answer was a loud snort. "Did you get that from a sociology textbook? Better dead than living by the expectations of others."

"Maybe it's easier for a man," she said, crossing her arms over her chest.

He raised a brow at her. "That's too weak to even call an argument. Besides, you look like you live according to your own code."

"What do you mean?"

He gestured toward her attire. "You don't care about current trends. You look old-fashioned."

"*What?*" Her little bee of fashion doubt buzzed loudly back to life.

"I like that. I like old things." He patted the dash of the van.

She looked down at her suit. If *he* thought this showed no care for fashion, what did everyone else think? Oh, heavens. Rebecca had been right. They were all going to laugh at her.

She felt a welling humiliation at the thought of mingling among the guests at the wedding reception. At least Trevor, by some miracle, hadn't seemed to notice her clothes.

"Brilliant!" Will suddenly declared. "A free parking space! Now, there's good luck for you."

She grimaced when she got out of the van, her feet having had more than enough of faux alligator pumps and hard sidewalks. Will tended to Sadie, and then they left the van, walked a couple minutes, came around a corner, and were in front of the Dorchester Hotel.

"Oh!" Katy exclaimed. "I know exactly where we are! I'm staying just a short walk from here." She'd seen the hotel during her ramblings yesterday afternoon.

"Where—" Will started to ask, but she grabbed his arm, pulling him through the front doors of the hotel. She wasn't going to tell *anyone* about the dump where she was staying.

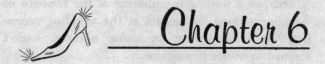

Chapter 6

The interior of the Dorchester was plush, all soft golds and greens, velvets and brocades. Katy and Will followed tasteful little signs to a ballroom off the main lobby, the place already half filled with guests. The chandelier-lit room bore just enough resemblance to her dream of the night before that she half expected to see her landlady wheeling in a poison-frosted wedding cake.

A reception line cut through the middle.

Ah, jeez. What was she supposed to say when she met the bride and groom? Or their parents? She was crashing their party, for heaven's sake!

Will led them into place at the end of the line.

Katy fidgeted. "The line's awfully long. Shall we get something to eat and come back when it's shorter?"

He wrinkled his brow at her. "The line's not long."

She chewed her lip and fidgeted some more.

"Do you need to use the loo?" he asked.

"What?"

"The W.C. The jakes. Do you need to go?"

"No! What a question! I'm not four years old."

"Sorry. It just looked like—" He stopped, apparently taking her warning look for what it was.

They took slow steps forward, giving Katy time to regret the bathroom denial. He probably would have waited by the door for her anyway, though, and escorted her right back into line.

They came to the first receivers in the line. Were they grandparents? A mother remarried to a second husband? Great uncle and aunt? Katy rubbed her sweaty palm on her skirt and forced a smile onto her face.

"Beautiful ceremony," Katy said, grasping a hand. "I'm so happy for them."

Blank eyes and a smiling nod answered her, and she was moving on. That wasn't so bad! Maybe she could do this. Behind her, Will greeted the same couple.

"William! It's so good to see you. It's been far too long. You *must* stop hiding yourself away like that."

Katy sneaked a look at the couple beaming up at Will. They seemed to adore him. Will shook the man's hand, kissed the woman on the cheek, and made a vaguely agreeable noise. The woman patted his shoulder, shaking her head slightly and smiling as if such was to be expected. The next two couples were clearly the parents of the bride and groom. Katy hurried through the greetings, trying to get a few steps ahead of Will so that he wouldn't figure out she knew nothing about either set. It was going well until she got to the last parent, a man. The person ahead of her was yakking away to the bride and groom, forcing Katy to stand and wait in front of this stranger with gentle, inquiring eyes.

Darn it.

"Are you a friend of Marjorie's?" he asked.

Katy didn't know if he was Marjorie's father or the father of the groom.

"Er, I came with Will," she said, nodding her head toward her escort, who was catching up with her.

Marjorie turned toward her, pretty brown eyes crinkling. "With Will? Oh, delightful!" She grasped Katy's hand and pulled her over. "I didn't know he was going to bring someone. I'm so pleased to meet you."

"It was a beautiful ceremony. Such a lovely location." Katy said. Whew! She'd dodged that bullet.

"Katy had never been to the Tower," Will said, joining them.

"No? You're American?" Marjorie asked.

Katy nodded.

"I'm dying to hear how the two of you met. Will has always been my favorite cousin, you know. He's been like a brother, always looking out for me." She turned to her husband, now free of well-wishers. "David, this is Katy. She's Will's girlfriend."

"It's a pleasure to meet you," David said, shaking her hand.

"Katy is one of your own guests," Will told David. "Her parents, Mr. and Mrs. Orville, couldn't make it."

"Pardon? Oh, oh yes." David's expression went through confusion and embarrassment to "make the best of it." He gave Katy that smile you give to somebody who knows your name but whose face you cannot remember. "I'm so sorry your parents couldn't be here."

"I'm sure they would have loved it," Katy said, her own smile back in place.

"But then, when did you two meet?" Marjorie asked, looking puzzled.

"Whoops, we're holding up the line. It was so nice to meet you," Katy said, and grabbed Will's hand, dragging him away much as he had dragged her. "I'm starving," she said to him. "Are they serving food yet?"

"There must be bits floating about," he said. "Wait, here's the seating chart. Let's see where they've put us."

"Seating chart?" she squeaked, staring in horror at the diagram and list of numbered names. There would be no party-crashing Orville on it. "No, no, I'm terribly thirsty. Let's find something to drink."

"Here I am," he said, pointing at a spot on the chart. "Now where are you . . . ?"

"Will!"

He looked at her, brows raised. "Hmm?"

"I'm thirsty. Really. Terribly." She tugged at his

sleeve. "Could you please find me something to drink? Be my hero?"

"Oh. Of course!"

"Thanks." She smiled in relief.

He left to fetch the requested drink, and she quickly put distance between herself and the chart.

Trevor saw a flash of yellow go by from the corner of his eye, and turned to look. There she was, the frumpy little American that his cousin was acting such a dolt over.

It was an honest, bone-deep pleasure to see Will at the mercy of another—especially when that other was a woman whose interests could be turned elsewhere. He snagged two glasses of champagne off the tray of a passing waiter and made his way over to her.

"You made it in one piece," he said from behind her.

She jumped, and then turned, wide-eyed. One hand went up to touch her lumpy twist of hair, her smile nervous.

"Here," he said, handing her one of the glasses. "I'm sure you can use this. Was Will a silent wart the whole drive over?"

"Will? No, not at all," she said, brow wrinkling.

"Really? Now there's a surprise! The beast can speak. Call the papers, put it in print! It's all most of us can do to get three words out of him. I was sure you'd be desperate for conversation by now. If you're all talked out, perhaps I should move on . . . ?"

"Oh, no! Don't do that."

"If the lady insists. So tell me, what did Will talk about to keep you so finely entertained?"

She took a cautious sip of her champagne, then darted the tip of her tongue out to catch a stray drop on her lip. She wasn't a bad-looking woman, really, if you could see past the hideous clothes and schoolteacher's hair. God knew it was a challenge.

"He talked about worms and dirt mostly."

Trevor laughed, surprised. "God love him! He knows how to capture the interest of a woman."

Katy raised her brows. "He talks about them with a lot of passion. Any topic can be interesting if the speaker loves it."

He couldn't quite tell if she was serious or having him on. "True enough," he answered cautiously, not wanting to risk misinterpreting.

"What do you do?"

"Your pardon?"

"What do you do for a living?"

Good Christ. What a stereotypical American question. Was she going to ask how much money he made, too? "I have an art and antiques gallery."

"Oh! One of my friends majored in art history and did an internship at Sotheby's. Do you do something like that?"

"Er, no. When you grow up around fine art, as I have, you learn everything you need to know by the time you're ten years old. Formal study isn't really necessary."

"Oh." She looked like she didn't know what to make of that. He wasn't surprised. She'd undoubtedly grown up shopping at chain stores and eating fast food, like every other American.

"How long are you going to be in London?" he asked, taking a sip of his champagne, and eager to change the subject. His gallery operated in the red, and he harbored fears that he might have to get a real job at some point. He received an allowance from the trust in his name, but it wasn't nearly enough to live on in style. He'd have to see if Mum could do something about that overdraft . . .

"I'll be here a few weeks."

"Visiting friends?"

She brushed her hand through the air, careless. "Oh, doing this and that. Whatever feels right."

"Free spirit, are you?" She didn't look it.

"Free enough," she said, with challenge in her voice.

He raised a brow. "Indeed." There might be a little more to her than met the eye. Not much more, but a little.

Will returned, a dainty glass of pink punch held in each enormous hand. His brows lowered, turning his stubbled face fierce.

"William Wallace, so good to see you off the battlefield," Trevor said. "Where's your claymore?"

If Will hadn't had the glasses of punch in his hands, Trevor thought, his cousin might have decked him. This was all too amusing.

"Thank you," Katy said, taking one of the cups from Will. Will hardly seemed to notice, his hard gaze on Trevor.

"Stay away from Katy," Will said. "I know what you're doing. Stop it, or I'll make you stop it."

"We're no longer children," Trevor said, lowering his own voice. "I'd like to see you try."

"Don't tempt me."

Trevor was aware of Katy's gaze flickering back and forth between them. The bird looked like she hadn't more than a single pebble rattling round her empty brainbox.

"William!" his Aunt Agatha said, joining them and interrupting the buildup of tension.

Trevor glanced at Katy and saw her eyes go even wider at this new arrival. She was actually gaping. Puzzled, Trevor looked at his aunt, but could see nothing in her pale perfection to cause alarm. As usual, her frosted hair was elegantly arranged, her diamond-and-pearl earrings sparkling with tasteful wealth.

"Aunt Agatha," Will said, kissing her on her tight cheek.

Katy ducked her face down, suddenly becoming fascinated by her glasses of champagne and punch.

Will made the introductions.

"Have we met before?" Agatha asked Katy.

Katy gave her no more than a quick glance and shook her head no. How very curious.

"I was certain we had. Odd, I usually remember faces." Agatha lifted her brows in a delicate shrug. She put her hand into the crook of Will's arm. "Do excuse us, will you, Miss Orville, Trevor? I need to steal William away for a moment."

Katy smiled and nodded.

Will gave Trevor a parting glower, then said to Katy, "I'll be back in a minute."

When he was out of earshot, Trevor said, "He probably will be, too, so I'd best take advantage of the moment."

"How do you mean?" Katy asked, half her attention clearly still on Will as Aunt Agatha maneuvered him toward Helena Dawby and Cynthia Smythe-Darling.

Poor Helena. Aunt Agatha was likely still trying to pair her up with Will. *That* would never work.

"Could I call you while you're here in London?" he asked.

That snapped her attention back. "What? Oh! Yes! Or, er, how about I give you my email address?" She rooted around in her purse. "I can't remember the number where I'm staying."

"Are you staying at a hotel? The name should be enough for me to reach you."

"Er, no, not a hotel. Just here in Mayfair." She scribbled her email address on the back of a crumpled receipt and handed it to him.

"Cheers," he said, pocketing it. There was quite a bit of fun to have here; he'd waited a long time for a chance to best Will. He finished his champagne and snagged a second glass from a passing waitress.

People were starting to fill up the tables. It must almost be time for the meal to start. "Can I show you to your seat?" he asked.

She stared at him as if he'd offered to show her to the guillotine. "If you'll excuse me, I have to go powder my nose."

"Certainly," he said, wondering what was going on under that beehive of red hair. "I'll talk to you later, then. Oh, and a word to the wise," he said, casting a glance over to where Will's head was visible above the rest. Damn the bastard for being tall and good-looking! Given the way he dressed, though, no one would ever guess that he was a duke. Nor would Will tell them. Trevor didn't know if Will was excessively modest, secretive, or if he just never thought about status.

"Yes?" She fidgeted, poised on the edge of flight.

"My cousin is not . . . the most even-keeled of men," Trevor said, widening his eyes and giving her a look of warning. "You might do best to avoid him."

Will broke away from his companions, his eyes finding Katy's from across the room. Then he moved purposefully toward her, like Genghis Khan sweeping aside the tribes of Asia in his march toward conquering the world. Trevor almost felt sorry for her.

Katy looked back at him, alarm in her eyes. "I'll keep that in mind. If you'll excuse me, I've got to go to the ladies' room." She fled.

Trevor smiled. Not a bad day's work.

Will followed Katy out of the ballroom, and caught a glimpse of her just as she went out the front doors of the hotel. Where was she going? Had she left something in his van?

He went after her, and was about to call out to her when she turned a corner *away* from the street where the van was parked.

Was she disoriented?

He took a moment to look around, making sure of his own bearings. She was definitely going the wrong direction. He followed her, then turned the same corner that she had.

The street was empty of pedestrians.

He stood, stunned, looking up and down the street, staring into shadows and patches of sunlight. What the hell?

He walked down the pavement she must have taken, looking at doorways. Everything looked like law offices and consulates, closed for the day. Across the street there was a car park, but even that showed no signs of activity.

"Katy?" he called into the quiet.

Nothing moved. The only sound was of cars on a cross street.

He stood a moment longer, then went down to the next cross street, peering up and down it for some sign of her. None. Puzzled, he waited several minutes in front of the car park to see if she would emerge in a vehicle, but all was silent. It was as if she'd disappeared into thin air. At a loss as to what else to do, he turned his steps back to the hotel.

Back in the ballroom, everyone was seated for the meal, the first course already on the tables. Will stopped at the seating chart and scanned it for Katy's name, so he'd know where to find her if she returned.

It wasn't there.

He went through it a second time, and then a third. There were no Orvilles listed, neither parents nor daughter. Maybe her mother had remarried and had a different name, he thought, trying to ease the strange twist of panic that was tightening in his chest. It could have been a stepfather she referred to when speaking of her parents, couldn't it? She would come back and sit at their place.

That didn't explain why she'd left, though. He sought out Trevor's name on the chart, then wove through the tables to where his cousin was holding court. He laid a heavy hand on Trevor's shoulder and forcibly turned him half around in his seat.

A flash of fear lit up Trevor's face, quickly covered with a blanket of charm. "Will! Didn't they give you enough food at your table? Have you come to take mine at swordpoint?"

"What did you say to her?"

"Whatever do you mean?"

He squeezed Trevor's shoulder. "Don't make me repeat myself."

Trevor's jaw tightened, and he gestured toward the others at the table, all watching intently, their expressions a mix of social discomfort and willing voyeurism. "You're spoiling everyone's soup."

"I doubt that. And you've forgotten with whom you are dealing, if you think I'd care. For the last time, what did you say to her?"

"I asked her how she would be spending her time

in London," Trevor said, voice low. "I made small talk. You've heard of that, haven't you? It's a species of civility."

"Nothing else?"

"What *should* I have said? And why don't you ask her yourself?"

Will eased his grip on Trevor's shoulder. "I can't. She's gone."

Trevor laughed, brushing Will's hand off his shoulder. "She went to the loo, is all. Good lord, Will, you needn't make a battle out of everything!"

"No, she's gone."

The look of surprise on Trevor's face was a little too Royal Shakespearean to be believeable, and there was a twitch in his cheek that hinted at a smug smile held tightly under control.

Will glanced at the other people at the table. Marjorie's wedding was not the place to make a scene. Any comeuppance he served to Trevor would have to come later.

He retreated to his own table, his emotions in violent foment. Rationality said he should drop the entire issue. If Katy had been truly interested in him she would have stayed, no matter what nonsense Trevor spilled in her ear. If she was such a bad judge of character that she preferred Trevor over Will, then he didn't want her anyway.

She'd seemed overly fascinated with titles, too.

And she lived in another country. That made dating nearly impossible, and he wasn't prepared to offer a woman anything more than dating.

He should just let it drop. It would be the wise thing to do.

He ate in silence as conversation flowed around him. He remembered the light pressure of Katy's hands on his shoulders as he'd slipped her shoe back on her perfect little foot. He remembered the touch of her fingertip on that bare space behind his ear. The memory sent a small shiver up his spine.

He'd enjoyed their conversation in the van, too. He had been comfortable with her in a way he couldn't remember being with any other woman. How was he supposed to forget about her?

On top of it all, being bested by Trevor ate at him. If he never saw Katy again, Trevor would have won a battle in their lifelong war. That was unthinkable.

There were a lot of things he could stomach in this life, but letting Trevor get the best of him wasn't one of them. He stabbed his fork into his chicken Kiev.

He'd have to find Katy and take her out to dinner.

Chapter 7

To: Rebecca Treinen
From: Katy Orville
Subject: Prince Charming?

Rebecca!

I finally found an Internet place (obviously), on Tottenham Court Road (pronounced TOT-num—and I thought the French were bad at not pronouncing all the letters!), and it is really something. You plunk coins into a touch-screen vending machine, and it spits out a piece of paper with a code on it. Then you go into this huge room FILLED with rows of monitors and keyboards. Pick a chair, log in with your code, and there you go! It's expensive, though. I think when I'm through I'll go to Sainsbury's (grocery store) and root round for lunch. I can't afford to eat out.

Anyway. Now for the real stuff: I've found myself a lordling! Can you believe it? His name's Trevor, and he's a viscount (??!), and looks like he could pose in Ralph Lauren ads. You know—absurdly handsome, with boyish features, perfectly silky hair that's longer on top and super short on the sides and back. He has my email address, and I'm waiting to see if he asks me out. Nothing so far . . .

I met him at a wedding I crashed at the Tower of London (!!!) yesterday, after almost getting run over by a lunatic faux Scot in an old van and a kilt. Long story. Will—the kilted madman—is a huge, rumpled guy who grows vegetables and is Trevor's cousin. A poor relation, obviously, from some twisted branch of the family tree. He seemed out of place at the wedding, and doesn't have many social skills. Doesn't seem to notice the lack, either. Trevor implied that he's unstable. I don't know if I believe that—they seem to hate each other, and I wouldn't take either's word about the other as being unbiased truth. Will wanted to take me for a drive in the country, but I slipped away before he could make me promise anything. Maybe if I'd gone, I'd have ended up murdered in the back of his van. (ha ha. not really! he grows organic lavender, for heaven's sake, and has a dog. how dangerous could he be?)

The one thing I'm worried about (besides anyone figuring out I wasn't really invited to that wedding) is my clothes. If Trevor DOES ask me out . . . I may *have to go shopping. What is hip and hot in London? I have no idea, and probably can't afford it, whatever it is. I don't want to look like a rube, though.*

    How goes the job search? Let me know how you're doing. I wish you were here. It's lonely at my B&B, and the place is run by a weird old witch. I think I mean that literally. The place is being renovated and I sometimes hear strange bumps in the night, but I never see a soul other than my landlady. It's freaky, I tell you.

Love,
Katy

http://www.oprah.com/email/reach/email__reach__
fromu.jhtml
Your Question:
Please do not exceed 2000 characters

———————————————

Dear Oprah,

I wanted to let you know how your show has touched my life. I'm an unemployed tech writer from Seattle, and have taken seriously your advice to discover my passion, and live my best life. Thanks to you, I am now in London, about to embark upon a love affair with a viscount. He's handsome and rich, and is going to give me the life I've always dreamed about. Fairy tales CAN come true! You just have to believe.

    I carry a picture of you, Oprah, around in my

purse. You really are my personal angel, and I say a little prayer to you every night before I go to bed.

> My thanks and love,
> Katherine Orville
> (SUBMIT)(CANCEL)

From: Rebecca Treinen
To: Katy Orville
Subject: Re: Prince Charming?

Dear Katy,

I can't believe it! I would have bet $1,000 that you wouldn't see any aristocratic bachelors, much less speak with one. You MUST let me know if he asks you out. Do you think he will? Why am I even asking? I imagine good-looking men in England are just as likely to be "I'll call you, really," jerks as the guys here. Who knows what goes on in their roast beef brains?

The issue of the handsome viscount aside, what's going on with this Will guy? You seem to know a lot more about him than about Trevor (and Gah! on the name. Trevor? You could marry a Trevor?). Are you sure you aren't just a little bit attracted to Will? He sounds more your type. No offense.

As for clothes: don't worry what Trevor will think. It's the women who run in his circle that will tear you to shreds, and they'll know if you're wearing knockoffs. *Stop being cheap for once and buy yourself a decent outfit. New.*

I've made it to the second round of interviews at one place, and have two more interviews scheduled elsewhere this week. Fingers crossed. I've also sent a resume to a place down in Oregon. God help me.

> Yours,
> Rebecca

P.S. *I found those M&M's in the coffee table drawer. I hope you don't mind, but I ate them.*

———————

From: Oprah.com
To: Katy Orville
Subject: Oprah.com has received your email

Dear Katy,

Thank you for your email! Your message is important to us. Unfortunately, due to the volume of email messages we receive every day, we cannot guarantee that you'll receive a personal response. Feel free to check out our Frequently Asked Questions for additional help.

Thanks again for writing to us!

> Sincerely,
> The Oprah.com Staff

———————

To: *Rebecca Treinen*
From: *Katy Orville*
Subject: *I think NOT!*

I am NOT attracted to William Eland, nutcase extra-ordinaire! He can't even support himself with his farming. I'd end up eating organic kale and cabbage for dinner for the rest of my life.

You should see Trevor. You wouldn't even suggest such a thing if you got a look at him. He's beautiful, and I'd be a viscountess if I married him (I had to look it up—yes, "viscountess" is the correct term).

It's okay that you ate the M&Ms. They have Smarties here, which are similar.

Katy

————————————

From: *Rebecca Treinen*
To: *Katy Orville*
Subject: *Re: I think NOT!*

Methinks the lady doth protest too much, about the farmer.

And besides, you'd better wait until Perfect Trevor asks you out before you start counting your viscountesses.

Rebecca

————————————

From: Trevor Mangold
To: Katy Orville
Subject: Thursday

Dear Katy,

Some friends and I are going to Charley Horse (St.
Martin's Lane) Thursday night, if you'd care to join
us. It's a private nightclub, but I'll put your name on
the list. Most of us should be there by 9:00.

   Not to worry, Will won't be there. ;)

Regards,
Trev

_____

To: Trevor Mangold
From: Katy Orville
Subject: Re: Thursday

Trevor,

I'd be delighted!
   :)

Katy

Chapter 8

Katy turned over the price tag on a brightly colored designer dress and groaned. £2,600? That was about $4,000. She could buy a car for that.

The dress didn't look like it was worth its price, but neither did it look like the mass-produced dresses in the cheaper stores she had visited. If even *she* could tell the difference in quality, Trevor's friends at the nightclub were certainly going to be able to tell.

She almost wished he hadn't asked her out. She could be riding double-decker red tour buses and that big ferris wheel, the London Eye, and eating crumpets and cakes instead of spending her day stressing about clothes she couldn't afford and people she didn't know how to deal with.

She had a flashback to meeting Trevor and

Will's aunt, and shuddered again at the mere thought. Aunt Agatha was the woman whose car she had mistaken for a cab outside Paddington Station. Angels be praised, she hadn't been able to recall who Katy was. Katy hoped she never would.

Agatha was one thing; Trevor was another. What in heaven's name was she supposed to talk about with a viscount? She still could hardly believe he'd asked her out.

Did this really qualify as a date though? She could imagine Rebecca's critical take on the situation: he wasn't picking her up; he wasn't buying her dinner; he wasn't taking her to a movie or a play or a symphony. He wasn't taking her *anywhere*.

Will was the one who had made a real offer.

Will, who might or might not be a lunatic, but was definitely poor. And built like a marine. Ohhh, those thigh muscles. . . .

She sighed, and wandered deeper into the vast designer collections at Selfridges, a department store on Oxford Street. She'd been to Harrods and Harvey Nichols earlier in the day, and been overwhelmed by the crowded goods and customers. She'd wanted to do nothing but escape. The displays at Selfridges were more spread out, the rooms quieter, and she could look at clothes here without feeling like security and half a dozen sales clerks were eyeballing her every move.

She couldn't even *see* a sales clerk, for that matter. She could hear two of them, though, just around an open doorway between display rooms. She inched closer, idly curious.

"I don't know where she gets off," one of the unseen clerks said, "making me work a ten-hour shift on Saturday, and a half day on Sunday. I haven't had a weekend off in three months!"

"Shhhh! Melanie, you're going to get yourself sacked."

"I'm almost beyond caring, I am. I'd like to see the cow find anyone else willing to work under her. I haven't had a pay raise in a year, and I bloody well deserve it. Need it, too."

"I know." The second woman made sounds of regret. "Sorry, sweetie, but my break's over and I've got to get back to cosmetics. See you later?"

"Yeah," the unseen Melanie said, still plainly angry with her supervisor.

"Stay out of trouble."

"Mm."

The worried friend sighed, and then there was quiet. A moment later the previously unseen Melanie came around the corner, stopping abruptly when she saw Katy staring at her.

"May I help you?" Melanie asked, her cheeks coloring, but her head raised in that arrogant, look-down-the-nose posture that Katy was beginning to find familiar in certain British women, department store sales clerks chief among them. Melanie had ash-blond curls, wide blue eyes, and the face of an ill-tempered Shirley Temple.

Katy tried to smile, intimidated despite herself. "Thanks, I'm just looking."

"Perhaps I can help you find something. Is there a special occasion you're shopping for?"

"No, I— Well . . . I was invited to a nightclub, and I don't have anything appropriate to wear."

"Which club is that?"

"Charley Horse."

Melanie made a moue of her lips, eyebrows rising, and gave Katy a look up and down. "I see." She cocked her head to the side. "Is there a particular look you want to go for?"

Katy told herself there was no reason to be scared of Melanie. She was just a sales clerk, not a wild cougar. "I just want something that won't make me look like an outsider, and that I can afford. This stuff," she said, gesturing at the room around her. "I can't afford *any* of this stuff."

"Well, neither can I, so we're equal there," Melanie said, her posture relaxing. A grin crooked the corner of her mouth, surprising Katy. "What's your price limit, if I might ask?"

"I was hoping to spend no more than a hundred fifty pounds," Katy said, anticipating the response her answer would get.

"I can find you a pair of designer knickers for that, darling, but not a frock."

"I know."

Melanie took the dress Katy had been looking at off the rack and held it up against Katy's body.

"Wrong colors, and too long for someone your size. You're American?"

Katy nodded, wondering why Melanie didn't go away. She'd made it clear there would be no fat commission earned here.

Melanie put the dress back on the rack and flipped through the other garments. "This store was founded by an American, did you know that? Gordon Selfridge. A millionaire from Chicago." Melanie held a pea green dress with ragged woolly trim up against Katy then wrinkled her nose and put it back on the rack.

"Really, I'm just looking," Katy said. "I can't afford anything."

"I know, darling. It can't hurt to try a few things on, though, can it? I can at least give you an idea of what styles look good on you."

"You don't mind?"

"Why should I mind? They're not *my* clothes."

"Okay . . . well, thanks. I can use all the help I can get."

"So how did you get invited to Charley Horse?" Melanie asked, picking clothes off the racks and hanging them over her arm. Katy trailed after her, like a little girl shopping with her mother, and told her story.

As they moved from designer section to designer section, Melanie managed to dig out every embarrassing detail of Katy's quixotic quest, and by the time they were back in the dressing room, trying and discarding dresses, blouses, and tight pants, Melanie was laughing so hard she had to sit down.

"Those brainless twits," Melanie said. "They haven't a bloody clue, have they?"

Katy shrugged, palms turned helplessly up, feeling a bit guilty that she had tricked the unsuspecting wedding guests.

"Trevor Mangold, of all the . . ." Melanie slouched in the dressing room chair. "I've seen him in *Hello!* and *Tatler*. He's sometimes in the *Mirror* and the *Sun*, too, with a supermodel or movie actress on his arm. Or with him on *their* arm—however you want to look at it. He's a well-known playboy."

"Really?" Katy asked, feeling a sick emotion she couldn't quite sort out. "He's out of my league, then, isn't he? With my looks, I don't have a chance."

"Maybe if you were filthy rich," Melanie said with ruthless honesty. "The aristos always like money, no matter that they pretend to be above talking about it."

"But I'm not rich, obviously."

Melanie narrowed her eyes at Katy, tilting her head to the side. "It doesn't *have* to be obvious, does it?"

Katy looked at the tag on the blouse she had on: £450. She shook her head, feeling hopeless. "Maybe the nightclub will be very dark, and they won't notice the knockoffs I have to buy."

"That's not what I meant," Melanie said, biting a hangnail. "Let me think a minute."

"Even if I *did* fool him, he'd have to find out

eventually that I have no money. He wouldn't be too happy to find out I'd lied."

"You're not going to lie. You're just going to refrain from sharing unnecessary information. Now, hush, sweetie, and let me think."

Katy bit her lip, frowning at herself in the mirror. She wasn't feeling too confident about the proposed charade. The truth would come out sooner or later, she was sure, and what would they think of her then?

In the mirror, Katy watched curly-headed Melanie as she squinted and schemed. If the clerk could come up with some way of dressing her up on the cheap, it *could* be an awful lot of fun. And when would she ever get another chance to go to an exclusive nightclub with a viscount? She'd be an idiot to pass this up out of fears of embarrassment. Even if she did end up humiliated, at least she'd have a story to tell afterward, when she was back in the cubicle.

And look at Will. All those snooty people accepted him despite how strangely he dressed.

She squelched the tiny part of her that piped up that Will had liked her Goodwill clothes just fine, and wouldn't have wanted her to change them. Will would probably even like her Wonder Woman nightshirt.

Or maybe not. Men were strange about lingerie. Maybe he'd want her to wear a pink lace teddy, with a thong up her behind. You never knew.

And why was she even thinking about it?

Without much enthusiasm, Katy took off the blouse and tried on a tight black Dolce & Gabbana dress. The shoulder straps and part of the bodice looked like a bra peeping out of the frock—a bra sadly empty of voluptuous flesh.

Melanie picked up the liquid-padded bra that Katy had discarded in order to try on the dress, holding it from a fingertip as if it were a rotten banana peel. "Why did you buy this thing?"

"I can't imagine!" Katy said, gesturing to her chest. She'd bought the bra especially for this trip, spending three times as much on it than she'd ever spent on a bra in her life. She'd wanted to look her best. "I don't even have a bosom to recommend me to Mr. Trevor Mangled Lord Whatever, who dates supermodels."

Melanie waved away her protest. "This is not Hollywood. You can be flat chested and even a little overweight, and no one cares as long as you're wearing the right clothes. It's the clothes, darling, that let them know who you are. You're going to a private London club with the aristos, not to the Playboy Mansion in Hollywood."

"Small blessing," Katy muttered.

"Chin up, sweetie. I think I have a plan," Melanie said, straightening up in the chair. "I'll let you *borrow* the outfits you need, and then you return them to me before the store opens in the morning. I'll reattach the security and price tags, and no one will ever know they were gone."

Katy gaped at her. "But— Won't you lose your job if you're caught?"

"It's not like no one here has ever done it before—I don't just mean the clerks, either. At least half the returns are by rich women who only wanted to wear a frock for a single night and didn't want to pay for it. And besides, it'll be worth the risk."

"Just to help me?"

She laughed. "No. Because you're going to do something for me, in return."

"What?" Katy asked, wary. Melanie was scaring her.

"Just don't spill anything on the clothes, for God's sake," Melanie said, ignoring the question. "And don't sweat. And don't wear this bra thing," she said, again holding up the offending piece of lingerie. "If it springs a leak, you'll have to pay for a two-thousand-pound dress. We'll get you some stick-on breast lifters instead."

Katy covered her small breasts with her hands, as if to protect them.

Melanie chewed the nail of her index finger, examining Katy. "We have to do something about your hair. I have a friend who's a stylist. She'll fix it. And I can have my friend in cosmetics do your makeup. We have to find a 'look' for you. Something to make you stand out, but in a posh way."

"But what do you want me to do in return?" Katy repeated. It felt like Melanie was rushing her toward a cliff, intent on throwing her off, and she didn't know whether there was a parachute strapped to her back. "I don't have to do anything illegal, do I?"

"Not to worry," Melanie said, with a wicked smile. "You'll get everything your ambitious American heart desires."

Somehow that didn't sound like such a good thing.

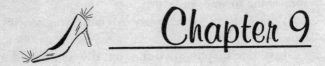# Chapter 9

Will put down the portable phone and stared blankly across his aunt's back garden. It was a pleasant late afternoon, white cumulus clouds drifting across a sky of deep turquoise, the small garden lush with leaves and flowers. His lawn chair was half in shade, half in sun; Sadie was napping on the small patch of grass; Aunt Agatha's housekeeper had just brought him a tray of tea and cakes; and he should have been content.

He was anything but.

He had talked to Marjorie's new mother-in-law, and neither she nor her husband had ever heard of Katy Orville. They had never heard of any Orvilles whatsoever. They did have American friends who had been invited to the ceremony and who had been unable to attend, but they did not live on the West

Coast, and to the best of her knowledge never had.

Will had called those Americans anyway, only to hear once again that no one had heard of Katy Orville.

He'd tried to search for her on the Internet, but quickly realized "Katy" could be spelled a variety of ways, and was likely short for another name anyway. She could be Katherine or Katharine or Kathleen or Kaitlin or Katerina, or all those names over again, spelled with a C.

He'd walked the streets of Mayfair, hoping to catch sight of her. He'd lingered on South Audley Street until a bobby had come and told him there'd been a report of a suspicious fellow loitering about and could he move along, please?

His last desperate ploy was to call the headquarters of Microsoft and ask if they had a Katy Orville in their employ. He'd been told that they did not give out information on their employees.

He was at a loss as to what to try next, but something inside him refused to let it go. It wasn't that he wouldn't give up on finding her; he *couldn't*. He didn't know if it was something about her, or the mystery of who she was, or his fury that Trevor had scared her off and he couldn't stand to let his cousin win.

Whatever it was that held him locked in this pursuit, he was powerless to escape it.

"William. William!"

He jerked out of his daze, turning to see Aunt Agatha looking at him with concern.

"Didn't you hear me calling you?" she asked.

"Sorry, no. My thoughts were elsewhere."

A wrinkle of worry creased between her brows, and she sat in another of the wrought-iron chairs. "I've never seen you like this, William—at least not over a girl. You were like this when you moved to Marreton House and started your little salad operation, and you nearly worked yourself into a collapse."

"Bollocks," he said without heat.

"It is *not* bol—It is not nonsense. You didn't eat and you lost weight, you were so focused on that one goal. Now you're doing it again, and it's not healthy."

"I thought you wanted me to get involved with a woman," he said, barely registering her concern, working on the problem of how to find Katy.

"You can't spend the entire summer wandering Mayfair. What about the farm?"

He blinked, and looked at her. "*You* are encouraging me to go back to the country? What about all your efforts to set me up with someone?"

"There are other 'someones' than one American girl you briefly met at a wedding. How about Helena? You enjoyed seeing her again, didn't you?"

"We have no interest in each other."

"Why ever not? I thought you got on well as children."

"That was a long, long time ago. No, I'd like to see Katy once more. Just once."

Aunt Agatha made a *tch* sound of dismissal with

her tongue. "You don't even know the girl. Such a fuss you're making, over a stranger."

A tickle of memory came back to him. "When I introduced her to you, didn't you say she seemed familiar?"

"Well, yes, for a moment—"

"Where had you seen her before? Can you remember?" he asked eagerly, sitting forward. "Please, Aunt Agatha, try to recall."

"I don't know. In a shop, perhaps? One sees hundreds of faces in a day if one goes out."

"We don't remember them, though. We take no note of them unless there is a reason for it."

"I don't think I was surprised that she was American, so I must have known that. . . ." She was quiet, her gaze focused inward, and then her lips parted, her eyebrows rising. "Oh! Oh, dear me, that must have been *she*."

"What? When?"

Aunt Agatha's mouth pursed in disapproval, her posture stiffening. "That horrible little girl who thought my car was a cab, outside Paddington Station. I was waiting to pick up Harold when the door opened and this . . . this . . . *girl* tried to get in."

Will laughed in surprise.

His aunt cast him a cold glance. "It gave me a terrible fright, having the door yanked open like that by a stranger."

"Oh, I'm sure," he said, nodding, lips pressed tightly together to contain himself.

"I don't know how she could have mistaken a Bentley for a taxicab. Really, I don't know at all."

"The light on the roof wasn't on?"

"It was not at all humorous, William. I had to make a long loop round the station to get away from her—she could have been a thief, for all I knew. Americans are so violent. Poor Harold had to wait fifteen minutes on the pavement until we could make our way back." She huffed out an offended breath. "It's just as well that you can't find the girl."

He looked his aunt in the eye, holding her gaze. "I *will* find her."

His aunt's gaze was steady, but then her eyes widened for a moment, as if something had occurred to her. She closed her lips and dropped her gaze, rubbing at an imagined spot on her immaculate skirt.

"What is it?" he asked.

"Hmm?"

"You looked like you were about to say something."

"Did I? No, I was just thinking that she is very lucky, this Katy, to have you so eager to find her. You're not a poor catch, dear boy. Some girls might even have the wrong motives in pursuing you. Americans have a long history of coming to England and shopping for a title."

"Katy very clearly is *not* pursuing me. She could have flown back to the States by now, for all I know."

"Perhaps she's clever," Aunt Agatha mused. "It's the mouse who runs who catches the eye of the cat."

Will gave her a stern look.

Aunt Agatha sighed. "Never mind me. I'm from a time of deeper social intrigues, and I'm almost afraid I miss them." She leaned forward and patted his knee. "If this means so much to you, of course I'll help. But do this for me: go back to Marreton and tend to your gardens for a few days. Rest. I will see what I can discover through friends. I know everyone. Someone surely will know of this Katy creature."

He leaned forward and kissed her on the forehead. "Thank you."

Will put a mug of steaming tea on the corner of his desk and sat down, switching on the computer. He was in his cluttered office, the house so quiet he could hear each breath of Sadie, lying on her cedar chip dog bed near his feet.

It had been a long drive through heavy traffic to get out of London, and he was relieved to be back in the quiet comfort of home. Aunt Agatha had been right about that: he needed time at Marreton for his own peace of mind.

He was beginning to wonder if Aunt Agatha hadn't been right about letting go of this whole Katy-pursuit business as well. Now that he was back home, there were a dozen other things that seemed more pressing. The house and farm needed his attention. He had several agricultural student interns to help with the chores—as close as you could get to free labor—but the farm didn't run itself.

A stray thought flitted through his mind: if no one could remember inviting Katy to the wedding, could that mean that she hadn't been invited at all? He suddenly realized that *he* had been the one who had assumed she was a guest.

But if that were so, then why had she gone along with the mistake? Was she nutty? A curious bystander?

Or maybe . . . maybe she *had* been a little interested in him? It seemed unlikely. He'd almost run her over and been dressed like a madman, after all.

He connected to the Internet and downloaded his email. There were a few notes from friends, a king's banquet of spam, and a note from Trevor.

A sour feeling seeped into his belly. He opened the message.

From: Trevor Mangold
To: William Eland
Subject: too bad

Dearest Cousin,

I hear you finally returned to your worm farm this afternoon. What a pity! Guess who's going to be at

Charley Horse later tonight with yours truly? I think she's quite looking forward to seeing me again.

Not to worry, I'll take good care of her.

Regards,
Trev

"Bastard!" Will said, slamming his fist on his desk, sloshing tea onto the antique surface. He rubbed at it with his sleeve, eyes going back to the hateful email.

The ass must have known how to find her this whole time!

He looked at the clock. Blast! It was nearly 8:00 P.M. Trevor must have been counting on him getting the message too late to do anything about it. Had the man had spies posted to watch his every movement?

He narrowed his eyes at the screen. If he took the motorway, it was only an hour to get to London. Another half hour at most to get into the city proper and park. They'd still be at the club, wouldn't they?

Most likely. He'd have to figure out a way to get in, though, since he wasn't a member and he knew Trevor would enjoy refusing him entrance.

A slow smile spread across his mouth, imagining the prat's face when he saw Will join his depraved little party.

He shut down the computer and ran up the stairs to his room, pulling off his frayed pullover as he went. Sadie followed after him, dark eyes curious.

He jerked open the door to his armoire and dug through the contents, looking for something, anything, to wear. The only choice was one of his too-small wool suits from his days in the city. He pulled a charcoal jacket off a hanger and forced it on. He could barely move his arms and it gaped open in front, but at least the length was right.

He remembered a dark green Italian shirt his aunt had bought him for Christmas a couple years ago and dug that out as well. It fit a little better, but had a greasy gravy stain on the front that he'd neglected to have cleaned.

Damn. Maybe the jacket would cover it.

The matching trousers still fit—a little loose in the waist, but a belt would take care of that—and his leather shoes. He pulled them on, threw a few things in an overnight bag, and dashed out of the room without so much as a glance in the mirror.

"Come, Sadie! We're off again to London!"

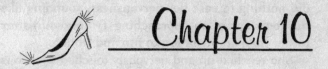 # Chapter 10

"Katy Orville," Katy said to the doorman, and shivered. Her arms were bare to the night air, and her chiffon halter dress dipped so low in the back that she was afraid a stray breeze might reveal the cleft of her buttocks.

The doorman checked his list and nodded, allowing her to pass through the starlit entryway. Carpet, walls, ceiling—all were black, lit by a scattering of tiny lights that resembled stars in the firmament. A dark blue Plexiglas path, lit from beneath to make it look like a river, led through the darkness. Katy followed it around a corner, treading carefully in her high-heeled sandals of muted gold.

The blue path led into a hallway with waterfalls for walls, the water sliding down glass panels. Behind the moving water a film of galloping wild horses played against the glass, hard to make out under the shifting water.

From ahead, the thumping bass of dance music carried down the corridor, echoing in her chest. It did nothing to ease her nervousness, sounding like the footsteps of an approaching *Tyrannosaurus rex* rather than an invitation to fun and frolic.

She reached up and nervously touched what was left of her hair, playing with the short wisps above her ear as if she could tug it out long again. Melanie's stylist friend had given her a pixie cut straight out of the early '70s, and then used a straightening solution to flatten Katy's curls. A deep auburn dye had followed. Katy thought she now looked like a redheaded Mia Farrow in *Rosemary's Baby*.

New eye makeup emphasized the big-eyed waif look, and the dress—worth nearly £5,000—made her feel like Tinker Bell in Disney's *Peter Pan*. It was dark green paisley, with a necklace of green malachite beads holding up the halter. The floaty chiffon skirt flowed loose and jagged to just above her knees.

With the stick-on breast lifters, only chiffon and a thin layer of sticky plastic separated her nipples from the eyes of the world.

She didn't feel like Katy Orville. She felt like a half-naked freak about to walk into a nest of vipers. More of the vipers were slithering down the corridor behind her, their voices loud.

A mirror at the end of the corridor reflected her new image. She stopped and stared, feeling disconnected from the girl in the mirror. That couldn't be her. That girl in the mirror was so pretty.

She moved her hand and touched her nose. The body parts seemed to be her own.

"Have you lost yourself?" a laughing male voice asked.

"I think so," she said, turning, and recognized Trevor. Relief surged through her. She was about to greet him, but then saw that his eyes were going over her dress, lingering on the nubs of her chilled nipples. She waited until his eyes rose again to her face, but when they did he just winked at her and moved past.

Her mouth dropped open, and she watched him sling his arm around the neck of a tall brunette and saunter with the rest of his group into the nightclub.

Trevor hadn't recognized her!

A smile curved her lips, delight simmering within. She felt deeply flattered. Trevor had ogled her as if she were a stranger worthy of his notice. Tonight she was not dowdy, clueless Katy Orville, beneath the notice of wealthy playboys. Tonight she was a trendy Somebody in a London hot spot.

She stepped into the club proper, and bumped shoulders with a man going by the other way. She glanced up into the face of Ioan Gruffudd, the Welsh actor she'd put all over her Life Map and seen in her Oprah dream. She gaped.

"Your pardon," he said, touching her briefly on her bare shoulder. And then he was gone.

She blinked after him, quickly losing sight of his head of dark curls. It was a message from Oprah. This was where she was meant to be.

Loud music, darkness, flashing lights, and pockets of illumination made a mass confusion of the nightclub. Movie screens high on the walls and slanting toward the ceilings showed silent films of more horses running free and of stallions fighting. The constant movement made her dizzy.

Tables and booths filled balconies and decks overlooking the dance floor on the lowest level. The place was full, but not yet packed. There were still a few empty tables, and the dancers had space to move. A DJ oversaw operations from his high-tech aerie against one wall.

Her silk drawstring purse bumped against her thigh, reminding her of what was inside: Melanie's price for the loan of the dress. She didn't know how she was going to pull it off. She was going to get kicked out of the club the moment she tried.

She spotted Trevor at a group of small tables that had been dragged together, a waitress already setting down drinks and a bottle.

She wove her way through chairs, narrowly missed getting a cigarette jammed into her thigh by a gesturing blond, and then was beside Trevor. He was talking loudly to one of his male buddies, oblivious.

She touched his upper arm. "Trevor."

His friend looked her over, and it was that diversion of attention that caught Trevor's own. He turned to her. "Hello again, darling!" He smiled, eyes flicking once again to her chest.

She felt conspicuous standing there, everyone's eyes slowly turning to her, conversation dying off. She snagged a nearby free chair and dragged it over, sitting by Trevor. His eyes widened. "Hello, hello!" he said.

"Don't you recognize me?" she half shouted over the noise of the club, a smile quivering on her lips.

For a moment he looked frightened, as if he might once have slept with her and forgotten her name. She again put her hand on his arm, leaning closer so that she need not shout. "It's Katy. Katy Orville."

He pulled back from her, staring, looking her over again. "Bloody hell! Damn, it *is*, isn't it? I say, Katy! Well done! Well done indeed!"

She laughed, savoring his shock, and leaned away so he could get a better look at her new self.

"I didn't know you. You look a completely different person," he said, plainly flabbergasted. "At the wedding you looked rather a frump, you know. I would never have guessed that this was what was hiding underneath that yellow suit and gaudy pin."

Her smile wavered. "One tries not to outshine the bride, you know."

"No fear of that! You looked rather a tip, and a suitable match for Wild Will, if you don't mind my saying. I'm glad to see the true Katy."

Her cheeks strained with the effort to keep smiling. She hadn't looked *that* bad, had she? That yellow outfit had felt more "her" than this one did. And at least she had chosen the yellow suit herself rather than been dressed like a passive doll, as she was now.

Trevor made the introductions round the table, and told everyone where he had met her. A few of them had been at the wedding as well. "Will Eland was running after her," Trevor added, "but he couldn't catch her."

"Is that why he was so cross?" one of the men asked, laughing.

"When isn't he cross?" Trevor answered. "The man is in a perpetual bad temper."

Glances were exchanged along the table, hinting at things unsaid. "He's not a bad sort, really," one of the women volunteered. "Just . . . eccentric."

"Like the rest of his family on his father's side," Trevor said. "He'll end up wearing his pajamas to the grocery, and that house is going to fall down around his ears."

"Well, I don't like him, either," another of the men said.

"Why not?" Katy asked, genuinely curious.

"Thinks himself a bit better than the rest of us."

"*Will?*" she cried in disbelief. "Have you seen that van he drives? I can't imagine he finds himself superior to *anyone.*"

"You saw the way he was dressed for the wedding, and what a mess he was," Trevor said. "It takes arrogance to appear like that at a formal occasion. You have to believe other people to be of lesser importance. It was his cousin's wedding, for God's sake. He could have made an effort."

She frowned at Trevor. "He probably couldn't afford to look any better."

"Couldn't afford to shave?" Trevor asked, his brow raised.

He had a point there. She still felt oddly disturbed by their criticism of Will, though. She wanted to defend him, but didn't know what else to say. These people clearly knew him much better than she did.

She looked round at the group. The women all had that high-headed posture that Katy found so annoying, even when they were lolling with drinks and cigarettes. They wore their clothes with the casual disregard that Melanie had coached her to affect herself, but Katy found it impossible to forget the cost of the garment lying against her skin. The women's hair was almost universally shoulder length and straight, some with highlights, none of it obviously styled.

A few of the youngest men looked to be no more than boys—one even had the full cheeks and small teeth of a child, though he must have been at least twenty. They were casual and beautiful and wealthy, and Katy wanted both to be accepted into their midst, and to push them all over the balcony rail for being self-satisfied snobs who had been born with everything and worked for nothing.

It felt like high school, and like she was sitting on the edge of the popular crowd. She was embarrassed that she wanted to be one of them, but there it was. She wanted their easy grace and their confidence. She wanted to be swept along in their midst as if it were her natural place, and she wanted to forget that she was a mere duck dressed as a swan.

Well, she would leave her duck self far behind, with Will, who was himself a duck if there ever was one. He seemed to like Plain Katy. Awkward Katy. Clumsy in the Crosswalk Katy.

The conversation flowed in voices raised to be heard above the thumping music. The few initial questions directed Katy's way trickled off, and she felt like she was slowly becoming invisible. She didn't know the people they were talking about, or the places. Trevor filled a clean glass for her from the bottle on the table. It was vodka, she saw now.

She sipped it for lack of anything else to do, listening to the talk of the others. Trevor seemed to have forgotten she was there.

"Are you feeling all right?" the brunette on her right asked after a while. Helena, Katy thought her name was. "You're terribly quiet."

"Oh, I'm fine—just a bit of a headache. All the noise and smoke, you know. All the moving lights." She *was* getting a headache, and it was better than admitting she had nothing to say. The vodka was already making her muzzy-headed, killing off any bits of wit she might have possessed.

"I've got something to make you feel better," Helena said, opening her purse. She took out a small mother-of-pearl pillbox, opening it to reveal an assortment of colored tablets. "Here." Helena held out a white unmarked tablet.

"Thanks. Can I take it with this?" Katy asked, raising her tumbler.

Helena shrugged. "Shouldn't hurt."

She put it on her tongue and swallowed, chasing the bitter, chalky pill with vodka.

Across the table, one of the other women ducked her head, putting something to her nose. She tossed her head back, breathing deeply. Katy's eyes widened. Was she using *drugs*?

A cold panic washed over her body. She turned back to Helena. "What was that?" Katy asked, voice trembling. "That tablet you gave me?"

"Only the best paracetamol money can buy," Helena said, laughing.

Cripes! What the heck was paracetamol? Was that some sort of amphetamine? Something like Ecstasy? She knew nothing about drugs, and hadn't even tried marijuana while in college. Her heart started to gallop. Should she try to throw it up? Where was the bathroom?

Helena took two more of the tablets out of her box, and swallowed them.

"You're taking *two*?" Katy asked.

"Did you want another?"

"No!"

"One barely does anything for me. Two doesn't do much, either." She poked through her pillbox, finding another couple of tablets. She took them.

"It's not like there's any risk of overdose at this level," she said, smiling almost apologetically.

Helena must have a terrible drug habit.

Katy sat motionless, trying to feel the effects the tablet was having on her system. Was she a little more light-headed? Were the lights swirling a little faster? Sounds getting fuzzier?

Helena stood and came around behind Trevor, wrapping her arms around his shoulders. "Come dance with me. I'm not going to sit on my ass all night."

He got up, peeling her arms from his shoulders and holding her hand. Katy felt like she was being abandoned, and right when she was in the throes of her first drug experience! She stared after them, willing Trevor to come back with all the passion of a dog with an attachment disorder.

Helena and Trevor had only taken a few steps when something or someone elsewhere in the club caught Trevor's eye. He stopped, stiffening, his face going slack with surprise. He dropped Helena's hand and turned back to Katy.

"How rude of me. Your first time here, and I leave you alone amongst strangers. Helena, you won't mind, will you? Let me break Katy's dance-floor virginity."

Helena looked like she did mind, very much, but she tossed her head and grabbed the arm of the baby-faced man, pulling him out of his seat. "Come, George, you've your own virginity to lose." He stumbled after her, his composure slipping.

Trevor held out his hand to Katy and a panicky sweat broke out all over her body. She was a horrible dancer. She knew that, she didn't need to gyrate in public among aristocrats, actors, and supermodels to have it confirmed.

Her hand shook as she put it in his and rose. She could smell her own fear sweat as she lifted her arm, no antiperspirant on earth being powerful enough to withstand it.

"Are you nervous about something?" he asked.

"Happy!" she lied, the thumping music banging on her head like drumsticks. At least she shouldn't be able to lose the beat.

Trevor led her down to the dance floor, pulling her into the midst of the crowd. He raised his arms and fell into synch with the other dancers, hips moving smoothly, torso undulating with the ease of a Chippendale dancer.

Katy fell back on the moves she'd learned at middle-school dances and shifted from foot to foot, moving her arms like a jogger in slow motion. The drug she'd taken seemed to be making her dizzy—or maybe it was the vodka. The floor seemed to tilt beneath her, and she bumped up against a woman her own height.

The face that turned to frown at her was Madonna's. Madonna watched Katy dance for a moment, raised a skeptical eyebrow, and turned away. Katy wanted to sink into the floor in embarrassment. Another wash of sweat broke out over her body. Oh, lord, she'd ruin the dress!

"Loosen up!" Trevor said, thrusting his pelvis at her.

Katy tried to move like Madonna was, but her shoulders felt disjointed from her body, her knees stiff and unbending. Her head bounced like a bobble-headed doll on a dashboard, her limbs jerking out of time with the beat.

Trevor put his hands on her hips and tried to get her to thrust and sway in tandem with him.

All she felt was a horrible embarrassment, their bodies failing to move together, and she knew his hands on her hips must be feeling every tense muscle and mistimed step.

When would the music end? It was going on and on and on . . .

A large hand landed on Trevor's shoulder, pulling them apart. Katy looked past Trevor at the man's face, and after a moment of confused, out-of-context familiarity recognized. Will! A cleanly shaven Will, at that. A warm flood of relief soaked through her body. She wanted to fling herself against his broad chest and let him sweep her out of this noisy, crowded, humiliating place.

"Where is she?" Will asked Trevor, ignoring her.

Trevor laughed, stepped out from between them, and pointed his opened hand toward her as if presenting a work of art.

"Will?" Katy said.

He blinked, and looked her over in shock. His eyes went to her hair, lingering there with a growing look of devastation. "What have you done to her?" he asked Trevor.

The corners of Katy's mouth pulled down, and she suddenly wanted to cry. She felt naked, and ugly, and stupid. Will was looking at her as if Trevor had turned her into a vampiress, and she would forever be a member of the unholy undead.

But then Will's eyes met her own, and his expression softened. He moved toward her, the force of his presence enough to shunt Trevor off to the side. He seemed oblivious to the dancers undulating round them, his dark green eyes focused only on her.

She reached up with one hand and pulled at her shorn locks. "You hate it."

"I could never hate anything about you," he said softly, his deep voice somehow audible despite the blaring music. She heard Trevor snort in derision, but Will ignored him, a pest beneath contempt. He lightly touched her cheek, sending a shiver running through her. "You look like you could be the fairy Peaseblossom from *A Midsummer Night's Dream*. You carry magic with you."

Tears started in her eyes, and she sniffed them back. From the corner of her eyes she could see Trevor pulling faces, and she knew that Will was being uncool, corny. She was a little embarrassed herself.

He felt like shelter, though. A large, strong, caring shelter that would never bend to outside forces.

That paracetamol must be making her goofy.

"Will you dance with me?" he asked.

"You dance?" she asked in surprise.

"After a fashion."

"I don't. I'm awful." She looked hopelessly at the other dancers. "I can't keep a beat. I can't move like that," she said over the noise, tilting her head toward a supermodel whose beautiful body writhed to the music.

"Neither can I." He took both her hands, standing in front of her. "Do you know how to swing dance?"

"I took a beginner's ballroom class once, but . . . I don't remember much." She glanced nervously round her, her cheeks heating. "We can't do that *here*."

"It's a dance floor, isn't it?"

"But—"

"Mirror my steps," he said, and started to move.

She looked down at her feet. Memory clicked in, and a couple of eight counts later, the basics were fresh in her mind. She looked up into his face. "We can't do this here!"

"You're embarrassed," he stated, still moving, still leading her along with him.

"Yes! I can't dance anyway, and now you're making me do the wrong one!"

"Stare at my chin."

"What?"

He waggled his chin back and forth, catching her gaze. There was a dimple in it. She hadn't noticed that before. How did guys shave dimples like that?

Her feet kept moving, and with her mind distracted, her body unconsciously shifted directions in response to the cues his hands gave her. Why did he want her to look at his chin, anyway?

He spun her outward, pulled her back in, and twirled her. She laughed, surprised, and looked up into his eyes. Clean-shaven, she could see how handsome his features really were. They were cut from a more masculine cloth than those of the pretty boys at the club. He even smelled different. Those *boys,* even Trevor, did not have the same scent as a full-grown *male.*

Suddenly she began to feel a little shy. Maybe Will wasn't the safe, easy refuge she had thought. She was self-consciously aware of how much larger he was, how much stronger, how much in control he could be of her physically, if that was what he wished. And she'd seen already that he was someone who did exactly as he wished, the opinions of others be damned.

He frowned at her, and waggled his chin again.

She obeyed, and was comforted by the silliness.

Her gaze slipped down to the lapel of his jacket, and she saw that there was a moth hole in it. A smile curled her lips. No, there was nothing to be afraid of here.

She was enjoying herself. With Will leading, she didn't have to find the beat herself. She didn't have to gyrate and reveal her lack of freeform dancing talent. She simply followed and abandoned thought. Focused on his dimpled chin, she let herself shut out the presence of the other dancers. The noise and lights mingled with the vodka and whatever else was in her blood, forming a muzzy cocoon around her brain. Sense of herself was lost, and she happily let it go.

The music morphed, shifting beat and tempo, and she didn't know if it was her imagination or the paracetamol, but it sounded like "In the Mood"—that 1940s hit that was the music for every swing dance scene in World War II movies.

It was music her body understood and she spun and rocked, her feet moving without conscious intention. She looked up into his face and laughed, feeling a joy far greater than any she'd ever felt dancing before.

The music morphed back into a modern dance mix, and Will spun her toward the edge of the floor, then led her off it. She was breathing heavily, her face damp with perspiration—a good perspiration, this time.

"I'm going to take you someplace quieter," he said.

"What? No, I'm having fun. And what about Trevor?"

"He'll be fine."

Katy looked back among the dancers, and saw him enjoying the thrusting closeness of Helena. He glanced over at her and Will and smiled tauntingly, running his hand over Helena's buttocks.

How stupid of her to have thought tonight was any sort of date with Trevor. It was only what he'd stated in his email: an invitation to join a group of people at a nightclub.

Some of the magic of the evening dribbled away, her joy fading under that taunting bump and grind.

"Sure, let's go," she said flatly. "I need to use the ladies' room first, though." The vodka had worked its wiles on her bladder.

"I'll wait for you here."

She left Will, wondering now if the music really *had* changed to "In the Mood." Was the paracetamol playing tricks on her mind, making a moment feel more magical than it really was? Maybe it was what was making her feel so fragile now, too.

She got directions from a waitress to the bathroom, which was way down a dark hallway. She pushed her way through the door to the ladies' room and blinked against the bright lights. The room smelled of disinfectant and cigarette smoke, and was the same mustard yellow enamel she remembered from her high school's restrooms.

A look in the mirror under the fluorescent lights made her wince. Her eye makeup had smudged and her lipstick was all but gone. She made some touch-ups, then went into a stall.

As she hung her little drawstring purse on the hook, she remembered what was inside it: a camera phone.

Ah, fudge it all. As if the night couldn't get any worse, she still had *that* to do.

Cameras were not allowed in Charley Horse, to better allow celebrities and the aristos to let loose.

The rule did not cover camera phones, though, which were now often the only style of phone that Charley Horse's patrons carried. Melanie's price had been photos of the club and any famous faces. She'd given Katy a stack of tabloid magazines to study, to familiarize herself with the A-list of London.

The faces had meant nothing to her. The British celebrities looked no more special than the average young person on the street and no more beautiful, and their names had slipped entirely from her mind. Except for Madonna and Ioan Gruffudd, she didn't know if she'd seen a single well-known person.

She'd successfully forgotten about taking the pictures for most of the evening. It felt like spying, and she had vague worries about why, exactly, Melanie wanted the images so much. Was she a stalker? Or just a rabid fan?

It was probably harmless. After all, Melanie had taken several photos of Katy herself once her make-over had been completed.

Katy put her face in her hands, feeling ill. She'd be glad to get out of the club, go back to her B&B, and bury herself under the blankets in her dingy room.

Some women had come into the restroom while she was isolated in her stall, and now voices broke into her contemplation.

"He's looking for her right now," the first complained. It sounded a little like Helena.

Katy leaned to the right until she could see through the gap between stall door and frame. Yes, that was her. She could see both Helena and . . .

Cynthia, that was the other one. A tall, thin blonde with even thinner lips.

"I don't know why he bothers," Cynthia said. "She's like a frightened child, saying nothing, watching us with those big blank eyes."

Katy got a sinking feeling that they were talking about her. She silently pulled up her undies and inched closer to the door.

"You'd think she'd spent her life on a farm somewhere and this was her first trip to a city," Cynthia went on.

"I doubt it," Helena said sourly. "Did you notice her dress?"

"How could I miss it? It barely covers her."

"Her family must have money if she can shop that designer," Helena said.

"Do you think that's what attracts Trevor, the money?" Cynthia asked.

"I don't know what else it could be. She's not much to look at, and doesn't have the wits of a dead cow. She can't even dance, and you know what that says about how she'd be in bed."

Katy's face burned.

"What *was* that she was doing with Will Eland?" Cynthia asked. "*Swing* dancing? And I never thought I'd see *him* at a nightclub. I thought he preferred the company of vegetable marrows."

"Maybe that's why he likes Katy," Helena said, and laughed.

A tear spilled out of Katy's eye. She wiped it away and set her jaw against the threat of more. She slipped the camera phone out of her silk purse, positioning the tiny lens in front of the gap beside the door. The flip-up screen that faced her showed a perfect shot of the two women, both bending over the sinks, their faces reflected in the mirror. Helena was using a fingernail to scrape at something inside her nose.

Katy silently pressed the button to capture the image. There was no shutter, so there was no sound to give her away.

Cynthia raised her arm, sniffing at her pit.

Click click.

"I've never understood why you want Trevor so badly," Cynthia said, turning contemplative as she poked at a zit. *Click click.* "He treats you like crap half the time."

"He has commitment issues. We get close, things go well, then he gets frightened."

"Mm-hm."

"He's just not ready yet to settle down," Helena said, defensive. She adjusted her thong. *Click.*

"Or maybe not ready to settle down with *you*."

"How kind of you to say so," Helena said.

"Sweetie, you know I've thought all along that you could do better. I've never understood what you see in him, beyond the good looks. He's a woman-izer and thinks far too much of himself."

"You don't know him like I do. There's more to him than that," Helena protested.

"You think there's a heart hidden in there? I doubt

it. I don't know that he's ever loved anyone at all, and certainly none of the women he's slept with." Cynthia picked at her teeth, digging out a bit of food and examining it. *Click click click.* "He's had it too easy, women fawning on him all his life. It's spoiled him."

"You think he'd be more attracted to me if he had to work for it?" Helena asked.

"He's a man. They only value what they've had to fight for. I still don't think he's worth it, though. Someone like Will would treat you better."

Helena laughed. "Me, a farmer's wife? I don't think so. His idea of conversation is one grunt for 'No,' two for 'Yes.' I'd go mad. I'd go mad out in the country, too."

"Didn't he inherit his uncle's house?" Cynthia asked.

"Yeah. I haven't seen it, but I hear it's a wreck." Helena picked an eyelash out of her eye. "His aunt would like to see us together, though. She's always trying to force us into each other's company."

"Did you ever think that maybe Will was the force behind that? Maybe he's interested in you, and asked her to set things up."

Helena snorted, but Cynthia's words planted a seed of worry in Katy's brain. That taunting dance that Trevor had done, his hand on Helena's buttocks—had that been a message for Will as much as for her? Was she Will's second choice?

"You have to admit there's something kind of sexy about Will, though," Cynthia said.

"Clothes that don't fit? Long stretches of silence while he broods and looks disapproving?"

Cynthia leaned her hip against the counter, arms crossed over her chest. "Yeah, but look at the size of him. You've got to wonder what it'd be like to have someone that big and strong taking a ride between your legs. And he has a certain . . . focused determination about him. If he was intent on shagging you, he'd do a thorough job of it."

Helena chuckled but it sounded forced, like maybe the thought of Will hiking her legs around his hips held appeal.

A jealousy ruffled inside her. *Helena can't have him. He's* my *admirer. Stay away!* So what if she didn't really want him? He was hers.

"Just don't start telling me to shave my head, like that American leprechaun," Helena said. "Trevor and Will both, chasing after her like dogs. Who'd have thought?"

"Men always have been idiots," Cynthia said as they headed for the door. "And you know the type of crap that dogs will eat."

Katy held back a sob. Not even in junior high had she heard such cruel words spoken about herself, and she'd thought that to be the nadir of her existence.

She left the ladies' room a minute later, camera phone tucked into her hand. Hurt and anger boiled in her blood. She stepped out into the noise and throbbing lights, hating everyone in the nightclub. They were all extensions of Helena and Cynthia. She wanted everyone to suffer.

As she picked her way back to where she'd left Will, she paused again and again to take pictures of strangers, careful to appear only as if she were dialing a number. She had no idea who any of them were, but she caught them slouching, smoking, laughing drunkenly, hands roving inside each other's clothing, and even one sorry fellow passed out, sprawled on a red leather banquette, saliva dribbling out his mouth, a stain of vomit on his shirt.

She spotted Trevor, standing still and peering about. She didn't know if he was looking for her or for Helena, and she wasn't going to stay around to find out.

She put the camera in her purse as she reached Will. Relief was plain in his face when he spotted her.

"I thought you'd done another runner, like at the wedding reception," he said.

"Sorry I took so long. Ladies' rooms always seem to exist in a time warp."

"Are you ready to go?"

"More than you can possibly imagine."

Chapter 11

Will noticed Katy shivering as soon as they stepped out into the night air. He took off his jacket and draped it over her shoulders.

She looked up at him in surprise. "You'll get cold."

He shook his head. "Not at all." He had the burning fires of victory to keep him warm. He'd caught the prize and was dragging her away from his enemy. He was the lion with an antelope in his jaws, stealing it from the hyena; he was the alpha wolf. He was the victor.

He'd savor for years to come the look of surprise on Trevor's face when he'd appeared on the dance floor. Trevor had probably had plans to seduce Katy, if only to spite Will. It was deeply satisfying to have foiled any such plot, both because it saved Katy from hurt and because it meant he'd won the battle.

Trevor's fondling of Helena on the dance floor had been but the pouty gesture of the defeated.

Will glanced at Katy. She was gripping the lapels of his jacket from inside, snuggling down into it, nearly disappearing. Her eyes were on the pavement, although he doubted she even saw it. It looked as though her thoughts were directed inward.

Will had noticed how her spirits had fallen after seeing Trevor dancing with Helena. How that slimy bastard could have wormed his way into Katy's heart so quickly, he didn't know. It occurred to him that he should say something to get her mind off the wanker. He didn't know what, though. Maybe she needed a few minutes of quiet to work through whatever she was feeling.

One good thing: at least Trevor had shown her his true colors. Will needn't worry about competition from *that* quarter any longer. The field was clear should he wish to pursue his deer before she fled into the night.

Poor little deer. Someone had shorn her beautiful hair. She was lovely even with it gone, the cheekbones of her face and the blue-green of her eyes brought that much more to the fore. But he would have liked to dig his hands into that mass of red curls. He would never tell her of his disappointment, of course: some things a man was wise to keep to himself. And for the moment he was content just to have her by his side, walking down a quiet street, away from Trevor.

As Katy stayed silent, though, he began to worry.

Was she just unhappy or was she unwell? "Are you feeling all right?" he asked.

"I don't know. I think Helena drugged me."

"What!"

She looked up at him, woebegone. "She gave me a para—Paracet— Oh, I can't remember what it was called!"

"Paracetamol?"

"Yes, that's it! She gave me one of those but didn't tell me what it was until I'd already swallowed it. Now I feel all muzzy-headed and funny. I think I started hallucinating while we were dancing."

He choked on a burst of laughter. "Had you been drinking, too?"

"Does that make the effects worse?" she looked almost ready to cry.

"Depends what you mean by 'worse.' I think it intensifies the effect a bit."

"Ohhhh," she moaned. "I never even tried pot in college. Helena hates me. She wants to get me addicted to para—Para—Whatever."

"Katy, paracetamol is a pain reliever."

"Prescription? Illegally obtained?"

"No," he said, trying not to laugh again. "It's the same thing as, what do you call it in the U.S.? Acetaminophen?"

She looked at him in disbelief. "Tylenol?"

"Yes."

She put her free hand over her face. "Oh, jeez. I am such an idiot."

He mimicked a concerned father. "Now remember, darling, you don't have to give in to peer pressure and pop pills just because your friends do. It's always all right to say no."

She punched his arm. "It's not funny!"

"Was I laughing? I'm curious about your hallucinations, though. I'm not familiar with paracetamol 'trips,' not being a drug addict myself. What did you think you saw?"

"Shut up! And I'm not telling." A wry smile was beginning to curl her lips, though. "Oh, man. I'll have to email my friend Rebecca about this. I am *such* an idiot."

"It was an easy enough mistake to make," he said, laughter still vibrating in his voice.

She rolled her eyes.

He shrugged. "Just trying to make you feel better."

Now that he thought about it, though, maybe it wasn't so funny. Part of the reason he'd long ago lost interest in parties was because of the free-floating drugs. Katy was lucky that it *had* just been a paracetamol.

Katy looked around, taking note of their surroundings. "Where are we going?"

"I left Sadie in the van and want to get her. After that, I thought we might go to a pub I know with outdoor seating and a good view. Does that sound all right to you?"

"Sadie's with you?" she asked, brightening.

He nodded. At least she liked his dog. He wasn't so sure what her verdict on him was.

Katy released the lapels of his jacket and put it on properly, slipping her arms into the sleeves, then took hold of his elbow. "I love dogs. My last one died while I was in high school. A German shepherd. You've never seen such a wimpy dog—she was afraid of the cat and used to try to hide behind the toilet during thunderstorms. She didn't fit, of course, so I'd go in the bathroom and see this fat rump sticking out from under the tank."

"She and Sadie were soul sisters, then." He steered her down a dimly lit alley to where the garden of a church sat in shadowed quiet behind a wrought-iron fence, its path and garden beds empty of visitors.

Katy clung a little tighter to his arm, stopping to look into the churchyard. Her voice was hushed. "What is this place?"

"The back of St. Paul's. Covent Garden is on the other side. This side feels lost in time, doesn't it? These lamps are gaslights, and the churchyard is supposed to be haunted."

"I can believe it." She shivered, snuggling a little closer. "Why did you bring me here?"

"I thought you might enjoy it. I'd heard Americans love ghost stories." The snuggling was an extra bonus.

"We're so predictable, then?"

"Only sometimes, I assure you." They moved on. "Have you seen much of London since the wedding?" he asked.

"Some. I saw the Changing of the Guard at Buckingham Palace—doesn't every visitor to London have to do that? I walked through Hyde Park, looking for the statue of Peter Pan I'd heard was along the bank of the Serpentine, but couldn't find it."

"It's on the bank of the Long Water—same lake, but it changes its name when it goes into Kensington Gardens."

"Why did they put a statue of Peter Pan there?"

"The author, J. M. Barrie, lived near the gardens. Kensington Gardens was where Peter Pan flew away to as a baby. He didn't want to grow up to be a city man and work in an office."

She squeezed his arm. "Is that what you did? Fly away to a garden?"

"I tried the city, first."

"Really? What did you do?"

"I was a stockbroker."

She stopped walking. "No!"

"Yes, I promise you. And every minute of it was a slow death. Peter Pan was smart."

She shook her head, walking again. "They *say* money can't buy you happiness."

"And money can't buy you love."

"Are you quoting the Beatles to me? I don't know that I agree. Money can buy a chance for love to thrive."

"I pity the man or woman who makes such a purchase," he said with feeling. "It will turn out to be no bargain."

"And I pity the woman who marries a man with debts and no job," she retorted. "Unless she has a fortune of her own."

"That would be a slow death of another kind, for the man she married."

"What do you mean?" Katy asked. "You're not going to spout something chauvinistic about how the man has to be the breadwinner, are you?"

"It's not chauvinistic. Why do you American women all assume that basic male–female differences have something to do with chauvinism or inequality?"

"It seems pretty obvious to me that that's what this is."

"Call it what you wish," Will said. "The truth remains that no man who cares to call himself one likes to have his wife be the provider."

"There are plenty of men who earn less than their wives and are very happily married."

"I'm sure there are. But if you asked one if he *liked* it being that way, you'd get a different answer."

"I don't see why," she said, sounding prim and affronted.

A perverse part of him enjoyed getting a rise out of her, the debate getting his blood flowing. "Be honest with me. Be honest with *yourself*. Given the choice, wouldn't you rather have a husband who could provide for you? Wouldn't you find that more appealing than having to support *him*?"

Her expression was tight. "You're probably going to say now that a woman should be dumber than her husband, too, and not bother her pretty little head with complicated things like bank accounts."

He felt a slow smile spread across his face. "You're not answering the question."

"I don't *know* what the answer is, all right?" she said, her voice rising. She glared up at him. "We're force fed 'Girls and boys are equal, girls and boys can do everything the same' growing up, while there are social rules that say otherwise. Am I supposed to be self-sufficient or dependent? Both? How am I supposed to be both? How do I know where to be one and where the other?"

"Are you still expecting me to tell you things that you have to discover for yourself?"

"What's the use of your vast life experience if you don't share it with poor, ignorant fools like myself?"

"Where else did you go, besides Hyde Park and Buckingham Palace?" he asked.

"Are you changing the subject?"

"Did you go to the British Museum? The Victoria and Albert? The National Gallery?"

"You're a stubborn piece of work, you know that?"

"So I've been told—usually when someone doesn't succeed in making me do as they wish."

She made threatening sounds and waved her clenched fist in front of him. "There are ways to make you talk," she said.

"There are more persuasive uses for a hand than punching," Will said.

Her mouth made an 'O' of surprise. He was a little shocked at himself, too. His mind must be in the gutter.

"Will! You, you . . . ! Oh!" She moved as if to punch his arm, but then shook her hand open. She looked at it, at him, at it. Then, while he was still watching that hand, wondering what she'd do with it, she goosed him from behind with the other one.

He yelped, rising up on his toes. "That is *not* a persuasive use of the hand!"

She grinned at him and took his arm again. "I went to a few art museums," she said, as if nothing had happened. "Like the Tate Modern. I'd heard that was where all the people 'in the know' liked to go."

"What did you think?" he asked, trying to regain his composure and mostly failing. He hadn't been expecting an attack from that quarter.

"I think I must not know much about art. I hated everything there except Rodin's statue *The Kiss*, which for some reason is hidden away by the coat check counter on the lower level."

"You like Rodin?" he asked, the sculptor having always been a favorite of his own. He knew the piece she spoke of, and it was putting ideas into his head.

"He had such . . . passion. That sculpture, you look at it and you can feel what that man and woman are feeling. You want to climb right up there and take part."

"I know exactly what you mean," he said, feeling a tingling stir of arousal.

"I wanted to strip off my clothes, push that woman out of the way, and let myself be ravished by that hungry man."

"I'm sure he would have appreciated the offer," he choked out.

"Would he?" she asked, blinking innocently up at him. "I mean, does it really turn guys on to hear a woman say, 'Take me! I'm yours!' " She flung her arms out to the side as if making such an offering of herself.

His mouth went dry. Was she naked under that dress?

"Does it?" she asked again.

"What?"

"Turn them on?"

"Yes, damn it! What did you think?" God willing, she wouldn't look below his waist and see the evidence of his answer. He threw her question back at her. "Do women want to be ravished?"

"Sometimes. Depends on by whom." She laughed. "How unsophisticated of me, to like Rodin for the kink factor. I guess I like a bit of porn in my art."

"Who doesn't?" he said past his dry throat.

They walked by The Savoy hotel and turned onto the deserted lane running along the Victoria Embankment Gardens. The lane was his "secret" parking place in London.

"If I can ask," he said, trying to firmly shove thoughts of ravishment down, "why did you leave the wedding reception so abruptly?"

She was quiet. He looked down at her and saw her chewing her lower lip.

"You don't have to answer," he said.

She glanced up, flashing a nervous smile. Her eyes were large and luminous under the jagged fringe of her hair. "I don't really have a good answer to give. I didn't belong there. I didn't know anyone. I was embarrassed." She shrugged.

"You really *didn't* know anyone, did you?" he asked.

Her eyes went wide and then she looked away. Was that a confirmation that she was not an actual guest?

"I told you I didn't know anyone," she said. "I told you that at the Tower."

"I know."

She was tense now, closing herself off, and he didn't want that. Whether or not she was invited didn't really matter anyway, did it? He'd rather she was not one of that crowd. He'd rather that she was a true outsider. "My aunt recognized you."

Her lips parted, and even in the dim light he could see her face redden. He loved watching her emotions cross her face. She didn't seem to know how to hide them, or to even consider trying. It was a conversation without words.

"It took her a couple days, but she finally remembered seeing you outside Paddington Station. You tried to get into her car."

"Oh, don't remind me!" she cried, putting her hands to her cheeks.

He laughed. "She's quite recovered from the shock, I assure you. You did her a favor, really—I think it's the most excitement she's had in years. She's told all her friends about it."

Katy groaned.

"Her husband got a good chuckle out of it."

"Did she tell your parents about it, too? Were they at the wedding?"

"My parents died in a plane crash when I was eighteen."

Her lips parted in surprise, just as everyone's always did upon hearing that statement. Many didn't know how to react and tried to skip over the topic altogether.

Katy laid her hand on his arm. "I'm so sorry. My mother died three years ago, of cancer. It keeps right on hurting, doesn't it?"

Again, she had surprised him. "Yes, it does. And your father?"

She shrugged, and gave a crooked smile. "They divorced when I was small. He appears now and then, but we've never been close."

"I'm sorry."

"It doesn't matter. I've learned to take care of myself."

Somehow he found that the saddest thing she'd said. Despite the rich clothes she wore, he felt certain that she had not been a sheltered and coddled child. He'd known plenty of wealthy parents who had turned the raising of their children over to nannies and boarding schools, and wondered if her upbringing had been the same.

"Oh, there's your van. Sadie must be dying to get out."

She hurried ahead of him, putting her hands against the side as she peered through the partly opened window. The van shook and he knew Sadie was leaping from seat to seat, excited to see them. He came up beside Katy, watching her watch his dog.

"She's such a beauty!" Katy smiled up at him, and when she met his eyes, something seemed to change in hers. She stilled, uncertainty on her face.

The sexual tension that had momentarily died down sprang back to life. He moved closer and brought his hand along the side of her neck, his thumb brushing her jaw. Her skin was soft, and cool from the night air, but it warmed quickly under his touch. She tilted her face against his palm, into the shelter of his hand, her eyes closing. Her lips parted, and when her eyes slowly opened her pupils were large dark pools, inviting him closer. He leaned down, feeling her breath on his lips.

Sadie barked loud, her claws scrabbling on the glass. Startled, Katy jerked away.

Will frowned at his dog. Sadie panted and wagged, still scratching at the glass.

"You'd better let her out," Katy said, pulling his jacket closed as if suddenly chilled.

Cursing silently, he unlocked the door and opened it. Sadie leaped out and set off in bounding circles around Katy, her tail going like an eggbeater. When she finally settled down, she sat and leaned against Katy's leg, looking up at her with adoration, licking her hand.

"Bad dog," Will muttered. "Very bad dog."

Katy sipped her half pint of cider, hoping it would calm her. She'd almost kissed Will. Will! The madman with moth holes in his jackets and a questionable stain in the middle of his green shirt.

Sexual tension was humming between them, and she didn't know what to do with it. This was not who she wanted! Her body, though, was ready to tackle him in the shrubberies and have her way with him.

Even when he teased her or got all difficult, she still found pleasure in his company. She didn't know if it was because she knew he was attracted to her, which was a constant unspoken flattery, or whether she just admired the way he didn't give a fig what anyone thought of him. Maybe it was both.

They were seated outdoors at a pub along the south bank of the Thames, which they'd crossed via a pedestrian footbridge. They had a view of the city across the water, and the occasional lights of moving boats on the river.

Her hard cider was a vast improvement over the bitter beer she'd tried a couple times while eating at pubs—and it hardly even tasted alcoholic. She could grow fond of the stuff.

The waitress was waiting to take their food order.

"Nothing for me," Katy said.

Will narrowed his gaze at her. "I heard your stomach rumbling. Go ahead, order something."

"No, really, I'm fine." He'd insisted on paying for the cider—she'd only ordered a half pint, knowing that he might do so—and she didn't want him wasting any more of his scarce money on her. If she ordered, he'd insist on paying, there'd be a scene—it was easier to go hungry.

"What do you think, should I have the roast beef or the salmon?" he asked Katy.

"Salmon is hard to mess up."

"The salmon, then," he told the waitress. "And afterward, the apple tart with custard sauce. Make it two of each."

The waitress was gone before Katy could protest. "I said I wasn't hungry!"

"Who said any of that was for you?"

"Oh, like you're going to sit there and eat all that on your own."

His lips quirked.

"I don't need a man ordering my food for me," she groused.

"Apparently, tonight you did."

She lowered her brows. "You are being less than charming."

"Stubborn, perhaps?"

"Boorish." She tried not to smile.

"Because I don't like hungry young women stealing food off my plate?"

"I would never!" she protested.

"Your stomach would growl, and you'd give me that same woebegone, long-suffering look that Sadie does."

Katy crossed her arms over her chest, the action only serving to remind her that she still wore his jacket. She was being put in a decidedly dependent position. She wasn't quite sure that she entirely disliked it. "At least let me pay for my meal."

He locked eyes with her. "No."

"But—"

"No. Leave it there, Katy. I don't care how modern American men are: an English gentleman pays for his lady's supper."

She nibbled the corner of her mouth, then shrugged. She'd tried to save him the money. She'd made her point for womankind. What more could she do?

When the food came, her hunger belied her protests. She did love salmon. Her plate was empty long before Will's, and her eyes kept going to the door into the pub, searching for that waitress with the promised dessert.

To his credit, Will did no more than raise a brow at her vacuumlike inhalation of food. She twirled her fork and pretended to survey the choice morsels still on his plate.

"Don't even," he said.

Resigned to waiting for more food, she sat back. "So, are you a member of Charley Horse?"

"What? No, of course not!"

"How did you get in, then? Trevor said you wouldn't be there, so I assume he didn't put you on the list."

"He said that, did he?" She thought she heard him mutter something foul under his breath. "I went through the back, through the kitchens. I brought a box of greens with me. They're excellent camouflage."

"So you just walked in?"

"Kitchens are busy places. Who's going to bother stopping a man with a box of produce? Obviously he's supposed to be there."

"I would never have the guts to do something like that," she said in awe, forgetting her crashing of the wedding. "I'd be certain I'd be caught."

"By whom? The kitchen police? The people who work there don't care if an extra toff gets in. I'm sure they feel the lot of us could go to the devil."

"Do you feel like one of those, er, 'toffs'?" she asked carefully. "I mean, I know Trevor is your cousin, but you don't seem to fit in with that crowd."

"Thank you."

She didn't know if that was in answer to her question or to the waitress, who finally appeared with the tarts with custard sauce.

The sauce was like warm liquid vanilla pudding. Katy purred in pleasure when she tasted it. "Why do you dislike those people so much?" she asked, licking her spoon.

"I don't dislike most of them."

"Just Trevor?"

"You noticed that?" he asked.

"It's hard not to. What's so despicable about him? He doesn't seem much different from the others, except for being none too fond of you, either."

"We've never gotten along. Then, too, when we were sixteen I gave him a bit of a thrashing. He hasn't forgiven me."

"You beat him up?"

"Once or twice. I sometimes think of doing it again, for old time's sake." He looked like the thought gave him pleasure.

"But why'd you do it in the first place?"

"Someone had to."

"Why? What did Trevor do?" She was distressed by this violent streak. Did he just randomly pound on people he didn't like?

"He dealt in an ungentlemanly manner with a young woman."

Her brows drew together. "What do you mean, exactly?"

"Suffice it to say that even at that age he had a reputation for womanizing. I feel sorry for any woman who gives her heart to him."

"Poor Helena, then."

He looked at her in surprise. "Helena? Is she in love with him?"

"I don't know if she's in love, but certainly interested."

He shook his head. "She should know better."

"Who ever knows better?" Katy asked. "I don't think that's how it works."

He appeared distracted by her tidbit of gossip, and again an ember of jealousy flared to life. Had there been some interest between the two of them before she had arrived?

She didn't want to think about it. She slipped Sadie a bit of tart crust under the table.

"You'll make a beggar out of her," Will said.

"Ha. I already saw you give her some."

He looked at his watch. "Are you done? There's something I'd like you to see."

"Now?" It must have been nearly midnight.

"It's one of the great sights and sounds of London."

"Okay."

They walked some ways down the waterfront, Sadie trotting contentedly at their side, her leash on Katy's wrist. Katy's feet hurt in the high-heeled sandals she had purchased, knowing they'd be unreturnable after an evening out, but curiosity about this London "sight" drove her on.

They climbed cement steps up to a bridge over the river, and she suddenly realized where they were. "It's Big Ben!" she cried, clutching at Will's arm. "And, and . . . this bridge!"

"Westminster Bridge," he said, leading her down the sidewalk until they were above the middle of the Thames.

The view of the clock tower was the same one she'd seen a thousand times in ads and movies, its face glowing ivory against a blue-black sky. The streetlamps of the bridge were in an ornate Victorian style, three lamps to each post, waiting for a good pea-souper of a fog to roll in.

"It makes me think of the Disney version of *Peter Pan*," she said, "where Peter takes the children flying past Big Ben."

The clock hands reached midnight, and the chimes in the tower started to ring in a melody familiar to her from every grandfather clock she'd ever heard. A shiver ran through her, and Will pulled her gently into the circle of his arms.

She looked up into his eyes just as the deep bell began to toll the hour: *bong . . . bong . . . bong . . .*

Oh, goodness, was he going to . . . ?

Without a by-your-leave, he bent his head down to hers, his lips capturing her own. The kiss was warm and tender and she felt weak in his arms, something going liquid and helpless inside her.

. . . *bong* . . . *bong* . . . *bong* . . . *bong* . . .

The bell vibrated through her as the kiss deepened. She made a soft sound in the back of her throat, bringing her arms up around his neck. Will's hand on the small of her back pressed her close to him, his mouth moving on hers, coaxing her lips apart.

. . . *bong* . . . *bong* . . . *bong* . . . *bong* . . .

The skilled invasion of his tongue brought an answering rush lower in her body. Her legs were going weak, her senses wanting only to continue this forever. She felt the hard ridge of him against her belly and moaned into his mouth, wanting him to take her right there, against the railing of the bridge.

Bong.

The final peal of the bell echoed into the night, and Will pulled away. She almost whimpered, wanting to pull him close again and drink more deeply of pleasure.

"Come with me tomorrow, out into the countryside," he said. "If it's castles you want, I'll take you to one where you can still see where the knights used to joust."

At that moment she would have agreed to anything, her mind in a haze of unsated desire. "Yes, all right."

"I'll pick you up at about nine?"

A bit of sense fluttered back into her brain. "Ah, no . . . I have a few errands I have to run." She had to return the dress to Melanie, and she still didn't want anyone to see the sorry little B&B where she was staying. "I'll meet you at ten, in front of the Dorchester."

A cab was coming down the bridge, its roof light on. She waved to it, and it pulled over.

"I'll drive you home," Will said.

"My feet would never make it back to the van," she said by way of excuse. She ruffled Sadie's ears and handed the leash back to Will.

He caught her around the waist and kissed her again, hard and quick, stealing her breath from her.

When he released her, her body cried out in protest. He opened the door for her, and she all but fell inside. He handed money to the cabbie before she could protest, and gave her a long look before closing the door.

The cab pulled away from the curb and Katy put her hands to her lips, as if to hold his kiss there.

"To Titania's Bower," she told the driver.

"Titania's what? You're having me on. No such place in London."

"South Audley Street," she said. "I'll show you."

She leaned back against the seat and tried to make sense of it all.

Chapter 12

"Well done, Katy," Melanie said, going through the images stored on the phone. "There's Helena Dawby picking her nose—she's the granddaughter of a royal duke, and her mother was an Italian countess. And look at the heir of the Marquis of Salingford, sprawled like a drunkard! Brilliant! And *Madonna*? A bit passé, but still grabbing attention."

Katy felt slightly ill about what she'd just handed over. They were sitting in a busy coffee shop a couple blocks from Selfridges. The green dress was in a bag on the floor between them, like a briefcase to be passed between two spies.

Melanie pressed buttons on the camera phone and sent the pictures to an email address.

"What are you going to do with the pictures?" Katy asked, not sure she wanted to know. The anger and loathing she had felt for the people at the club last night had faded, other emotions having since overwhelmed her.

"I'm not going to blackmail anyone. Don't worry." The upload completed, Melanie slid the phone back across the table to Katy, along with a charger. "I forgot to give you that before. I wouldn't want your batteries to go dead."

Katy nudged the phone back toward her. "I don't think I'll need it. I don't think I'm going to get invited to any more clubs."

"Why not?" Melanie asked.

"They thought I was boring."

"Darling, 'boring' isn't going to matter anymore."

"What? Why?"

Melanie sipped her coffee, a wicked smile playing on her lips. "Tomorrow, pick up a copy of the *Weekly Moon*."

"Is that a tabloid?" Katy asked in apprehension.

"A very well-paying one," Melanie said.

"What did you do?" Katy whispered in horror.

Melanie made a face. "Oh, pish, don't make such a fuss. I've served you well, is what I've done. There won't be any questions about party invitations after that paper comes out."

"What did you tell them about me?" Katy cried.

"You'll just have to wait and see," Melanie said primly. Then she shrugged. "I don't know what they'll decide to print. I didn't write the article myself, after all."

Katy dropped her face into her hands and groaned.

"Stop that. And take the phone. You never know what interesting things you may come across."

"I don't want to do this again," Katy said. "No more pictures."

"Never say never, darling. Feel free to use the phone to make calls—consider that my little gift to you."

"A gift with a thousand strings attached."

"Nothing in this world is free."

Katy looked at her watch, leaving the phone on the table. "I've got to go."

"Where?"

"No place of interest to you."

"Getting touchy, are we?"

Katy sighed, and decided to be civil. It was her own fault she was in this situation, after all. "A friend is going to drive me out into the countryside, to see a castle."

"A rich, titled friend?" Melanie teased.

"I wish. Well, I'm off."

"Take the phone," Melanie coaxed.

Katy reluctantly slipped it into her purse. It wouldn't hurt to have her own phone number while she was here, after all.

She left the café and headed for the Dorchester, glad to be wearing comfortable clothes again. She had on her favorite turquoise capri pants with daisies embroidered around the hems and a light green cotton/spandex T-shirt. On her feet were red canvas tennis shoes. They didn't match the pants but they were her favorites, and bliss to walk in after last night's high heels.

Her only spot of discomfort was her bra. The stick-ons of last night had refused to come off, except to peel up a bit at the edges. Her liquid-padded bra felt strange over the stick-ons, and she kept wanting to reach in and scratch at the peeling sheets of plastic.

She surreptitiously dug her thumb into the side of her bra, while her mind went back to Will and his chosen profession. What a change from being a stockbroker. The possibilities might have been so different if he'd stayed in that job.

She'd gone to sleep last night trying to think her way around Will's lack of income. She had imagined the two of them living in the tumbledown hovel Trevor and the others had mentioned, subsisting on beans she'd canned during the summer, and had tried to find something appealing about that scenario. But she knew what it was like to be poor and couldn't romanticize it in her mind.

Of course, if by some odd chance she and Will eventually married, she assumed she'd be legally able to work in the UK. But what type of job could she get out in the sticks? Nothing that paid well. Most likely she'd end up helping him on his organic farm, which sounded like a lot of hard physical work. She was used to making her money using her brain and couldn't talk herself into thinking she'd enjoy weeding vegetables all day.

Financially, they'd be worse off together than

they were apart. They'd never be able to afford children, and what type of fairy tale ending was *that?*

Money couldn't buy love, but it could buy groceries.

He'd kissed her, that was all. She was hungry for physical affection, and that was the only reason she reacted to his touch. Which meant it would be wise not to see him again. Accepting future invitations would only encourage him.

She came around the corner of the Dorchester and saw Will standing with Sadie near the entrance. Her heart picked up, and her impulse was to rush toward them—but she checked herself, remembering her resolution to keep her distance. She'd be pleasant, but she wasn't going to give him false ideas.

She'd behave like a proper young lady. No more kisses.

Will glanced over at Katy, the breeze through the open window ruffling her hair as he drove the B roads. She seemed distant, preoccupied, but no less lovely for that. She sat with one red tennis shoe propped on the dashboard of the van. He blamed himself for the mental shield she seemed to have erected around herself; it was probably a reaction to his behavior last night.

Not that he was going to apologize for it. He wasn't a man who lied, and he wasn't sorry for what he'd done.

Something vibrant was thrumming to life within him. He didn't know how he could have been content with composting techniques and rare tulip bulbs for so long. What type of life was that compared to the one where there was a woman by your side: a beautiful woman who made you laugh, and who moaned into your mouth when you kissed her?

His body responded to the memory with a warm rush of arousal. He wanted to do much more than just kiss her.

"How much farther is it?" she asked, breaking the silence.

"Almost there."

She slapped her hands on her thighs in a rapid rat-a-tat. "I really am looking forward to this. My first castle!" Her enthusiasm sounded forced, as if trying to drum up some excitement.

"There are dozens and dozens more."

"I'd love to see them all."

"It might take you a decade. A lifetime if you threw in the great houses as well."

"But what a fun life."

He cocked a brow at her, remembering her confusion about her career. "Maybe you should move over here and lead tours."

"Oh, I couldn't. I wouldn't know where to start."

"If you did know where to start, would you want to do that?"

"I don't know." She was quiet for a minute as she stared out the windscreen. "You know what would be really fun? Having a B and B in an old house, a really old house, where you could tell the guests there were ghosts and all sorts of legends." She started talking faster, her eyes sparkling. "And then you could lead day tours for them. Themed tours. You know, ghosts or flower gardens or places in famous novels."

"You sound excited by the idea."

She looked at him in surprise. "I am. Huh—go figure."

"Maybe you've found that career calling you were looking for."

She made a moue of dissatisfaction. "Yeah, and I picked a real practical one, didn't I? I don't know how I could ever get there from where I am now."

"Don't you believe you could do it?"

"Well, no. I can't believe . . ." She trailed off, frowning.

"You can't believe what?"

She shook her head. "Nothing."

Plainly it was something. He wasn't going to push her, though. She had the look of someone who needed to chew on a new idea for a while and see how it tasted. He didn't know if she had the means to start a B&B, or the desire to work for a tour company, but at least both prospects had engaged her interest. And her shield had dropped, and she was behaving more normally.

It occurred to him that Marreton House would be perfect for what she was talking about. But he would never be able to stomach the idea of letting a bunch of tourists stay in his house, sticking their noses into private places and making messes.

If Katy had a dream to make real, she'd have to do

it herself. Working to make it come true would make the dream all the more precious to her, in a way that having it handed to her would not. He'd learned that truth himself, with his farm. Whims passed with the first efforts made. Soul-deep desires had you sacrificing anything to achieve them.

He sneaked another look at Katy. Which of those two would she turn out to be for him?

"Is it always this beautiful here in June?" Katy asked.

They were walking along a narrow road between tall hedgerows thick with flowers, leaves, bees, and birds. They'd seen a hare disappear into the base of one, and a fox darting from the shelter of the living wall on one side of the road to the other. Sadie trotted ahead of them off the leash, tongue lolling.

"It's not always this nice, but here in the south it's not uncommon."

Katy turned her face up to the gentle sun, the warmth feeling like an extension of the contentment reaching through her body. Bodiam Castle had been great, if only for the lovely picture it made rising out of its moat. Who could resist a moat? The castle itself was little more than a pretty shell, though, because not much of the interior had survived the six centuries since it had been built.

They'd gone to lunch at a pub afterward, the place oddly decorated with stuffed foxes—some in glass cases, others gathering dust and moths on shelves. The pack of them bared their needlelike teeth in perpetual growls at the pub's patrons. Katy had elected to eat in the pub's garden, out back.

Now they'd left the van in a small lay-by along the narrow road and were walking to an Iron Age fort Will knew about. She was full of cider, warm sunshine, good conversation, and beautiful countryside. All her concerns seemed miles away.

"You were right about me needing to see more than just London," Katy said. "I wouldn't have missed this day for anything. Thank you."

Will smiled, saying nothing.

Katy thought he was looking better than she'd ever seen him. He was wearing old jeans washed to pale softness, which fit close enough that she could finally check out his butt. It was a view worth revisiting, and she'd done so at every chance.

His tan T-shirt, when touched by the occasional breeze, plastered itself against his well-defined chest, revealing a set of pectorals that would make worthy pillows for any sleeping princess. His forearms were bare and tanned, with fine dark hair dusting the toned muscles that changed shape with every movement of his hand.

In short, he was as fine a piece of manhood as she could ever hope to lay her eager hands on.

Down, Katy, down! she scolded herself. *No touch!* She wished she weren't enjoying herself so much, it was making it difficult to keep up her defenses.

"I'm beginning to feel like a rat in a maze," she said, walking on tiptoe for a few steps. "I can't see where we're going, or what's beyond these bushes."

She brushed her fingers through the outer leaves of the hedgerow. It was taller than she was.

"Here, climb up," he said, squatting down and patting one of his shoulders.

It took a moment for her to understand the invitation. "Oh. Oh, no, I'm not riding on your shoulders. I haven't done that since I was a small child."

"Come on, don't be afraid," he said.

"I'm too big."

He laughed. "Right. I promise, if you get too heavy, I'll put you down."

There *was* a certain temptation to it, not the least of which was the excuse to be touching him.

"Just don't drop me," she said, and cautiously climbed aboard. As he stood, she grabbed hold of his hair, struggling to find her balance.

"Ow!"

"Sorry." She let go and tucked her feet around his sides, the tops of her feet against his back, and repositioned her weight. He held tight to her shins.

"All right up there?"

"I think so." Then she looked around. "Oh! Glorious!" Her head cleared the top of the hedgerows by over a foot, and she could now see rolling green hills dotted with sheep and pockets of woodland. "It doesn't look anything like the countryside at home."

"No?" he said, resuming walking.

"I mean, it does in that everything is green, but here . . . it all looks so *organic*." She put her hands back on his head for stability as she swayed with his steps. She liked touching his hair; it was silky and warm from the sun. "It's as if the hedgerows grew straight out of the earth. Well, I guess they did, but the houses—I can see a farmhouse over there—look as if they grew out of the earth, too."

"They probably did, in a way," he said.

She bent forward to hear him better, aware that his head was, more or less, right between her legs. What an interesting place for it to be, and what interesting thoughts it stirred.

"Most of the houses are built from local stones," he went on. "As you move from place to place, you can see the geology change by looking at the walls of houses."

"Fascinating." She wasn't really listening, being more interested in playing with his hair.

He lightly slapped her leg in punishment for her inattention.

"Bad camel!" she said, and ran her hands down to the front of his neck, making a feint at choking him. She let her fingertips rest harmlessly against the crew collar of his shirt, where they tingled with the desire to reach inside.

He'd made no move to kiss her so far today. She'd given him a couple opportunities at Bodiam, moving into his personal space and standing still, feeling *shudders* of excitement each time she thought he might be leaning toward her. She shouldn't have done it, but he smelled so good, and was so tall and warm and sexy, she had had a hard time behaving herself.

They came to a wood fence with a small pedestrian gate to be passed through. Will reached up to her, her heart skipping a beat as his warm hands grasped her own. But all he did was steady her as he knelt to let her dismount from his shoulders.

The gate was attached to the fence on one edge while its unhinged side protruded into the mouth of a U of fencing, the unhinged edge swinging freely inside the U. There was no latch. Will and Sadie passed through it, pausing at the bottom of the U to swing the gate past them, then exited the other side of it.

"Neat!" Katy said. "We don't have these at home." The benefit was clear—people could go in and out without bothering with a latch; but no animal would get through on its own.

"No? It's called a 'kissing gate,' " he said, waiting for her.

She met his eyes, but there was nothing there to suggest she was going to get lucky. She passed through the gate unkissed and disappointed.

Sheep grazed at the far end of the field, and she realized they must be on private land. "We aren't trespassing?"

"The footpaths are all open to the public."

"Everywhere?"

"Just about."

"You're kidding," she said. "You'd risk some hoary old farmer coming after you with a shotgun in the States."

He gaped at her. "You're exaggerating."

"Actually, in some places, no."

They talked about countryside differences as

they followed the path up the side of a hill and around it to another. "I should show you around Washington someday," she found herself saying. "It's so different."

"Do you like it better than here?"

"In some ways. It feels . . . wilder at home. More primeval, which is kind of freeing. But then, this is comfortable," she said, gesturing over the rolling fields.

"Do you ever think about living elsewhere?" Will asked.

"Sometimes," she admitted. "Not elsewhere in the U.S., but if it were someplace interesting, like England, I think I could do it. Probably not just for the heck of it, though. I'd miss my family and friends too much," she said, her voice trailing off. Saying that made her realize she was already feeling it.

"Are you homesick?"

She had to bite the inside of her cheek to keep from getting teary. "A little."

He ruffled the hair on the back of her head, then pulled her close and kissed her on the crown. "I'll try to keep you distracted," he said, releasing her.

He'd have to give her more than a brotherly peck on her head to do that, she grumbled silently. Some real physical consolation would be nice.

"So where's this fort?" she asked with forced brightness.

"We're standing on it," he said, stopping. "See the ridges ringing the hill? That's what's left of the fort."

"Huh." It was going to take more imagination

than she possessed to turn this into a fortress.

He climbed up the slope behind them to the next ring, and sat in the grass. She joined him. Sadie found a spot a few feet away and lay down with paws crossed before her, surveying the land as if it were her own.

Katy absentmindedly dug her thumb into the edge of her bra, through her shirt, to scratch at the stick-on, which had been feeling weird. Something oily met her touch. She looked down, pulling the shirt out to see. A big dark patch had spread across her shirt, looking like a monstrous sweat stain. She gasped.

"What is it?" Will asked.

She let go of her shirt and sat up straight. "Nothing." Would he notice?

"I thought maybe a bug had bitten you."

"No."

He lay back against the grass, arms folded behind his head, and closed his eyes. Excellent!

She dug her thumb back into her bra and felt an oozing.

Oh no. She'd sprung a leak.

She glanced at Will to make sure he still had his eyes closed, then turned so her back was to him and reached up inside her shirt from below, feeling around for damage. The liquid from the bra seemed to be loosening the hold of the stick-on, a whole edge of it came up.

She pulled her neckline away from her skin, looking down her shirt to see what was going on.

One of the stick-ons was peeling off like a sheet of sunburned skin. It took some maneuvering and struggle, but she managed to pull it off. She whipped it out from beneath her shirt, holding it out in the sunlight for examination.

"What the hell *is* that?"

She gasped, turning to Will with wide eyes. He was sitting up, looking at the shiny thing in her hand as if she'd just pulled a dead jellyfish out of her shirt.

"Half a bra?" she said weakly.

"*That?*"

She explained the workings of a stick-on, rambling in her embarrassment, detailing the necessity of it under the green dress and the trouble she'd had removing the things in the shower.

"But why's it wet now?"

"I'm leaking," she squeaked, turning so he could see the big stain.

"Leaking *what?*" he asked in horror.

"I'm not sure."

"Oh my God," he cried, jumping to his feet. "We've got to get you to hospital!"

"No! Jeez! It's nothing deadly." She rubbed two greasy fingers together and sniffed them. "Feels like baby oil, actually."

He was staring at her chest as if aliens were birthing from it. "That can't be healthy. Aren't you in pain?"

"It's not like they'd put acid in them. They have to know there's a risk of them breaking. It seems to be a good solvent for adhesives, whatever it is." She reached inside her shirt and squeezed some of the oil out into her hand, carefully withdrawing it so he could see. "What do you think it is?"

He whimpered, his face going pale.

Katy rubbed some of it on the back of her hand. "Huh. It might make a good massage oil. What a convenient second use—and rather appropriate, too, don't you think? They should just put a valve on the edge of the things so you can take some out whenever you need it." She sniffed the back of her hand. "No smell. Want to feel it?" She held her hand up to him.

He swayed on his feet.

"Will?"

"We—We should get you a plaster—"

"A 'plaster'? Oh, a Band-Aid? You have a first-aid kit in your van?"

He nodded weakly.

"I suppose that might help a little bit. . . . But you know what would be even better? Duct tape! That would fix me right up! Duct tape can do anything!"

"Surely not—"

"Do you know, they did a study and found that it cures warts?"

He made weak motions with his hands. "Don't you need more help than just tape?"

She poked at the half-deflated cup of her bra. "You know, I don't think it's worth saving. If you have a pocketknife, I could cut out the sac and be done with it." She cupped her other false breast with her hand. "I'd have to do both, of course, to look even."

A strange gurgling sound came from his throat, and he sat down suddenly on the grass, as if his legs had collapsed beneath him. "I think . . . I think a professional should handle it."

"Pooh. I'm a self-sufficient American woman, remember?" She held out her hand. "Knife! Rip, rip, and I'll be done!"

"No . . ."

"If you have a sewing kit in the van, I could even stitch the things up afterward."

He looked at her disbelievingly. "You're serious, aren't you?"

"Well, yeah. *Do* you have a knife?"

"I can't let you do it," he said, his jaw setting in a hard line. I'm taking you to the doctor."

She tucked her hands away from his reach. *"Why?"*

"You shouldn't be doing surgery on yourself. It's just not right, Katy. It's dangerous."

"Surg—Danger—*What?*" It took a moment for the coin to drop, but then she made the connection. A chuckle started deep in her belly. "Oh, Will. Oh, you silly man! I don't have implants!" She looked at his pale, strained face and started to laugh. "It's not my breast that's leaking, you nut, it's my bra!"

"What?"

She doubled over, laughing. "It's a push-up bra, with liquid pads," she sputtered out. "You know, for cleavage. For girls who don't have any."

His expression slowly cleared, and the color came rushing back to his face. He slowly sat back down on the grass, back stiff with offended dignity. "You nearly gave me a heart attack."

"Ohh, my stomach hurts." She held her arms over her gut as she giggled.

"How was I supposed to know?"

"The fact that I wasn't screaming in agony, maybe?"

"What are you wearing a padded bra for anyway?" he grumbled.

She rolled her eyes, trying to hide her embarrassment. It was one thing to wear a padded bra and another to be caught in it, like a guy with a sock in his pants. "What a silly question."

"Your breasts looked fine to me last night."

"You were looking?"

"I'm male. I can't help it," he said.

"You probably shouldn't admit it."

"The male part or the looking?"

"I figured out the first part early on, although it was a little difficult, what with you wearing a skirt and all."

"A kilt is a manly piece of attire," he said with mock pomposity.

"Mm." She reached up the back of her shirt and unhooked her bra.

"What are you doing now?"

"Taking off my bra. My shirt's going to be soaked unless I drain the rest of it. Don't worry, I'll be covered the whole time."

He grinned. "Too bad."

She reached through her sleeves to pull the

straps off, then whisked the whole thing out from under her shirt.

"I didn't know women could do that."

"Can't you men do the same with your underpants?"

"No." He caught on belatedly that she was joking. "Imp."

She checked the label on her bra. "Mineral oil. Nothing to worry about." She glanced down at her chest, one breast still lifted higher by the stubborn stick-on bra. The things had been driving her crazy. She looked out at the empty countryside, populated only by sheep. "Do you think we're going to be alone for a bit?"

"Probably." He looked interested in her reasons for asking.

"Close your eyes, okay?"

"What are you going to do?" He sounded hopeful.

"Take off my shirt. I want to get that other stick-on off. Promise not to look?"

He groaned, and covered his eyes with his hands. She squinted doubtfully at him, then twisted so her back was to him and pulled off her shirt. She used some of the oil to rub at the edges of the plastic and gradually eased it off her skin. A little more of the oil, rubbed over both breasts, took up the last remaining streaks of adhesive.

A gentle touch in the small of her back sent a shiver up her spine, and she straightened. She looked over her shoulder. Will's eyes were open, his gaze fastened on her back.

"You're not supposed to look," she said.

His eyes met hers. "Is your back forbidden?" He flattened his hand on her back and moved it slowly upward.

Her eyes closed of their own volition, and she shivered again. It felt too good to resist. As his hand moved up, she tilted her head down to expose all of her neck. His broad hand traced up her spine, brushing the edges of her shoulder blades, and then moved up her nape.

His fingertips stroked softly up to the bare skin behind her ear, then back down again, along her neck, to her shoulder. He followed that line out to her arm, then dropped down her side, over her ribs, his fingertips reaching around her sides to where they just brushed the edge of her breast.

She closed her eyes, her chest rising and falling with her breath, waiting to feel what he would do next. Her breasts tingled, waiting to be touched.

His hand slid around her waist, then up her rib cage, and he let the edge of his finger trace where the underwire of her bra had left a line under her breast. He ran his finger along that line once, twice, then followed it forward to the center of her chest and traced his fingertips up her sternum, the palm of his hand raised just high enough to escape touching her breast, although she felt the passing heat of his skin.

He retraced his route, his hand returning to her back, and then both his palms were on her, rising up her rib cage and over her shoulder blades. He cupped her shoulders in his hands, then ran his hands down over her arms, lifting them as he went until they were straight out to the sides, his own arms lying against and supporting them, his hands holding hers, his chest touching her back.

He lowered his head to the bend of her neck and kissed her, lightly. He feathered a second kiss on her neck, and a third, tracing upward to the place behind her ear.

He crossed her arms before her, his own matching their movement, until they both had their arms wrapped around her body. It was the skin of her own arm that touched her breasts, his body a shield around her.

His mouth moved back into the crook of her neck, kissing harder this time, sending a shot of arousal straight down to her loins. Her muscles there contracted, and a warm fullness stole through her body.

"I didn't look," he whispered, and slowly released her as he pulled away.

She didn't move, half hoping and half frightened that he might do more. She could feel him watching her, feel his eyes almost touching her back, and a sudden shyness possessed her. Her breasts were small, her skin pale and freckled. The full light of day exposed her flaws too clearly. She couldn't turn to him without encouragement; she needed reassurance that he would find her beautiful.

She willed him to give her that reassurance; to touch her again, to say her name. To encourage her to turn and offer herself.

The moment stretched, and then suddenly her nerves could take no more. She grabbed for her shirt, glancing over her shoulder to see that his hand was raised, stretched toward her. But the moment was already lost, anticipation replaced by awkwardness, and feeling flustered, she scrambled into her shirt.

When she turned back to him, his gaze was out over the horizon, and his hand was stroking Sadie's silky ears.

There was an uncomfortable quiet between them as they drove back toward London through the dusk. They had haltingly resumed conversation, but hanging between them was the sexual advance that might or might not have been rejected. Or accepted.

Katy didn't know what he was thinking and couldn't bring herself to ask him point-blank: Did you want to do more? Did I mess up? Are you thinking that I rejected you? Maybe I should have, but I didn't mean to.

She chewed a hangnail, frowning fiercely.

If it turned out they really liked each other, and wanted to be together, could they make it work?

If Will couldn't support her financially, she'd have to support herself. It was almost impossible to work here as an American. She could work for the UK branch of a multinational company if she was hired in the U.S. But which company would that be, and how long would it be before they consented to transfer her here?

She could go back to the U.S., work for a year and save all the money she could, and then come back here. She could live near (or with) Will, and see how they got on together.

But that meant going home for a year.

"Do you ever think of moving out of the country?" she asked into the silence between them.

"Me?" He sounded surprised.

"Yeah. Like moving your farm operation to someplace else? Organics are big on the West Coast."

He studied her for a moment before looking back at the road. "You'd want me to do that?"

"No! I didn't say that. Why would I want you to do that? I was just wondering. I'll be going home in a couple weeks, and five thousand miles is a bit of a hike. Long-distance relationships don't seem to work well. Not that we *have* a relationship, of course," she quickly said. Gawd, guys hated the *R* word.

"I mean, we hardly *know* each other," she went on, unable to stop herself. "I mean, jeez, it's only been a week! It's not like we're going to stop seeing other people."

He gave her a dark, questioning look. "If you want me to—"

"So . . ." she interrupted, not wanting to get into that discussion. "*Do* you ever think of moving? Away from England, I mean."

"I couldn't leave my farm. The land has been in the family for generations."

"Ah." One of those. She'd seen farmers like that in the U.S., on TV. They'd be hundreds of thousands of dollars in debt to banks, but still hang on to the bitter end, not wanting to give up their land. "Was your father a farmer, too?"

He shook his head. "Stockbroker. He loved working in the city."

"Do you ever think of going back to it?"

He shook his head.

"Not even part-time, or online?"

"Why would I?"

She shrugged. "For the money. The security of a job that pays."

"Money isn't worth doing work you hate."

"It is if it means survival."

"I'm surviving perfectly well."

"In a general sense, I mean. What if you had no money and then had a child—would you do work you hated then?"

"I wouldn't have the child unless I knew I could support it," he said.

"So if you couldn't afford children, you wouldn't have them, even if it meant you'd die childless?"

"Even if. I won't have a child of mine raised in poverty." he said brusquely.

While she agreed with his sentiment, his answer saddened her. "Accidents happen. No birth control is a hundred percent effective. What then?"

That earned her another dark look. "Accidents don't happen to me."

Was that why he had gone no farther with her at the fort? "You can't go through life with your pants always on. You can't keep yourself wrapped up tight in hopes that nothing ever escapes your control."

"What are you *talking* about? I never said I lived that way!"

"You didn't have to say it—you showed it. And don't yell at me!" She felt tears start in her eyes.

"I'm not yelling! I want to know what the hell you're thinking, is all! Ah, damn it, now I *am* yelling. I'm sorry. And sorry for whatever else I did wrong." He was quiet a moment while she snuffled. "What *did* I do wrong?"

She shook her head. "Nothing."

What was she supposed to say to him? She couldn't tell him that she didn't want to get involved with a sweet, good-looking guy who knew how to kiss just because he was a dirt-poor farmer who would never be able to afford children. Money wasn't supposed to matter in affairs of the heart. Practicalities were supposed to be thought of another day. Love conquered all, etc.

But it was only going to conquer all if it prompted her to figure out a way to make a bucketful of cash.

Maybe the B&B idea would work, in his house, depending on how big it was. Maybe that would bring in enough money to make being together feasible. She could go home to Seattle, work like a fiend, come back and fix up his house, where they could live happily ever after, taking in guests and raising their children.

She remembered their conversation that night after Charley Horse. He'd insisted he didn't want to be supported by a woman. But maybe he wouldn't mind her putting her own money into his house if it were an investment in a B&B business. That wasn't the same as being supported.

She cleared her throat. "I heard someone say that your house needs some, er . . . repairs." Trevor actually had said Will's house was "going to fall down around his ears." "Does it need lots of them?"

He laughed a bit, looking uncertain about this change in topic but relieved. "Extensive. It's livable, but the kitchen is an embarrassment."

"By 'extensive,' I take it you mean that it needs more than new paint."

"Well, there's the dry rot."

"Oh? That sounds bad."

"And the roof. It's slate and copper, and needs a lot of work done."

"That sounds expensive."

"Rather."

She did some mental arithmetic, based on the last time a friend had dealt with anything similar. But who in Seattle had slate and copper roofs? Depending, the total cost so far might be $10,000. She could maybe save that much in a year, if she lived super cheap.

"And the whole building really should be rewired," he said.

Electricians were expensive. Okay, so two years of tech writing at a high-paying job.

"I don't know what I'll do about heating. The plumbing in half the house seems to be doing all right, though hot water is an issue."

"And the plumbing in the other half of the house?"

"Doesn't exist."

"How long have you been living there?" she asked, appalled. She'd have to live with three or four roommates while she saved the money for that type of repairs. And take four years.

"Five years or so."

"And you've been okay with living in a house that's only half plumbed?"

"The place has character." He grinned at her. "It's not so bad. I was putting off getting things fixed because I was concentrating on the greenhouses. I had to get those going first."

She imagined so. At the rate he was going, though, it would be a century before he could get his house fixed on his own.

"Is the house very big?" she asked.

"About average for its type."

What did that mean? Two bedrooms? "Is there room for guests?"

"Of course. Or there will be, once things get cleaned up and some new loos are put in. Why?" He looked like he already knew the answer.

"Just wondering."

There was quiet between them again. There were so many obstacles to overcome, even to have enough time to know if something could be built between them that would last a lifetime.

It all seemed so impossible. She didn't want to lose her heart to someone with whom she could have no future.

If she were an heiress it would be little easier, even given his bias against being with a woman better off than himself. But if she had her own money, she could at least afford to stay in England for several more months and see if they were a good match.

She had to face facts. He was twenty-eight and in love with being an organic farmer. He was old enough to know what he wanted, and to chuck aside anyone who wanted different.

If they had a little fling, she would go back to the U.S., they'd exchange emails and a few phone calls, and their relationship would fade away bit by bit, doomed by distance.

There was no happy ending to be had with Will Eland, organic farmer.

"I could show the house to you if you like," he said after a few minutes of silence.

She tried to smile, but sadness weighed it down. "Maybe some other time."

"You'll have to direct me to the place you're staying," Will said. He had the feeling that something had gone wrong, but for the life of him he didn't know what it was. His ignorance, and the inability therefore to correct the problem, was creating an uncomfortable stir of anger and frustration in him.

He'd forgotten what it was like to get involved with a woman. One day you were perfectly in control of yourself and acting like a rational human being and the next the world has turned to chaos and you were stumbling round blindly in the dark, hoping some beast you couldn't see wasn't going to sneak up and rip your guts out.

Katy had been quiet for the past twenty minutes as they drove into the heart of London. His question stirred her out of her contemplation. "You can drop me at the Dorchester. That'll be easiest."

"It's dark now. I'd be more comfortable seeing you safely to your door."

"It's just a short walk from the hotel. Don't worry about it. This is Mayfair, after all."

"And thus a target for muggers."

"It'll be easier for *me*," she said, her voice getting tense, "if I don't have to try to figure out which streets you can or can't turn on, or where they are. Especially in the dark."

He gave up. For whatever reason, she didn't want him to know where she was staying. "How can I get in touch with you? Do you have a phone number you can give me?" He knew his voice held an edge; his frustration was leaking through.

She hesitated, then said, "How about email? Do you have access to a computer?"

"Yes."

She pulled a scrap of paper from her purse and wrote on it and handed it to him as they pulled into the drive of the Dorchester.

"Let me give you mine," he said, and took a piece of paper from the shelf behind him and wrote out all his contact information for both Marreton

House and his aunt's townhouse. "If you need anything, call me. Or even if you just want to say hello."

She glanced at the paper he handed her, then folded it and stuffed it into her purse. "Are you going back to your farm now?" she asked.

"I need to get back. I'll email you, though, and we'll set something up."

She smiled but didn't say anything.

Damn it. He'd just ask straight out. "Katy, what did I do to upset you?"

She shook her head. "Nothing. You've been perfect. Really."

If he'd been perfect, why was this day ending like this? He couldn't figure it out, and trying to was making his head hurt.

There was only one thing that he knew *was* right between them.

He lifted her chin with his fingertips, looking into her eyes. She looked back uncertainly, and for a moment he didn't know if she would let him kiss her. His heart beat hard in his chest, and he suddenly felt as callow and vulnerable as a schoolboy.

He brushed a short lock of hair behind her ear, and cupped the back of her head in his hand. Then he slowly lowered his mouth to hers, stopping a hair's breadth from her lips, their breath and body heat mingling.

She swayed toward him and closed the distance herself, her soft lips touching against his. He took full possession of her mouth, deepening the kiss, gently exploring with his tongue until she moaned, her hands gripping his shirt.

He pulled her off her seat and sideways into his lap, the steering wheel forcing her against his body, her back against his supporting arm as he kissed her, his other hand massaging her hip, her waist, and up to her ribs, his thumb brushing the underside of her breast. She wrapped her arms around his neck, her fingers digging into his hair.

Sadie growled, and then barked. Will glanced out the windshield at the approaching doorman and broke the kiss. "We're gathering an audience."

She blinked at him, then turned to look out the window. At sight of the doorman, she scrambled off his lap and back to her seat, straightening her shirt. Before he could stop her, she was opening her door.

"Thanks for a wonderful day," she said. "I had a great time."

"I did, too."

Why did they both sound like they were lying?

She smiled, but he thought he saw a sheen of tears in her eyes. She petted Sadie once and then was out the door.

The kiss had been right, yet had held no power to heal whatever had gone amiss between them.

Will slammed his hand on the edge of the steering wheel. Bloody, sodding hell!

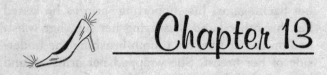

Chapter 13

Katy huddled on the sofa in the shadowy TV room of Titania's Bower, trying to find *Oprah*, knowing that it was probably hopeless on a Saturday.

The only light came from the TV screen and weak sconces on the walls. The room was bare except for the ancient Chippendale sofa on which she sat and the tiny color TV, a cable snaking out its back and through a hole drilled in the wall. The walls themselves were pale yellow with a faded, hand-painted oriental design of bare tree branches and colorful birds. A white plaster medallion on the high ceiling marked where a chandelier had once hung. It all hinted of a glorious past, now gone.

The landlady had said *Oprah* might show in the evenings on one of the satellite stations, and Katy was desperately in need of the comfort of her personal goddess. She kept flipping stations, trying to ignore the creepy feel that ghosts were watching from the dark corners of the room. She had yet to see another tenant at the B&B, but as freaky as that was, it was just fine with her at the moment.

The *Weekly Moon* had come out today. She'd picked up a copy along with a bag of nonperishable groceries at a small supermarket, and then scuttled back to the B&B to go into hiding.

There was one article. It wasn't long. It *was* horrifying. And the pictures were worse.

The glossy tabloid—it was a thin, oversized magazine heavy on photos—lay on the bare wood floor next to the sofa on which she huddled. Katy sank against the back of the sofa and tried to pretend the tabloid didn't exist.

She curled into the fetal position, falling to her side, her cheek smooshed against the dusty old brocade cushion, and flipped through endless stations of tennis, racing, and soccer. Where was Oprah when she needed her?

She felt utterly alone and deeply ashamed— shame of the cowering, pillow-over-the-head variety. She wanted to hide here until it was time to go back to the U.S. She never wanted to see anyone ever again.

What was Will going to think of her when he saw the tabloid with its made-up story? And those awful pictures—pictures *she* had taken. She felt guilt mingled with a terror that Will would figure out that she was the one responsible. What would happen *then*?

Not that she cared, of course. It didn't matter to her what Will thought. It didn't matter that he would lose all interest in her the moment he read what the tabloid said about her.

Maybe he wouldn't see the magazine. Maybe no one she'd met would. No one actually read that type of trash, did they? Or believed it?

Trevor dug his finger into his ear, chasing a glob of wax, and looked again at the story in the *Weekly Moon.* Who'd have thought it? He could kick himself for treating Katy so shabbily. He'd have to make amends there. It had been jolly good fun using her to torture Will, but apparently there was more to be had from her than revenge.

It was his own name on the cover of the tabloid that had caught his eye, in a small headline at the bottom of the cover: "Playboy Viscount Stanley Finds New Princess."

Have I? Good show! he'd thought, and bought the magazine to see whom he was dating now. It had been a couple months since he'd rated any space in its columns, which had been a sorry reflection on his romantic life. It was getting harder and harder to rate any time in the tabloids—all anyone cared about was movie and TV stars and the occasional athlete. You had to have a pop superstar on your arm to be worth attention, which was rather a poor state of affairs.

The article itself had been a bit of a shocker. Tucked away on the society page along with half a dozen photos of others there'd been an old picture of him—he'd been half plastered when it was taken, and a bloody good party that had been, too—and then a picture of Katy Orville in her new hair and that indecent green dress.

The article read:

> The newest bird to alight on the arm of
> Trevor Mangold, Viscount Stanley, is
> ultra-fashionable newcomer Katy Orville.
> An American rumoured to be a software
> princess worth hundreds of millions, Miss
> Orville was seen Friday night on the dance
> floor of Charley Horse with London's
> favourite playboy.
>
> It's Miss Orville's first visit to London
> from Seattle (home of Microsoft's Bill Gates),
> and all eyes are waiting to see if she's found
> the cream of the aristo crop to be to her
> taste. The naughty viscount may have met
> his match in this wild creature from the
> Silicon Forest. Can he hold her, or will she
> flit away to a more tempting arm?

Damn! Hundreds of millions! There'd be no more worrying about his meager allowance or his failure of a gallery with her as his wife.

He'd known plenty of fabulously wealthy women who were far more beautiful than Katy Orville, but they'd all seen him as the plaything he'd seen them. True, he'd be an earl someday, assuming the old man ever saw fit to die, but that just didn't count for what it used to. All the rich girls seemed to want to marry rock stars or athletes.

What fools. He sniffed in disdain. Katy, though— he could easily catch Katy, and all her hundreds of millions.

He glanced through the rest of the pictures on the page, several of which had been taken at Charley Horse by some sneaky bloke. There was Madonna, and the usual crop of young actors and models and pop singers, and best of all, Helena and Cynthia engaged in embarrassing acts of self-grooming.

He snorted with laughter and went to his computer.

To: Katy Orville
From: Trevor Mangold
Subject: races, anyone?

Dear Katy,

I'm sorry we didn't get to spend more time together at Charley Horse, and especially sorry that my cousin showed up and dragged you away. I'd wanted to steal you away myself.

Continuing the theme of horses, would you be interested in going to Royal Ascot with me Thursday next? My mother won't be going as she had planned, so we can sneak you in on her badge. You'll need a hat, of course! But you look the type who doesn't mind a bit of shopping, and does an excellent job of it. Your dress was stunning. As were you.

Do let me know.

He typed in his phone number, signed off with a jaunty "Regards, Trev," and hit "send."

A moment later, he remembered that he'd promised to go with Helena to Ascot on Thursday. They had a tradition of wandering the royal enclosure together, mocking the other racegoers and their clothes. It was great fun.

Ah, well; she'd understand. She always did. He opened a new email and started to write.

The ringing telephone woke Will from sleep. He grabbed for it, trying to clear his mind. The red figures on his clock said 2:00 A.M. Panic went through him, fearing an emergency.

"Hello?"

"Will! It's Helena. You won't believe what that bastard has done now!"

"Helena?" His foggy, scared brain tried to make sense of the hysterical voice on the other end of the line. "Who? What bastard?"

"Trevor! He's taking that stupid twit to Royal Ascot, when he'd promised to go with *me*. And what does he do? Sends me a friggin' email to tell me. He doesn't even have the courage to tell me to my face. Bastard!"

Will sat up and clicked on the bedside lamp. His brain was starting to get into gear, the panic fading.

"Helena, why are you calling me, of all people? You already know how I feel about him."

"Don't you care about Katy?"

His gut clenched. "You mean it's *Katy* he's taking?"

"Yes! Of course! Why else would I call you? We can't stand for it, Will, we just can't! It's because of her money, you know," she said in a lower voice. "Those hundreds of millions."

"What are you talking about?"

"You didn't see the *Weekly Moon*? I burned my copy," she said darkly. "If I ever catch the person who—"

"Helena, what are you on about?"

She gave him a summary of the article and photos. He sat in silence as she ranted about the pictures of her and Cynthia, but it was the information on Katy that he couldn't get out of his head.

She was a multimillionaire?

A sinking in his gut told him this was bad. A feeling of inadequacy crept through him. She could buy her own house for a B&B; she didn't need Marreton House. He suddenly realized that he'd been thinking of Marreton House as a prize that he might use to lure her to him, as if he were a weaver bird preparing a nest for his prospective mate. He'd thought it was his ace in the hole.

But why would Katy ever want to come live in his crumbling old manor house if she could live anywhere she pleased?

This must be why she had kept on about his becoming a stockbroker again. She must think she needed someone more presentable on her arm than an organic farmer. She must want a more upscale life than she thought he would want to share.

Well, he couldn't stand being the impoverished husband of a wealthy heiress. He wasn't going to be one of those aristrocrats from ages past who sold themselves to rich American women who had come to England shopping for a title.

Money can't buy me love. How much easier it would be if she were poor.

"Will? Will!"

"Pardon?"

"I was *saying*," Helena said, "you have to come with me to Ascot. Can you get a badge? Maybe your uncle Harold will let you have his. I'm not giving up without a fight! You aren't going to give up your pursuit, are you?"

"I didn't know I was pursuing anyone."

She snorted. "For God's sake, Will, it's clear enough you're crazy about her."

He didn't want to answer that. "Helena, why do you chase after Trevor, even now?"

"I'm *not* chasing. And neither are you, not anymore. It's time we turned the tables. Trevor treats me like his faithful dog. Not this time! He'll go mad when he sees me with you."

"He goes mad when he sees me at all. You're worth more than someone like him. You always have been."

"Brilliant, darling! Say something like that in his hearing."

There'd never been any dissuading Helena once she had her mind set on something. He heaved a heavy sigh.

"What?" Helena asked. "What are you making that noise about? You think I'm nutters? You do, don't you!"

"Only nutters in love. Who am I to say what's best for you?"

And now he was afraid he might be slipping down that same slope to amorous insanity, for why else would he be thinking about going along with Helena's plan? Damn it! He was losing all his common sense.

Helena chuckled wickedly. "All right then, it's to Ascot we go. And wear the right clothes, for God's sake. They won't let you in if you don't."

Katy dreamt.

Oprah sat atop the television, her vanilla skirts hiding the screen and muffling the sound of her theme song, coming through the speakers: *Oh-oh-oh-oh-OHP-rah!* She was wearing her tiny silver reading glasses again, and reading the *Weekly Moon*.

Ioan Gruffudd stood beside Oprah wearing nothing but tight jeans. His bare chest wasn't looking quite as appealing as she remembered; it was undeveloped compared to Will's. Ioan met Katy's eyes and winked.

She forced a fake smile and nibbled her lower lip, trying not to panic. This was a very bad time for Oprah to be reviewing her progress. Very bad! It was like being back in high school, faced with an exam for which she had forgotten to study. Oprah looked at Katy over the tops of her glasses, dropping the tabloid down onto her thighs. "Is this your best life, Katy Orville?"

"Ma'am?" Katy squeaked. She sat very still, hands clasped in her lap.

"Is this your best life, to take pictures of women sniffing their armpits and picking their noses?"

"No," Katy said. "I'm sorry I did it. Really."

"Really?" Oprah asked doubtfully.

"Well, maybe I'm not so sorry the pictures made it into the magazine."

"You mean you'd rather someone else had done your dirty work, but you'd want it done all the same?"

Katy thrust her jaw forward. "Those girls were mean to me."

"And you think that makes it okay?" Oprah tapped the magazine against her leg, shaking her head. "Is this your authentic self?" She held up the picture of Katy in her short hair and the green dress.

Katy shrugged. "I dunno."

"I have to say I'm disappointed in you, Katy Orville. I thought you were really onto something there. You seemed to have such a good start. What happened?"

"I've been trying to follow my Life Map, but it's not working. It's just messing me up. It's useless."

"The Life Map is a valuable tool!" Oprah said, voice rising as she stood. Her skirt billowed around her with a threatening rustle. Ioan's eyes went round.

"The Life Map is crap!" Katy protested stubbornly.

"Then you're not taking the right message from it. Your authentic self is in that Life Map. You need to look more carefully."

"I'm searching high and low for my authentic self, and I'm telling you, I can't find her!" Katy said, getting angry. "That map is just a bunch of pictures of things I'll never have. Some 'best life,' huh? Best fantasy life, maybe."

"You have to believe."

"I came here believing, but all that's done is get me in trouble, and made me do things I'm ashamed of. Bad memories and a broken heart are all I'm going to get out of this."

"You're afraid," Oprah said, putting her hand on her hip and nodding. "Afraid to truly find your authentic self."

"What a load of bull hockey!"

"Now you're defensive. That's when you've got to pay attention, when you're defensive. What are you trying to hide from yourself?"

Katy saw red. "Defensive? I'll *tell* you what you can do with defensive!" She could just pop Oprah—standing there telling her how to live her life, telling her she was hiding things from herself! "Come a little closer. I'll show you something you can believe in."

"What is going on in that little red head, Katy Orville?" Oprah asked with attitude.

Katy felt her muscles bunching. Oprah was asking for it, she really was! A talk show host shouldn't be playing mental health counselor to strangers, acting like she knew what was best for them.

"You wanted my help," Oprah went on. "You made me your goddess. You can't get rid of me now just because you don't like what I think of your behavior."

"*I don't care* what you think!" Katy gave a rebel yell and sprang off the sofa at Oprah in a flying tackle. Oprah's eyes went wide in shock, her arm rising to fend Katy off.

A hand on Katy's shoulder shook her awake, dissipating the dream midleap. Katy forced her eyes open, blinking in wide-eyed confusion into the gnomelike face of her landlady. The shocked face of Oprah was already flickering out of her memory.

On the television screen, tennis players batted a ball back and forth. A dim gray light was seeping through the windows.

"What time is it?" Katy asked, yawning and sitting up.

"It's five-thirty. You've been here all night." Millie fiddled with her crystal pendant, shaped like a crescent moon. "I hope the chanting from my women's group didn't drive you from your room. We were practicing for Midsummer's Eve, and the floor below yours is where we meet."

"No, I didn't hear you." Katy could smell a heavy scent of spices wafting off her landlady and wrinkled her nose. They must have been chanting in a fog of incense.

Millie held the tabloid out to Katy, her expression betraying nothing.

Katy shied away from the thing, as if she'd been offered a poison apple. "I don't want it."

"They're full of cruelty and lies, these things. Gossip and mischief and jealousy."

"No one believes them, do they?"

Millie folded the tabloid and stuck it under her arm. "Only those who want to believe."

Katy flashed her a look, but the landlady was already turning away.

Millie went toward the door and paused before going out. "In my women's group, we believe that the energy you send out comes back to you. It's a reminder to be good, even when tempted otherwise. Only wish good things on your friends as well as on your enemies." She nodded once, as if agreeing with her own statement. "You should go to bed."

Katy swallowed, feeling eerily certain that her landlady knew more than she should about the mischief Katy had been up to. "Thank you. I will."

She resolved to stay far away from Melanie and the tabloids, Trevor and Helena, and all the nasty goings-on of the young aristos. They brought out nothing but the worst in her.

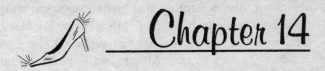# Chapter 14

"*I* can't breathe!" Katy complained.

"Hush. You can too," Melanie said, tightening the laces on the red satin corset. They were in the ladies' lounge off the lobby of the Dorchester, using it as a dressing room for Katy's day at Royal Ascot. Trevor would be picking her up out front in half an hour.

"This doesn't seem at all appropriate. I thought I was supposed to dress conservatively." *Oh why oh why had she let herself be drawn into this?* All her resolutions about staying away from the aristos had disappeared the moment they'd acted like they wanted her. She was weak and shallow, with no moral staying power.

But how was a poor girl from Seattle supposed to resist an invitation to Ascot? You might as well throw a two-pound bag of M&M's down in front of her while she was dieting.

That the invitation to Ascot had come at all was due to that stupid article in the *Weekly Moon*, she was sure. And accepting the invitation meant that she had to crawl back to that sartorial devil Melanie, and once again pay her evil price.

"No . . . no . . . no!" Melanie said, punctuating each *No* with a tug on the corset laces. "Royal Ascot is all about being *noticed*. It's about face time on the telly. You have to be so striking, every station and magazine covering the event will want your picture."

" 'Striking'? This is 'eighteenth century meets Victoria's Secret'! I'm going to look like I should be in a music video!"

"Exactly." Melanie stood back to examine her handiwork. "That looks brilliant on you, darling, if I do say so myself."

Katy looked in the mirror and widened her eyes at her reflection. Wowza! Was that her waist? She put her hands on it, admiring the new small size. Corsets. Cool. It rose high on her chest, her small breasts smooshed flat with only a small moon edge of flesh rising over the top. There was a cutaway red jacket with black details to wear over the corset, which would leave most of it exposed.

Katy felt a spurt of satisfied vanity. She'd be willing to do a little evil and suffer a bit of karmic punishment in exchange for the pleasure of looking this good. The only time she'd felt half as fabulous was while wearing that green dress at Charley Horse. For someone who'd spent most of her life feeling like a small mottled bird, it was a heady experience to look smashing and sexy.

The full skirt was the same brilliant red as the corset and jacket, only in sand-washed silk. It gathered high above one knee and would show off the boots Melanie had bought for her.

"You really aren't serious about the boots, are you?" Katy asked one last time. She'd paid Melanie back for them, but wasn't at all sure she should have. They were black vinyl platforms, high heeled and laced up to just below her kneecap.

"Of course I'm serious. I couldn't lend you anything from the store, what with all the muck you might be stepping in. These were cheap and they make a statement. Now sit. Let's get them on you."

Katy sat—or tried to. The corset forced her to sit stiffly upright, unable to bend at the waist. She stuck out her black stocking-clad foot for Melanie. "Just don't tell me you got them at a bondage shop. They look like dominatrix boots."

Melanie grinned.

Katy moaned.

"I'm here, I'm here," a young woman said, rushing into the ladies' lounge. It was Erica, Melanie's friend from the cosmetics department. She was carrying a makeup bag and an enormous hatbox.

"I was getting worried," Melanie said. "We've only fifteen minutes until he's supposed to pick her up!"

Katy closed her eyes and let Erica go to work on her face.

She felt like she was doing something wrong by going to Ascot. That she was betraying Will—even though that made no sense.

When she'd checked her email a couple days after the tabloid came out, she'd scanned the list of senders looking for Will's name. Right at the bottom, the newest message in her file, there he'd been. Hurrah!

But she wasn't supposed to be excited. It wasn't going to work with him. That way lay heartache.

Still, part of her heart quietly said, "Hurrah!"

The delight faded as soon as she opened his message.

To: *Katy Orville*
From: *William Eland*
Subject: *to the races*

Dear Katy,

I hear you're going to Royal Ascot with Trevor on Thursday. I do hope you have a good time. It's something everyone should see once, if they have the chance.
   Perhaps Helena and I will see you there.

Yours truly,
Will

Royal Ascot? With Trevor? What the . . . ? She'd scanned back up her list of mail and found Trevor's older message inviting her to Ascot. She finished reading it and sat back, stunned.

It only took a few moments for the anger to start seething inside. Who had told Will she was going to Ascot with Trevor before she had even read the invitation herself? And why hadn't Will asked her about this *himself* and gotten her side of the story before hying off with Helena? Helena, whom he *knew* she didn't like.

Arrrrrgh! The witch was trying to steal her man! Maybe there *had* been something between them in the past; maybe Will still *did* have a thing for Helena.

Or maybe Will was the fickle womanizer he had accused Trevor of being. It took one to know one, after all.

Not that it was supposed to matter to her.

Fine. Let Will go with Helena; *she* would go with Trevor. So he might be a womanizing jerk: so what? There were plenty of them floating around. At least she'd see the races and get to wear a cool hat. She'd show Will that she could do just fine without him, thank you very much!

She'd written a quick reply to Trevor accepting his invitation, and then given him the mobile number to Melanie's camera phone so they could make arrangements.

It was only after she'd sent the message and stomped off to treat herself to tea at Fortnum & Mason that she had second thoughts.

Royal Ascot meant once again asking Melanie for wardrobe help. It meant taking more pictures. It meant throwing herself once more into that mix of shallow, nasty rich people.

She'd sat alone at her table in one of the restaurants at Fortnum & Mason, ordered her tea, and when it came she slathered clotted cream and strawberry preserves onto a scone. She ate scones until she was stuffed, trying vainly not to think about anything else.

So here she was now, in a ladies' lounge, once again in borrowed clothing.

"Open," Erica said.

Katy opened her eyes and made a face at her reflection. Her eyes had a heavy layer of up-sloping liner, so she looked like a girl from the '60s. Her lips were blood red.

"You won't be able to ride in the car with the hat on. Just leave it in the box until you get there, but let me show you how to wear it," Erica said.

She took the lid off the box and lifted out a black tricorne hat with a rich cascade of black ostrich plumes falling from the underside in back. A wisp of black veil wrapped around the front.

Katy looked at it with trepidation. "It looks like an evil muppet."

"It's gorgeous!" Melanie helped Erica position it atop Katy's head. She slanted it down at a rakish angle, so that the front point of the tricorn was aimed over Katy's right eye. She arranged the veil so that it covered Katy's face just to the end of her nose, leaving her red lips exposed.

The black ostrich plumes gave the startling illusion that Katy was wearing a heavy set of long dark curls, like a lord in a wig from centuries past.

Katy again looked in the mirror and didn't recognize herself. No one *could*. She was a cross between a devil, an eighteenth-century equestrienne, and a prostitute. "Good gracious," she said under her breath.

"Good God!" Trevor shook his head, laughing. "I still can't believe it's you. Am I ever going to recognize you, or do you change with each new day?"

Katy merely smiled. They were wandering the royal enclosure—that section of the Ascot grandstand and grounds that were reserved for upper-class patrons who had received badges of admittance. Or so Trevor had explained.

The grandstand was actually a huge building much like one would find at any other racecourse, full of restaurants, snack counters, a shop, bars, bars, and more bars, and private boxes. Right next to the royal enclosure was the winner's enclosure, the ring where riders and horses received their prizes.

The racecourse itself was turf, something Katy had never seen. Of course, she'd only been to the races once before, in Tacoma. Races had always struck her as slightly tawdry, perhaps because of the gambling and quantities of beer.

Royal Ascot, at least in this rarefied part of the grounds, was anything but tawdry. From behind the screen of her veil, Katy stared in awed delight at all the people: at the men in gray or black morning suits, complete with top hats; at the women in everything from staid Queen Elizabeth—style suits and matching hats to boldly tailored pantsuits and chapeaux three feet across.

Trevor seemed to know everyone. He stopped yet again to talk, and she lightly held his arm as he chatted with the easy, slick charm of a salesman. Feeling secure behind her veil, Katy smiled when he introduced her.

"How do you do?" she said in her best imitation of Audrey Hepburn with marbles in her mouth in *My Fair Lady*. She said nothing more, deciding that being a Lady of Mystery was far better than saying something stupid.

The people to whom Trevor introduced her were not the ones she cared about.

Where were Will and Helena?

Trevor chatted, yakkety-yakkety-yakkety, but she tuned it out, her attention on the passing crowd as she scanned it for Will's dark head. All the men wore top hats, though, making them difficult to distinguish. Will must have had to rent an outfit to get in. How much had that cost him?

How much had the tickets cost him, for that matter? Maybe Helena was paying his way. The nasty tart seemed desperate enough.

"The Royal Procession will start soon. Do you want to see it?" Trevor asked.

"Sure," Katy said, wondering what it could possibly be.

They went around to the front of the grandstand, Katy's heels sinking into the ground with every step, and stood with dozens of others on a lawn that sloped down to the racecourse. A chest-high wall at the bottom of the slope separated the spectators from the track. High in the grandstand she could make out clusters of television crews, some of their cameras aimed down at the crowd in the Royal Enclosure.

A fanfare played, and on the course an open carriage appeared, drawn by four horses with outriders uniformed in red and gold.

"Who's that in the carriage?" Katy asked.

Trevor laughed. "It's the queen."

"The queen!"

Oh my God! The queen!

She dropped Trevor's arm and ran down the slope, shoving her way past the coolly dignified patrons, voices protesting "Oof" and "Your pardon!" trailing in her wake.

The queen! The queen! She was going to see the queen!

She used her small size to slither like an eel between morning suits and pastel ensembles.

The carriage had passed by the time she wormed her way to the wall, which reached to the bottom of her chin. She turned to the startled older man beside her. "Will they come back?" she asked anxiously.

"Presently."

"Oh good! I've never seen the queen before!"

He chuckled. "She does this same procession all four days of Royal Ascot. I've always thought she must feel a little silly, paraded back and forth like this." He shrugged. "Perhaps she is used to it."

Katy lifted her chin imperiously and held her hand up as if to wave, and turned it slowly back and forth, fingers together. "At home they tell everyone in parades to do this. They say it's what the queen does."

The man chuckled again, eyes twinkling.

She smiled back. Maybe all the aristocrats weren't so snooty after all.

"Katy," Trevor hissed behind her, and put his hand on her shoulder.

She glanced back at him. "Can you see the carriage? Have they turned around yet?" She bounced up and down on the balls of her feet, trying to see past all the hats.

Trevor took her arm and gently tugged. "Come away," he whispered harshly. "You're embarrassing me."

"Oh, pish," she said, shrugging off his hold. She tried to dig her toes into the mortared spaces between the bricks and pull herself up to see better, but her platform shoes wouldn't let her. "Are they coming?"

"They've just turned," the older man said.

Katy clapped her hands in excitement, then stuck her arm over the wall and waved. "Woo-ooo!" she cried.

"Katy!" Trevor jerked her away from the wall,

dragging her back several steps. "Stop it!" he hissed.

"She's going to pass twenty feet from us! I want to wave!" Katy protested, pulling against him, trying to get back to the wall.

"You're making a fool of yourself, and you're embarrassing me. Look around you. No one else is behaving like this."

The older man turned and stared at Trevor. "Young Stanley, isn't it?" he said coldly.

Trevor released her arm and stiffened. "Sir."

"You find waving to our queen an *embarrassment?*"

"No, sir. I just meant her leaping about and shouting. I thought it unbecoming. Sir."

The jovial man had turned steely and frightening. Katy watched the interchange wide-eyed.

"I find your attempts to stifle this young lady's enthusiasm *unbecoming,*" the man said.

"Sir, my apologies. I did not mean to offend."

The sound of hooves and the change in the mood of the crowd drew Katy's attention away from the men, and she turned back to the track. The carriage was just passing by. She rushed back to the wall, raising her arm to wave, but was a moment too late. She was behind the queen's line of sight.

Katy lowered her hand, and slumped as much as the corset would let her. She turned and glowered at Trevor, her mouth pulling down unhappily.

The older man raised an eloquent eyebrow to Trevor. "I believe you owe the young lady an apology. If I were you, I would make sure she enjoys the rest of her day."

"Yes, sir."

The older man turned his attention to her. "It was a pleasure meeting you . . ."

"Katy Orville," she supplied, and shook the hand he held out to her.

"Edward Wilton." He tipped his hat to her. "Enjoy your day at Ascot, Miss Orville." Then he leaned closer, and whispered to her, "Chin up! I've smacked the puppy's nose with a paper, and he should be minding his manners the rest of the day."

She bit her lips, hiding a smile as she glanced at the disgruntled Trevor. "Thank you."

Wilton winked, and ambled off.

Katy rejoined Trevor with reluctance. "Do you know him?" Katy asked.

"He's the Marquis of Palmerston," Trevor bit out. His face was red with anger and humiliation.

"A family friend?"

"He's acquainted with my father. The old bastard's never liked me. Fat old sod."

That nice man was a marquis? She would never have guessed. Rebecca would be stunned to hear she'd had a conversation with a marquis!

Would his wife be a marquissa?

Trevor put his elbow out for her, and she reluctantly took it for help climbing the grassy slope in her high-heeled platforms.

"The old sod was right, though. I do owe you an apology," Trevor said with smarmy insincerity.

Katy considered tripping him. The stupid, self-conscious clod had made her miss the queen! She'd like to walk all over him with her dominatrix boots.

"These boots are made for walkin' . . ." she sang under her breath.

"Pardon?"

"Nothing." *And that's just what they'll do . . .*

"Oh, Christ," Trevor groaned.

She looked up, sensing that his words weren't directed at her. "What?"

"What are *they* doing here? Bloody hell, are they *together?*"

"Who?" Katy asked, peering through the film of her veil.

"Helena and Will. Quick, let's go the other way."

"Didn't you know they were coming together?" she asked, refusing to turn with him, still trying to spot Will.

Trevor glanced down at her. "You knew?"

"Yes. Will emailed me. And *he* already knew I was coming here with you," she said accusingly.

"*Did* he, now. How very interesting."

Her lips parted in surprise. "I thought you'd told him yourself."

"No. I think it's the other one you need to look to for that."

"Helena?" Katy asked. Just then she spotted the two of them and her knees went weak.

Will took her breath away. He was in gray morning clothes, and the formal suit with its cutaway jacket and vest fit him perfectly. His shoulders looked even broader than usual, his hair darker, his jaw more square. He carried himself with the ease and grace of an aristocrat born to the role. Her loins went liquid.

Darn it. It hurt to look at him. Why did a future with him have to be impossible? It wasn't fair.

"She's trying to punish me for not escorting her today," Trevor was blithering on. "I can punish back, though, can't I?" He put his arm around Katy and pulled her close to his side.

Katy tried to push away, but her arm was caught between them and she was having trouble moving in her tight outfit and tottering shoes. She tried to writhe, then gave up and made herself stiff, like a walking cardboard cutout. Will would be able to tell she didn't want Trevor's attentions, wouldn't he?

Helena spotted them and grabbed Will's arm, talking and pointing. Will's gaze skimmed past Katy and went to Trevor, then snapped back to her. They approached.

She cringed, Trevor's arm around her feeling like a neon sign declaring her a faithless wench. A *scarlet* faithless wench, with these clothes. She lifted her free hand to waist height and gave a desperate little wave to Will.

"What's wrong with you?" Trevor said out the side of his mouth.

"I don't like the way you're holding me so close. What will they think?"

He squeezed her tighter. "Will's here with Helena, not you. Do you want him to think that bothers you? He's made his choice: he'd rather have Helena than fight for you. He's always been protective of Helena, you know."

That hurt. "So I'm Will's dregs?" Will couldn't have chosen Helena, could he? He was too good a guy to be with a witch like her. Helena would chew him up and spit him out like a wad of tobacco.

"I'd hardly call you 'dregs,' " Trevor said.

"Gee, thanks."

Will and Helena were almost up to them.

"Come on," Trevor said, shaking her a bit. "Be a sport."

Katy's jaw set in a hard line. She'd been wrong. Wearing a hat and seeing the races was *not* worth putting up with Trevor all day.

Her heart hurt so much that she wanted to cry, seeing Helena on Will's arm instead of being there herself.

This is what she got for driving out into the country with him. She had known better: she came to England with the goal of finding a man who could make all her fairy tale dreams come true. She should have stuck with her plan instead of allowing herself to get involved with a regular guy like Will.

Only he isn't regular, her heart protested.

She'd rather be poor and alone back in Seattle than marry someone like Trevor, though. She tried again to pull away, but his hand was clamped on her shoulder. He was stronger than he looked.

"Will, what a surprise!" Trevor said. "Helena! Good to see you!"

Katy met Will's eyes, though she couldn't be sure he could see hers through the veil. She parted her lips to say something, but could think of no words. Trevor squeezed her again, and her mouth pursed in discomfort.

Will's expression darkened. "Same as always, are you, Trev?"

"What's that?" Trevor asked.

"Preying on the vulnerable."

"You surely don't mean Katy. We've been having a delightful time, haven't we, darling?"

"Delightful," Katy muttered. Helena was glaring at her from under the brim of her nondescript pink hat. "Nice hat," Katy said to her.

Helena mouthed *Bitch*.

Trevor let his fingers drape down over Katy's collarbone, the tips brushing the tops of her breast. Katy gasped and shoved Trevor's hand away.

Will's eyes followed it all, his face turning purple.

Helena pulled on his arm. "Will, no. Not again."

"He wouldn't," Trevor said, and laughed. "He'd have no more right this time than he had with me and you."

"You and Helena?" Katy asked Trevor.

"Didn't he tell you?" Trevor said. "When we were teenagers, Almighty Will decreed that Helena and I were not to be together. He used his fists to make his point."

"Why did you care?" Katy asked Will, feeling suddenly set adrift. *Did* he care for Helena? Had he always?

"Helena?" Will asked. "I never have said anything, and I won't now without your permission."

Helena tossed her head. "I'll tell her myself. Will thought the age difference between Trevor and me too much. I was twelve, Trevor was sixteen. I was quite intent on losing my virginity, you see, and Will came upon us 'in the moment,' if you will. Pure overreaction on his part. I knew exactly what I was doing."

"Oh." Katy felt a quiver of fresh revulsion for Trevor. What type of perverted sixteen-year-old would have sex with a girl of twelve, however willing?

"Quite noble of him, though, don't you think?" Helena said, cuddling up against Will. "He enjoys championing those he sees as misfits or weak." She blinked and smiled at Katy.

Will seemed unaware of Helena's vinelike clinging, but Katy felt sick inside, and sicker still by his indifferent acceptance. He should be throwing Helena aside, cursing her for daring to lay a hand on him. He should be declaring that he was *Katy's* man. That he didn't do any of that felt like a slap in her face.

"Darling," Helena said, and turned Will's face toward hers. She stood on tiptoe and kissed him on the lips, digging her hand into his hair, holding his face to hers. She opened her mouth, and even Katy could tell that she'd forced her tongue into Will's mouth.

Trevor went stiff beside Katy. She looked up at him and saw that he was staring at Will and Helena even more intently than Katy had been. His nostrils were flaring. Katy was certain he'd forgotten that she was still trapped under his arm, but then he suddenly turned to her. He bent her back over his arm and clamped his mouth to hers, his tongue invading and scrubbing at her teeth like a Sonicare electric toothbrush.

She gurgled in protest and turned away from his kiss, thinking of him with a twelve-year-old Helena. She squirmed and shoved, thoroughly revolted.

There was an angry shout, then Trevor was torn away from her. She fell to the grass, plopping down on her rump.

Will and Trevor were grappling with each other, angry grunts and shouts coming from their throats as they punched and headlocked and twisted around with the type of hand-to-hand fury she hadn't seen since the yell of "Fight! Fight!" had echoed in the halls of her high school.

And just like in high school, a crowd quickly formed a circle around the combatants. Even aristos, apparently, had a love of blood sport.

The two combatants fell to the ground, top hats coming off, gray suits smearing with mud and grass. Streaks of blood appeared on both their faces.

A man Katy didn't know helped her get back to her feet. His wife brushed at her skirt, but Katy's frozen attention was on the fight. The shock of such violence made her incapable of thought, and she almost felt that she didn't know either of those two men. She could only watch and gasp.

A sharp whistle broke through her awareness.

Uniformed men in black rushed into the melee and pulled Will and Trevor apart. The two men struggled for a moment to be free, but then Will seemed to realize what was going on and stopped. He searched the crowd with his eyes until he saw her. Regret washed over his features, and a deep sadness of loss, almost of grief.

It made her heart ache.

Trevor was ranting, shouting curses at Will and leaping against the restraining arms of the police as if he were a mad dog on a leash. There were grass blades stuck in his hair, and clod of mud on his forehead. The police dragged him away.

One of the police said something to Will, he nodded, and then they escorted him away under his own power, he somehow managing to look dignified and unruffled despite his stained clothes.

Katy watched them go. Will didn't look back.

Helena came up to her. "Well done, Katy," she sneered. "I hope you enjoy what the papers will write about you after *this*." She walked away.

Katy was at an utter loss. She had no ride home. She had no one to stand or sit with. She was in a crowd of upper-crust strangers in a brilliant red dress designed to catch every eye.

The first race of the day began, and all eyes now turned to the course.

Katy thought about slinking away to hide in a bathroom until she could figure out how she was going to get back to London. Will's lost look haunted her, and a feeling of guilt welled up inside her.

As she stood there, her eyes idly followed the horses. After a minute more, she started to pay attention. Wow. They were fast. She had to watch *one* race, didn't she? She couldn't leave Ascot without seeing a single horse cross the finish line—which was right in front of the royal enclosure.

She set her jaw against the misery inside her. Men sucked—she hoped Trevor and Will both spent the night in a puke-scented cell. Or maybe just Trevor.

She would watch the races, treat herself to lunch in one of those posh restaurants in the grandstand, and have a fine time of it. This was *Ascot*, for heaven's sake, and she'd never again have a chance like this. Maybe she'd even place a bet or two. She could save the ticket for her scrapbook.

The thought of Will still tugged at her heart, but she stuffed the emotions away in the same pigeon-hole where she'd tried to stuff his cutely kilted self, and set about making the best of her day.

She was down by the wall, cheering on her losing horse, when a man behind her said, "Miss Orville?"

She turned and saw one of the police officers. "Yes?" she asked in some trepidation. Were they going to kick her out? Was she supposed to go see Trevor?

"Will you come with me, miss?"

"Okay." Where were they going? Cowardice won out and she didn't ask.

They went into the grandstand, and he led her past security barriers and up a staircase, and then to a set of elegant dark wood doors. *Nice police quarters,* Katy thought.

There was pair of guards on duty to either side, and they nodded to the policeman and let him open the door. "Please wait here a moment," he told her.

He disappeared inside, then a moment later emerged with Edward Wilton, the marquis of Palmerston.

"Oh, hello!" Katy said, relieved to see a friendly face amidst all the severity.

"Hello, my dear," he said, coming forward and taking one of her hands between his own. "You've had quite a day of it, haven't you?"

She sniffled, suddenly on the verge of tears in the face of such kindness. "I don't know how I'm going to get home," she squeaked.

He patted her hand. "Not to worry. Are you staying in London?"

She nodded.

"You can ride back in my car if you like. But I have a surprise for you. Come," he said, and led her into the room.

It was a private box, luxuriously appointed, one whole wall made of window glass overlooking the racecourse. And in a chair near that wall of glass sat Elizabeth II, queen of England.

Katy turned to the marquis, her lips round in a silent *Oh!*

The queen looked up and smiled at Katy. "You must be Miss Orville. Welcome to Ascot. Is this your first time here?"

"Yes, Your Majesty." Somehow Katy managed not to faint.

"Are you enjoying the races?"

"Very much! I hadn't realized that the horses were so beautiful." Katy held up her losing ticket, and made a "poor me" face. "I placed a bet on number six, but I'm afraid I didn't win."

The queen smiled. "We share the same misplaced faith. You bet on a horse from my own stables."

A few stunned minutes later, Katy found herself posing beside the gently smiling queen as the marquis of Palmerston took her picture with the camera phone.

Rebecca would never believe this. Never!

Chapter 15

"Mmm," Aunt Agatha protested deep in her throat, and cast Will yet another disappointed look over the breakfast table. "Mmm mmm."

Uncle Harold's lips twitched.

Will sneaked a piece of bacon under the table to Sadie. "No charges were filed. There's really nothing to be upset about."

Aunt Agatha dropped her fork onto her plate with a clatter and put her hand over her heart. "You were on *television!* Can you imagine my shock when they showed the police breaking up the fight and I saw *your* face?"

Harold chortled.

Agatha flashed a glare at him.

Harold cleared his throat and pretended to cough. "A bit of something caught."

"And then they said your name. Ohhh," Agatha moaned. "You have been like a son to me, William. Do you know how it hurt me to hear your name spoken in such a context?"

Will caught Harold's eye. Harold let a snort of laughter sneak out, and another followed. Will choked on a laugh.

"You men!" Agatha sniffed, standing up and tossing down her napkin. "I don't know how you can take this so lightly. Trevor has been hurt! The family name has been besmirched!"

Tears started to roll down Harold's cheeks, his belly vibrating with suppressed laughter. Agatha huffed angrily and swept from the room, casting them one last censorious glare before going out the door. "You're like a pair of twelve-year-old boys!"

The laughter let loose at that. They laughed for another good two minutes until they wore themselves out. Will wiped a tear from the corner of his eye. He'd needed the release. He'd been a miserable mess since Helena had first called him about Ascot.

God, he was sorry that he'd acted without thinking, agreeing to go with her. He wasn't sorry that he'd pummeled Trevor, the ass, but he was sorry that Katy had been involved.

"Your aunt went white as a sheet, you know, when your face came up on the screen," Harold said. "She had to have a glass of whisky and a nap. I think she'd burst a vessel if she ever saw *this*." From the bottom cabinet of the buffet, he took out a copy of the *Weekly Moon* and tossed it to Will.

The front cover was a color shot of him attacking Trevor, with Katy falling to the ground in a spreading pool of crimson fabric. Helena was reaching after him with a look of anguish on her face, lending the scene the flavor of a tragic Italian painting. All that was missing was a rearing stallion in the background and a couple of bloody bodies strewn about the ground. Will felt his face reddening.

With great reluctance he opened the tabloid. There were more pictures of him and Trevor fighting (they'd caught Will landing a good blow on Trevor's jaw, he was glad to see) and then being led away by the police; one of Helena making hissing cat faces at a rigid Katy; and then a final one of Katy standing beside the queen in her private box.

Will stared in shock at that last photo, then gathered his wits enough to read the caption beneath it: *Miss Orville may not have a friend in the tawdry Miss Dawby, but she has the queen's favor to console her for the lack.*

Who *was* Katy Orville? Despite the discovery that she was a rich woman, he realized he'd still been thinking of her as the lost-looking, awkward girl he'd almost run over outside St. Paul's Cathedral. Never would he have guessed that she would be invited into the private box of the Queen of England. Who *was* she, really?

He found the beginning of the article and started to read.

Royal Ascot—The rarefied air of the Royal
Enclosure had a rude wind blown through it
Thursday when a bloody brawl broke out
between infamous playboy Trevor Mangold,
Viscount Stanley, and William Eland, the
Duke of Marreton. We hear that not a few
bets were made over the outcome, with
three-to-one odds favoring the duke.

The cause of the fracas was that new
darling of the social set, American software
heiress Katy Orville. Both Stanley and
Marreton appear set on winning the heart
of the multimillionaire, and in true stag
fashion sought to settle the matter with a
battle. The police broke up the fight before
a winner could be declared, but there
seemed little question that the duke had
the upper hand.

And let us not forget the unfortunate
Helena Dawby, granddaughter of the Earl
of Stowe, on-again, off-again girlfriend of
Stanley, on whom neither man shed a
glance. Miss Dawby was but a faded rose
compared to the fiery Miss Orville, whose
smashing ensemble displayed a level of
fashion wit to which the dowdy Dawby
could only dream of aspiring. (And the
the*Weekly Moon* advises Miss Dawby to
cease the public displays of nose-picking,
should she hope to regain her place in the
fashionable heavens.)

Miss Orville appeared unimpressed by the show of machismo of her suitors, however, and after a long visit with the queen in her private box was seen stepping into the car of the Marquis of Palmerston.

Our English roses had best polish their petals: there's a new flower in London, and she's stealing the show.

Will sighed. He hoped Katy never saw the article; she'd wonder why he hadn't told her that he really was a duke, not just the Duke of Lavender. He'd look like a fool if he told her that he'd not wanted her to be impressed by his title. She was on friendly terms with the queen, for God's sake! She wouldn't have been unduly impressed by His Farming Grace.

"Ah, God," he groaned. He ran his fingers into his hair, then scrubbed madly at his scalp and pulled his hair straight outward, leaving it in rumpled disorder. "What a mess I've made of things."

Harold spread marmalade on a slice of toast. "More of a mess of Trevor, I'd say. I never did like that boy. Thrash him again if you get the chance, could you?"

"Only if it's not on camera. What am I supposed to do now?"

"Sue the tabloid?" Harold asked around a mouthful of toast.

"Not about that—about Katy."

"Ah."

Will frowned down at his plate, as if he'd find the

words he needed hiding amid the remains of his eggs. He wasn't one to talk about his private thoughts and feelings, but he was in over his head here. He needed the outside view of someone older and wiser.

"I like this girl," he began haltingly. "I feel like . . . It's like I've been shown a bulb I've never seen before."

"Eh?"

"A flower bulb. It's like someone showed me an exotic flower bulb, but didn't tell me what type of flower it would be, or what I would need to do to make it grow. All I know is that it *looks* like it could be very interesting; it *looks* like it could turn out to be a flower that I'd want to have in my garden for a very long time. Every time I try to reach for the bulb, though, it disappears. So what do I do?"

"Buy tulips you can count on?"

Will shook his head. "I can't forget about this bulb. I think about it all the time, and it makes me do crazy things."

"Are we talking about a woman or something illegal?"

Will smiled. "A woman."

"If you want the wisdom of my years, then don't call her a bulb the next time you see her. Women don't like that type of talk. They always think you're referring to the shape of their buttocks."

"Thanks for the tip," Will said drily.

"You could do worse than to remember it. I forgot once . . ." Harold trailed off, his eyes taking on the glaze of distant memory. He shuddered violently, then looked back at Will. "Sorry. Ah, yes, your little flower. There's only one thing to do, really."

Will sat up straighter. "Yes?"

"Kiss her senseless, of course."

Will snorted. "I tried that."

"Did you do a bad job of it?"

"I'd like to think it was better than average."

"Apparently it wasn't. Trust me, you've got to kiss her silly. Women can't help it—they fall in love with men who give them a thorough kissing. It's this chemical in their brains that does it."

Harold tapped a folded newspaper on the table. "Read about it last week, about a new study they'd done. But I knew it already—it worked like a charm on your aunt. Still does, when she starts getting temperamental."

Will shuddered at the image of Aunt Agatha overcome by sexual passion. He didn't want that picture following him to bed at night. "I don't believe it."

"Look at James Bond. It works for him in all those movies. One minute he's doing jujitsu with a beauty, the next minute they're tangled together on the floor and she's looking at him with doe eyes saying, 'Kiss me, James!'"

"I'm not James Bond. And I'd just as likely have the police called on me if I tried to kiss anyone into submission. These are different days."

"Pah. Women are still the same. Kiss her until she can't think straight. Then feed her chocolate."

Will frowned at his uncle.

"It was in the article! More of those chemicals. There's a reason that chocolates are lover's gifts."

Perhaps for lack of sensible alternatives, Will was beginning to find Harold's plan appealing. It was simple. Basic. *Organic*. And there was brain chemistry supporting it. Who was he to argue with science? "I'd have to find her first."

Even as he spoke, his gaze lit on the *Weekly Moon*. The Marquis of Palmerston must know where Katy was staying.

He felt his heart lighten. Perhaps there was hope after all. True, the kissing hadn't worked after his day in the country with Katy, but maybe he hadn't kept at it long enough. This time, if she tried to get away, he'd just kiss her again.

How could it fail?

Chapter 16

Three, four, five . . . To Katy's shock, interspersed amid the spam for penis enlargement and home mortgage refinancing, there were six different emails inviting her to gatherings and parties, plus a message from Trevor.

It was obviously the disaster at Ascot, and the media attention it had gotten that made her so suddenly popular. She supposed she'd have to thank Melanie as well—Melanie had said she would send the photo of Katy with the queen to the *Weekly Moon*, and Katy had been unable to protest. A deal was a deal: clothes for photos.

A sneaky little part of Katy enjoyed knowing that everyone would see her with the queen; but at the same time, she hadn't had the courage to buy a copy of the *Weekly Moon* to see what they had to say about the trouble at Ascot, nor had she watched the news coverage. She felt like a marked woman, as if everyone on the street knew that she was the scarlet woman who had caused a fight in the Royal Enclosure at Ascot.

She glanced around the Internet café. No one seemed the least bit interested in her.

If she was honest with herself, she felt a smidgen of perverse glee at having been part of the action at Ascot. She'd never been on TV before.

No one had ever fought for her before, either, as Will had. It was barbaric and uncivilized, and politically incorrect . . . and sexy in a primal way. Smashing a fist into Trevor's face wasn't sticking a head on a pike and carrying it home to the princess in the castle, but it was as close as a girl could get these days, without her knight serving ten to life.

As flattering as Will's manly display had been, though, he was off limits. He was not part of the Life Map.

But Will's attacking Trevor had led to this flood of invitations, which meant that the dream of marrying a lord and living the life of a lady of the manor was once again alive. True, there was the slight issue of her having no billions, but surely a rich nobleman would have no need of her fictitious money. Prince Charming didn't reject Cinderella when he found out she was a merchant's daughter, did he?

She opened the message from Trevor, wondering what the jerk had to say for himself.

To: *Katy Orville*
From: *Trevor Mangold*
Subject: *fighting for milady*

Dear Katy,

I told you Will was unstable, and now you have the proof of it! The man ought to be locked up. He sprained my arm, and now I'm in a sling for God knows how long. I'm lucky he didn't do more serious damage.

I'm not too poorly off for dinner, though. Let's go to the theatre and have dinner Thursday night. I'll pick you up early and show you my gallery as well.

Looking forward to seeing you, my darling,

Trev

Katy gagged and deleted the message. Presumptuous twit.

She read through the invitations next, and one in particular caught her attention.

To: *Katy Orville*
From: *George Tremayne*
Subject: *Party*

Dear Katy,

George here—you remember, we met at Charley Horse? I was wondering if you might like to come to my party this Saturday, at Carleton Hall in Norfolk

*(click here for a map). Sorry I couldn't send a proper
invitation, but no one seems to know your address in
London. It's my annual A Midsummer Night's Dream
party. Yes, I am shamelessly stealing the idea from
your own countryman, but who am I to argue with
brilliance? Do say you can come.*

*A bit of an embarrassment, that stir at Ascot, eh? I
can't say that I was sorry to see ol' Trev get taken
down a peg. Lips sealed, don't tell a soul I said that!*

Hope to see you 8:00 p.m. Saturday.

> *Yours,*
> *George*

A Midsummer Night's Dream. Millie would agree
that it sounded auspicious. Katy didn't understand
the reference to *her* countryman, but maybe
George was a bit of a dunce and didn't know that
Shakespeare had written that play, and that he was
most definitely English. She remembered that he
was the baby-faced man with the small teeth who
looked like he still needed a sitter.

She shrugged. The party sounded like it could be
fun, dopey host notwithstanding. Maybe Melanie
could drive her to it. Katy felt like she was already
on the path to damnation, having sold her soul to
the curly-headed salesclerk, so why not complete
the ride?

Katy zipped off a reply to George, then discovered two new messages in her inbox. The first was
from Rebecca. The second was from Will.

She put her fingertips over her mouth and sat back, staring at Will's name in the "from" column. A welter of emotions rose within her, shame and regret strongest among them. She didn't know what accusations he might make against her, either for playing him false or for not telling him about her "millions." She couldn't tell him that this was all a charade; he would feel no compunction about letting everyone know of her lies.

More than that, though, she didn't want him to think poorly of her. It would hurt too much. She'd rather not hear from him at all than hear that he had been disillusioned about her, and judged her to be as low as Trevor.

Feeling ill, she opened Rebecca's message instead. The day after Ascot, Katy had emailed her friend all the gory details.

To: *Katy Orville*
From: *Rebecca Treinen*
Subject: *I don't believe it!*

NO way. NO FRICKIN' WAY! You took that picture at Madame Tussaud's, didn't you? Tell me you did. Do NOT tell me that you met the queen.

But you must have. The rest of your story—you don't have that good of an imagination. I can't believe it! And you know what? One of those fashion shows on E! is going to have a segment on Ascot, and I think I saw you in the preview. God, I'm glad I didn't cancel the cable.

Trevor sounds like a louse, by the way. Good riddance.

I'm of mixed opinion about Farmer Will. He sounds like he has a violent temper, and that's never a good thing. On the other hand, he was saving you from being mauled by scumboy. Maybe it would be best to stay away from him, though, if you are serious about pursuing an aristocrat. You don't want anyone thinking you're already taken, and don't want men fearing that Will will come after them if they make a pass at you.

I still think this is a crazy plan, though. It doesn't sound as if you like many of the people you've met. Why would you want to spend the rest of your life amongst them? And they're going to find out sooner or later that you're no software tycoon.

Okay, I'll shut up now. You've surprised me this far, so maybe I'll be surprised again.

Take care of yourself.

                                        Rebecca

Katy reread Rebecca's email, trying to savor Rebecca's amazement that she'd met the queen, but to no avail. She felt unsettled and ashamed.

She looked at the line with Will's unopened email, curiosity and hope warring with fear inside her. She couldn't keep thinking about him, making herself miserable over what could not be and what he might think of her. No matter how it hurt, she had to cut the tie.

She moved the cursor over the delete button beside Will's message, and before she could second-guess herself, she deleted it, then emptied her "trash" folder.

The moment she finished, she felt a horrid, sinking certainty that she'd just made a huge mistake. She would likely never see or talk to Will again. She dropped her face into her hands, shutting her eyes tight against a sting of tears, trying not to picture him with his ragged hair and sexy kilt. Her head knew she had made the right choice, but her heart was not happy.

What was she doing here? She just wanted to go back to her cubicle.

Chapter 17

"If you're wrong about this outfit, I'm going to kill you," Katy said. "I don't mean that figuratively, either."

"I'm not wrong." Melanie turned the car down a long driveway lined with lights strung in the trees. Carleton Hall was at the end, warm light blazing from dozens of windows. Twilight was turning the sky a charcoal blue, and the yellow moon was low over the horizon.

"And I'm not wrong about that warning I gave you," Melanie went on. "Do *not* stay past midnight. This party is notorious, and if you stay too late you're going to get into trouble. Meet me at the car at midnight, and we'll get out of here."

"You're scaring me."

"Good. I care about what happens to you, you

know. I don't want you getting into more trouble like what happened at Ascot. Or worse."

Before today, Katy might have doubted the claim, but Melanie had offered to lend her the expensive lingerie and drive her to the party without the usual spy photo fee, saying that she felt bad about what had happened to Katy at Ascot and that she wanted to do something nice for her.

Melanie glanced at Katy, a mischievous twist to her lips. "You're sure that the duke won't be here to look after you?"

"I wish you'd stop calling him that," Katy said crossly. "Being the Duke of Lavender wasn't his idea."

Melanie laughed under her breath. *"The Duke of Lavender."*

"It's not that funny." Katy crossed her arms over her chest and cast Melanie a sidelong glare. She was getting the distinct feeling that there was some piece of information about this lavender business that she was missing but that Melanie found amusing.

Melanie stopped the car in front of the house, and a uniformed man opened the car door for Katy. The cool summer night air hit Katy's bare legs, and she had another moment of deep doubt. "You're sure my butt doesn't look too big?"

"You look adorable, darling. They'll think you're scrumptious."

Katy put her pink mule-clad feet on the gravel drive, the marabou feathers on the vamps waving in the breeze, and reluctantly got out of the car, her thighs unpeeling with a sticking sound from the

vinyl seat. She wore nothing but pink underpants
with ruffles across the butt, a floaty spaghetti-strap
top with ruffles on the bralike bust, and the results
of a Brazilian bikini waxing. The bikini waxing had
been a traumatic new experience, and she'd rather
have the hairy inner thighs of an ape than go
through anything like it ever again.

As for this party—she couldn't believe that she
was putting herself through this at all.

When George Tremayne had said he'd stolen the
idea of his party from one of Katy's countrymen, he'd
meant Hugh Hefner and the annual Midsummer's
Night Dream party held at the Playboy Mansion,
where all the guests were required to attend in nightwear. Melanie had explained it all to her with relish.

As Katy walked into the grand entry hall of
Carleton Hall, she was overcome by the embarrassing absurdity of it all. Never, ever, would she have
guessed back in Seattle that she would attend a
party at a stately home while wearing nothing but
£350 lingerie. The only good thing about this was
that there was no chance Will would be here to wit-
ness her shame.

She heard music up ahead and saw other female
partygoers heading toward the back of the house—
all of them in nightwear and lingerie like her, thank
God, although their thighs looked as well toned as
if they spent every day riding horses.

She folded her arms over her chest, feeling naked
and vulnerable, and very much alone. Something
told her that going to this party was *not* something

that Oprah Would Do. Oprah had better sense than to stand in public in a pair of frilly-butt undies and think that she might thus catch Prince Charming.

The only thing a girl could catch at a party like this was a boatload of embarrassment and a socially transmitted disease.

Helena came into the house from the back terrace and gardens, and stopped in her spike-heeled tracks. It was *her*. The American. Katy Orville, the stupid little moo-cow who had stolen Trevor and turned Helena into a laughingstock.

Dowdy Dawby. Not worth a glance from either Trevor or Will. Public nose-picker. That's what the tabloids said about her, while they fawned on Katy and gushed about how much the queen—the frickin' queen!—adored Katy. Katy with the cutting-edge fashion sense, Katy drawing the eyes of all the men, Katy with her high-tech fortune.

Could there *be* anyone who was more *nouveau riche* than a software heiress? It was new money of the worst sort. She was a plain little thing, too, all freckled and pasty, with no tits to speak of.

None of that was stopping Trev, of course. It was the money that drew him; that, and besting Will. He couldn't *really* want the girl.

Helena knew she could change Trev's mind; she could make him remember what they had together. That's why she'd come to George's party. After hearing that Trevor would be here, she had taken the train to Paris and hunted down the sexiest lingerie that the City of Light had to offer: a flesh-toned lace cat suit with black lace roses twined over strategic points on her body. Her shoes had Lucite soles and clear straps, making it look like she was walking on nothing but her toes. She thought she looked like a sexy Eve in the garden.

Katy started to turn toward her, and instinct had Helena ducking into an alcove, behind a curtain. She cursed, angry at the cowardly move, and was about to step out and face her nemesis when George appeared. *Damn.* She'd look like she had been skulking if she came out now. She pulled aside an edge of curtain and spied on them.

"Katy! Hello!" George said, rearranging his burgundy bathrobe as if he'd just finished going to the bathroom.

"Hello," Katy said in her squeaky voice. *Mewling twit.*

Helena thought George was looking particularly unattractive this evening, his face puffy, his belly protruding with hints of his future middle-aged self. George took Katy's hand and patted the back of it. Helena doubted he had washed his own.

"I'm so very pleased to see you," George said. "We get so bored for lack of new faces, it's a true pleasure to have someone fresh, and so *interesting* in our midst."

"Oh, ah?" Moo-cow said.

"The Affair at Ascot has been on everyone's lips." He put her hand into the crook of his arm, leading her toward the back doors and thus closer to

Helena's hiding spot. "Will has hardly been seen or heard of in the past few years, and it's so very *intriguing* that you've managed to lure him out of his beloved vegetable patch. And a brawl with Trev—you don't know how many people that has delighted! Everyone is *dying* to talk to you, you know. You're such a mystery! And of course we're all expecting exciting things to happen, now that you're here."

Helena wrinkled her nose. George was easily amused if he found that dull creature fascinating. And look at the way Katy was dressed! With all those pink ruffles, she looked like a plastic baby doll that would pee when you squeezed it.

"Tell me true, darling," George went on. "Are you and Will together? Or is it Trev for whom you have a *tendre?*"

Helena clung tighter to the bit of curtain shielding her, her eye pressed close to the gap. She held her breath.

"Neither," Katy said.

Liar! Helena silently screamed.

George smiled, showing his gums and small teeth. "Brilliant!" He snuggled Katy's arm a little closer to his side. "Let me get you a drink and introduce you to everyone. I'll keep you away from Helena, though. I know you two are far from ready to play nice together."

He had that right.

"Great," Katy said without any apparent enthusiasm. George led her through the doors to the back terrace, and thence to the gardens where the party was being held.

When they were gone, Helena stepped out of her hiding place. Trevor wasn't here yet, and she wished she had a way to get rid of the moo-cow before he arrived. The way Trevor had been led astray by Katy's billions, he might even find the American attractive in her horrid pink outfit.

"What's so special about *her?*" a young woman asked, coming up beside Helena. "Does she think that money makes her one of us?"

Helena looked in surprise at the woman. She had curly blond hair and an upturned nose, and Helena had never seen her before. Her accent had something of the Midlands in it, but she was wearing a blue silk nightdress, so she must be a guest. "Do you mean Katy?" Helena asked warily.

The woman nodded. "She doesn't think much of you, you know. I heard her saying some nasty things. And she's after Trevor, no matter that she might say otherwise."

Helena flushed. The girl seemed to know an awful lot about her business. But then, who didn't, after the tabloids?

The girl lowered her voice to a confidential level. "I have my own reasons for being none too fond of Miss Orville. Trevor won't be the first boyfriend she's stolen."

"The *bitch!*"

"I have an idea for bringing her down a peg or two, though, if you're interested."

"Oh, I'm interested," Helena said.

"Fabulous! My name's Melanie, by the way."

Helena shook the offered hand. "It's a true pleasure to meet you."

Will came out onto the back terrace of Carleton Hall and looked with dismay upon the Bacchanalian revels below. Good lord. What did Tremayne think he was doing, reviving the Hellfire Club? He snorted.

The place didn't look much like the wood outside Athens, where the characters in *A Midsummer Night's Dream* meet for their romantic adventures. It looked like a drunken university party, with whorish beer babes as the entertainment. The women all wore scanty lingerie while the men imitated Hugh Hefner, sporting silk bathrobes and smugly contented attitudes. A band in boxer shorts played dance music as the half-naked guests writhed on the outdoor dance floor and a freestanding bar served up a steady stream of alcohol.

There was something depressingly juvenile and unoriginal about it, although he suspected that everyone thought they were being daring.

A young woman noticed him and clutched at her friend's arm, whispering fiercely. The other turned to stare at him, eyes wide, then both their gazes skimmed over his body.

Will glowered at them, and barely kept himself from reaching up and pulling his pajama top closed. Hadn't they ever seen a man's chest before?

He surveyed the males below. Maybe they

hadn't. All he saw were a bunch of boys wrapped up in bathrobes, their bodies still lanky with the dregs of adolescence. They looked like they could be broken over his knee—except for the plump ones; those he could just sit on if they needed subduing.

He was in the mood to do whatever subduing might be necessary. It had been a frustrating five days as he tried and failed, tried and failed again to find Katy. The Marquis of Palmerston had told him he'd let her off in front of the Dorchester, and had assumed that's where she was staying. Plainly, she wasn't.

He'd sent her an email, but she hadn't responsed. Had she even read it?

As a last resort, he'd contacted his cousin Marjorie, and had her put her circle of friends to work discovering where Katy had been invited and where she might show up. As a consequence, Will had attended three parties in a row, each of them more awful than the next, and now his frustration was at a peak.

The only reason he was *here*, at this bad joke of an event, was because some woman whose voice he didn't know had called him and said that Katy would be here. She'd rung off before he could ask her name, and he didn't know if she'd been lying or telling the truth.

It didn't help his mood any that he was wearing bloody *pajamas*. At least they were new—a former girlfriend had given them to him years ago, but he'd never worn them. The top was too small, of course, so he'd left the dark green silk unbuttoned. He felt like a kung fu master without the serenity.

Out of the hubbub below a chiming laugh caught his ear, sending his heart tripping. Katy? He tried to pick her out of the crowd, and then he saw her, in a flash of pink.

It was the last sort of party he would have expected her to attend. Had he been wrong about her, about her character and personality? But no. She was sitting on a bench, a male on either side of her, and one standing in front. She looked overwhelmed, as if all this was more than she knew what to do with. It was that air of vulnerability that undoubtedly drew the predators. They all leaned toward her like wolves around a sheep, sly smiles on their faces as they planned their attacks.

But there was only one wolf who was going to lay claim to that sheep.

Will ran down the terrace stairs and made a direct path toward Katy, a gold box of Katy bait in his hand. One of the wolf puppies saw him coming, his eyes going wide. Will lowered his head and turned an eye of impending death and pummeling upon him. The puppy jumped up and scampered away.

Katy looked after her departing suitor in puzzlement. Some atavistic sense of danger made one of the remaining young men turn to see what had spooked his friend. When he saw Will he cringed, and if he'd had a tail it would have tucked between his legs. He looked ready to roll onto his back and wet himself.

The third man chatted on, unaware, his back still to Will.

Katy slowly turned her head, and when she saw him her eyes widened. Her gaze drifted down over his chest and then lower before snapping back up to his face. Her cheeks colored, her lips parting. She looked stunned to see him.

The puppy next to her grimaced a smile at him, then murmured something to Katy and slunk away. The third man finally realized something was amiss and turned. His face lit up with delight when he saw Will.

"Will! Good to see you, my man!"

Damn. It was Thomas Wentworth, the future Earl of Linwood. He was passably attractive, fabulously wealthy, and worst of all, a solidly good fellow with a jovial temperament. Everyone liked him, and he was considered one of the country's most eligible bachelors, if not exactly the most exciting.

"Tom. I wouldn't think to find you here."

"Likewise! But I'm as helpless as the rest of the male half of the species when offered a chance to see beautiful women in their nightclothes." He cast a genuine smile at Katy, his good nature stealing away any hint of salaciousness. He seemed like an uncommonly well mannered boy in a candy shop, content to look and not touch, the abundance of beauty around him more than enough to satisfy his appetite.

"Katy," Will said in way of greeting.

"Hi." She looked at a loss for what else to say or do, and looked deliciously helpless in her fluffy pink lingerie. A fierce fire of hunger lit inside him, and he suddenly burned to carry her out of here, away from the eyes of others, and secrete her in his lair, where he could have his way with her and howl at the moon when he was done. He'd have to get rid of Tom first, though.

Tom sat down next to Katy on the bench with a sigh. "I thought those two would never leave!"

Will growled in frustration.

"They seemed like nice boys," Katy said, looking nervously at her knees, one of which started to bounce. She took a gulp of her drink.

"Yes, but my feet hurt. My arches don't like walking around in slippers." Tom lifted one foot and rotated it at the ankle. Katy smiled. Tom smiled back.

The man was making himself altogether too comfortable. "I'd like to have a private word with Katy," Will said.

Katy's sea-green eyes looked up at him in alarm.

"Let me rest a moment first," Tom said.

Was there a bit of challenge in Tom's voice? A hint of protectiveness? Will narrowed his eyes, noting how closely Tom sat to Katy. Katy's unaffected, approachable nature made her just the sort of woman to whom Tom would be attracted. He would feel at ease with her, and unthreatened. Her spritely figure didn't hurt, either: even Tom, who was no giant, would feel manly next to her.

"Perhaps I'll rest as well," Will said, and sat down on the other side of Katy, close enough to brush her bare arm with his. She shivered.

Will put the gold box on his lap, shaking it slightly so the rustle of paper and small solid things could be heard.

Katy's gaze went to the box, then away, then back again. She resisted, but then the question came. "What's in there?"

"Do you want to see?"

She took another sip of her drink, hesitated, then nodded.

"I say, are those chocolates?" Tom asked eagerly as Will started to lift the lid.

Will ground his teeth. "Yes."

His frustration was washed away when he heard Katy's "Ahhh!" as the lid came off.

"Chocolate-covered strawberries—oh, I love those," she said. She leaned closer to him, hand lifting, gaze lovingly on the strawberries. Then she looked up at him, her eyes huge. "May I?"

"Will you come talk with me?"

"May I have one?" Tom asked, leaning around Katy, hand reaching.

Will moved the box out of Tom's reach. "Come talk with me?" he asked Katy again.

She glanced down at the box, as if weighing the worth of the treat. She swayed slightly, her glass tilting enough for a drop of liquid to spill onto her thigh, and he realized she was probably a little drunk.

"The strawberries are from my own hothouses. It's Belgian chocolate. Here, taste one." He lifted a strawberry by its stem and let her take it.

"Thank you," she murmured, then took a bite,

watching him with the caution of a wild animal. As her teeth sank into the berry, though, her eyes closed and a soft moan of pleasure purred deep in her throat. Her chin lifted, and her back arched as if someone were touching her far lower than her lips. "Mmmmm. . . ."

Will swallowed, his whole body reacting to the sound of her moan. He saw that Tom, too, was staring at Katy with a new intensity, his body rigid.

Katy nibbled the rest of the berry off its stem, then licked her lips and looked at Will with glowing eyes. "Oh, my God. I've never tasted anything that good."

"There's more," he said past a dry throat. "Come away with me."

Tom grasped Katy's hand. "You don't have to go. Will, don't make her beg for sweets. Be a gentleman and leave her the box."

"No." Then more softly, to Katy, "Come away."

She shook her head slowly. "I shouldn't. I can't. There's nothing for us to say."

He lifted another strawberry by the stem. "We'll talk. Just talk."

"I . . . I have a driver here. I can't leave with you." Her eyes were focused on the strawberry. She wet her lips, and then her gaze slipped down to his chest again, lingering there before coming back to the berry.

He nodded toward the strawberry, inviting her to take it. "We'll walk in the gardens, and talk. That's all. There's plenty to say. We're friends, aren't we?"

He wasn't above stretching the truth about his intentions. All's fair in love and war, after all.

She tugged her hand out of Tom's and reached for the strawberry. "Just talk? Just friends?"

"There are sweets being served inside," Tom said, desperation in his voice. "I'm sure I saw some chocolate cakes."

"Just talk. And eat." *Say yes, say yes, say yes,* Will silently urged her.

Katy turned to Tom. "You don't mind, do you? I'll be back soon."

Yes! Will tried to keep his reaction from showing on his face. He could see the effort it took for Tom to smile, though.

"Of course, my dear," Tom said. "I'll be waiting for you."

"Thank you. You're a sweetie." She patted his knee.

Tom smiled shyly, then scowled at Will. "Bring her back soon."

Will stood and held out his hand to Katy. She put her hand in his and rose, and he started leading her into the gardens. He wanted to get her alone, away from distractions and curious eyes. This was his chance with her, and he wasn't going to let it slip through his grasp.

"May I have another strawberry?" Katy asked as Will dragged her away from the noisy party. He held the box out to her and she nabbed another of the delicacies, happy to think of the treat and nothing else.

She was feeling strangely dissociated from her body, the shadowed garden looking like a dream as Will pulled her through it. She knew that she was a bit tipsy, and wasn't sorry for it. If she'd been sober, she'd be scared to death of Will right now.

Or more accurately, scared to death of herself and what she might do. Sweet heaven, his chest was better developed than she had imagined, and a thin, dark trail of hair led from his navel down into the waistband of his pajama bottoms, encouraging her to imagine what lay below. Alcohol usually made her horny, and this moment was no exception. She had warm tinglings going on.

"Are we going into a maze?" she asked as he pulled her through a gateway in a yew hedge.

"It will be quiet in here."

A few steps later, the sounds from the party were all but inaudible. The pathway was deep with shadows, their way made clear only by the moonlight above.

"Won't we get lost?" she asked.

"No. There's a trick to finding your way."

"I've never been in a maze." It was cool there and she felt goose bumps rising on her flesh. A sudden, eerie sense that they were being followed made her cast a glance over her shoulder. *There*, was that a movement? She stared hard into the darkness.

No, just shadows.

She faced front again and Will glanced at her, the moonlight giving a devilish glint to his eye. She felt a fresh chill of danger run through her. He didn't look like either the charmingly grumpy or the pleasantly good-natured Will she had seen before. He looked . . . bent on trouble. She should have been frightened of him, but she let him lead her deeper into the maze anyway.

"You said you wanted to talk to me," she said. Lascivious thoughts filled her mind, and she half wished he would push her to the ground right here and do as he would. She didn't want to think anymore; she wanted to *feel*.

"Yes, talk," he said.

"What did you want to talk about?"

"You."

"Oh."

"Us," he said.

"There is no 'us.' "

"I don't remember discussing it before."

"Well, no, but clearly it's impossible."

He put his finger to his lips. "Hush," he whispered. He led her around a corner in the maze, and then another.

Katy thought she heard someone behind her, and again looked over her shoulder. "I don't think we're alone," she whispered.

Will glanced behind them. "I'll lose them." He hurried her around several more bends, so quickly that she had to cling to his arm to stay on her feet in the high heeled slippers. Then suddenly they were in a dead end.

"I thought you knew your way," Katy said.

"I do. Whoever was behind us was on the way to

the center. No one will disturb us here, in this hidden spot." He sat on the grass and tugged her down after him.

"I'm not sure I should be here," she said.

"Shhhh." He gave her another strawberry.

"I didn't read your email," she blurted out around a mouthful of chocolate and berry.

"Shhhh." He touched her cheek, then let his fingertips trace lightly down her neck.

She shivered.

"Are you cold?" he asked softly.

"No."

His warm palm slid behind her neck, and he gently pulled her forward. She could barely see him in the dark, but she felt when his face was close to hers. A tingling filled her breasts, rushing down to her loins. Her whole body wanted to be touched by him.

He didn't kiss her. Instead she felt the warmth of his breath on her lips, and then he brought his mouth to the space behind her ear. The tip of his tongue touched her and then withdrew, leaving a damp spot that made her shiver again as she felt his breath on it. She leaned toward him, heart racing. This time his tongue traced a slow circle on her skin.

She grasped his arm and thigh, holding on to him as she closed her eyes and felt the world sway.

His mouth moved down her neck, settling in the bend where it met her shoulder. He sucked gently, his tongue pressing hard into her flesh in rapid short strokes. Her body imagined the same touch down below, and her inner muscles contracted in pleasure and yearning desire.

"*Will*," she breathed.

His hand went to her waist, slipping beneath the hem of her camisole. His palm was rough against her skin. It slid up her side to her ribs, the top of his thumb brushing against her breast. She bent her head forward until her lips pressed against the crook of his neck, her whole inward focus on the movement of his hand, urging it upward. She tasted him with her tongue, his skin smooth and slightly salty.

His hand slid around to her back, fingertips brushing her spine, then tracing upward between her shoulder blades, his hand spreading out to span most of her back and press her toward him.

His lips brushed up her neck and at last found her mouth, kissing her gently at first, in soft, glancing caresses, then taking her lower lip between his own and stroking it lightly with his tongue. She arched toward him, and at her urging his mouth took possession with commanding confidence.

She wrapped her arms around his neck, gripping the back of his head as she opened her mouth against his, welcoming his tongue, her breasts flattening against his chest.

Both his hands went beneath her camisole and rose up her sides. Before she even knew what was happening, he was unfastening the clasp in back and easing it over her head. He pushed her down onto the grass, his hand supporting her as he lay her on the ground. He braced his elbows on either side of her body, looking down on her with the moonlight behind him.

She was bare to him, breasts exposed in the chill air, her skin warm with desire. She pushed at his pajama top, shoving it off his shoulders, and the garment fell into the darkness. He lowered his bare chest against her own. She let her hands roam over his back, warm and silky, the muscles flexing under her palms.

He lifted up and kissed her again. One hand cupped a breast, then caught the nipple between two fingers, pinching gently. His mouth moved down her neck, sucking at the hollows, teeth scraping along her collarbone, and then her nipple was in his mouth, the warm, wet heat making her arch her back and hold his head against her.

His hand moved down her side and held tight at her hip, massaging, then moving beneath her to squeeze her buttocks. Then his hand was working at the band of her panties, easing them down.

Faint alarm went through her, and she touched the side of his face to get his attention. "Will."

He lifted his mouth for a moment, looking at her with eyes unreadable in the dark, pure male animal.

"I'm not on birth control," she said. "We can't . . ."

"I'm not going to." He came up to capture her mouth again with his own, kissing her hard and deep as his hand eased the panties down her hips. He rose up to devote both hands and all his attention to stripping her bare.

"What are you doing?" she asked nervously, feeling what was left of her control of the situation skittering out of reach. She put her hands over her panties.

"Tell me to stop and I will." His thumb stroked lightly over her sex, through the soft curls; sending her inner muscles clenched and she grew moist. He stroked again, and she didn't care what he had in mind anymore.

She lifted her hips and let him slide the panties down her legs, kicking off her slippers herself. His pajama bottoms still on, he eased her back in the grass, the blades tickling her skin all down her body, cool beneath her.

He settled between her parted thighs, the silk of his pajamas against her open sex, his hard ridge of desire pressing against her. She felt vulnerable, defenseless. She was exposed to the sky, to the earth, and to the raw force that Will had become.

He worked his way back down her body, laving at her breasts, flicking the ends of her nipples with his tongue. He moved downward again, dipping into her navel, tracing kisses to the side of her waist. And then she felt the warmth of his breath through her curls, her flesh already warm and swollen with arousal, tingling in anticipation of his touch.

He tilted his face to the side and kissed the inside of her thigh. She parted her legs farther, giving him access, and he used his tongue to paint a trail down toward her knee.

She throbbed with thwarted desire.

He moved to her other leg, his mouth nipping her

soft flesh and painting a new trail up to the top, where he played in the hollow where thigh joined torso. His fingertip drew a circle around the entrance to her sex, then up the outside of her mound.

She squirmed, shifting position to trick him into touching her where she most wanted.

His fingertip brushed lightly over her nether lips and down to her entrance, resting there with a gentle pressure. Her inner muscles contracted and she felt her hidden opening kiss at his fingertip, as if she could draw him inside.

He gently parted her curls and then his mouth hovered over her flesh, his breath touching her. She tilted her hips toward him and was rewarded with the barest touch of his tongue. She moaned in frustration and desire, and clenched her fists in the grass.

Then finally he licked her, the full length of her, ending atop the peak of her desire. He took her into his mouth and sucked gently, his tongue working her. His fingertip at her opening drew tiny circles, the pad of his fingertip just barely piercing her entrance.

Her mind was filled with the pleasures coursing through her body, and the building tension that insisted his tongue go faster, harder, and most of all, that he press his finger all the way inside her. All her muscles tensed, waiting for the moment she could feel coming.

He slowly slid the tip of his finger inside her, thrusting gently, moving more deeply and then touching a place she didn't know existed, stroking the spot as his mouth worked her from above. Her climax washed over her, throbbing through her, all her being focused on the sparkling pleasure shimmering through her body.

And in that moment she saw a bright flash of light, searing her retina. And then another, and another.

Will's hand pulled from her, his mouth lifting as a roar of anger rose from his throat. Stunned and confused, she tried to sit up even as more flashes came. She saw Will moving in the strobe of light, frozen moments of rage as he turned toward the source of the light.

Before he could gain his feet, the light stopped. There was a confusion of sound—breathing, footsteps, cursing, the rustle of branches. Will charged into the darkness but she could see nothing, the flashes of light having stolen her vision.

She reached blindly for her discarded clothes, trying to make sense of what had just occurred. As she found Will's pajama top and pulled it on, the answer came to her.

Camera flashes. That strobing light had been the flash of a camera.

Icy panic poured through her body. She had a vision of Janet Jackson's boob flash at the Super Bowl; Paris Hilton's nightvision sex tape; Pamela Anderson's infamous video; the tabloid photos of a topless Sarah Ferguson on vacation. Katy didn't want pictures of her naked self downloaded a hundred thousand times onto the computers of adolescent boys and perverted men. She didn't want people to think of those pictures forever after whenever they heard her name or saw her face.

Dizzy and sick, she stumbled down the path of the maze. She had to get out of here; get out of these gardens; get out of England.

"Stop!" Will shouted somewhere in the maze.

A desperate hope sprang to life inside her. Maybe Will would catch the photographer!

Melanie. It must be her. Katy began to run, wanting to catch the betrayer herself before Will did. Her bare feet were silent on the grass, but she careened noisily into the yew walls of the maze. She hit a dead end and backtracked, hit another dead end, and then after another half-dozen turns hit another.

Her desperation to catch Melanie grew as she realized that she was lost in the maze. But surely if she kept moving, she'd eventually find her way out.

"Got you!" Will shouted behind her.

Katy shrieked in surprise, just before she was tackled. "*Ooomph!*" The air left her lungs, and she lay stunned beneath him.

He rolled off her and turned her over. "Katy?"

The breath knocked out of her, she couldn't so much as wheeze.

"Ah, Christ, Katy, I'm sorry!" He swept her up into his arms. "Are you all right? Katy? Say something!"

At last her breath returned, and she took a long deep gasp of air. ". . . catch her?" she squeaked.

"No, damn it! There are other people in the

maze, and half a dozen at the entrance. None of them was carrying a camera that I could see."

She shook her head, still gulping for air. "Camera *phone*."

"Damn, you may be right! No, wait—the phones don't have flashes, do they?"

Melanie's didn't. But if it hadn't been Melanie, who *was* it? She had to be sure. "Parking lot," she said.

"What?"

"Where the cars are parked!"

"To see if someone is rushing off? Good idea!" He rose up with her in his arms, then put her on her feet. "You all right now?"

"Better if we get the pictures."

He took her hand. "Follow me." Then he was off, pulling her along so quickly that her toes barely touched the ground. It was all she could do to stay on her feet.

"Excuse me! Pardon!" he said, rushing them past other maze-explorers, their faces pale blurs in the dark. Then they were out in the gardens once again, the thumping, screeching music an assault on her ears, the lights threatening exposure and embarrassment. Will pulled her away from the crowd and around the side of the massive house.

The path they followed turned to gravel, and Katy let out a yelp as her feet hit the sharp stones. Despite his own bare feet, Will scooped her up in his arms, carrying her with no more effort than if she were a piece of firewood.

They came around the house to where the cars were parked. Will set her down on the smooth cobbles of the drive. A group of valet parking attendants and personal drivers were hanging around, smoking and talking. Melanie was one of them, seated on the edge of a planter, smoking and chatting. She didn't look like she'd been running through a maze.

"Pardon me," Will said to the group. "Did any of you notice who it was that just left?"

They all looked at him in surprise. There was a murmuring, then one said, "No one's left, mate. The party's just starting, isn't it? Don't know why anyone'd want to be leaving *this* party." There were knowing assents from his fellows.

Katy walked over to Melanie, wary and suspicious. "How long have you been out here?"

Melanie finished off her cigarette and stubbed it out in the planter. "Since we got here. Well, almost. I followed you in to use the loo, but I've been out here with this sorry lot the rest of the time. Seemed better than waiting in the car. Why?"

"Someone took a picture of me."

"So?"

Was that a look of eager glee in Melanie's eyes?

"It wasn't the type of picture I'd want anyone to see."

"Well, I didn't take it. Hey," Melanie called to the guys, "how long have I been out here with all of you?"

One of them looked at his watch. "Nearly an hour."

"And I've been here the whole time, right?"

Several of them shrugged, giving her a funny look. "Yeah. What of it?"

Melanie looked back at Katy, raising her brows as if to ask if that was proof enough.

Damn.

With hope of retrieving the photos gone, panicked embarrassment again flooded through Katy and she felt tears stinging her eyes. *Damn damn damn damn.*

"Sweetie, it can't be *that* bad, can it?" Melanie asked.

Will put his arm around her before she could answer and pulled her away, out of earshot of the group.

"We'll call your lawyers and have them contact every tabloid in town and threaten lawsuits should the photos appear in their pages. It's an invasion of privacy, and the tabloids have lost enough lawsuits lately that they'll think twice about inviting another one, especially from someone who can hire the best. Their pockets do have bottoms."

"But so do mine." She shook her head, the tears spilling over her cheeks. "I can't fight them."

"Of course you can. They're not invincible."

"No, you don't understand." She blinked through her tears, his face swimming in and out of focus. She had nothing left to lose—no secrets to protect, no castle to hope for. It didn't matter who knew the truth, because no titled, rich aristocrat would want her after those pictures came out. "I don't have any money. I'm an unemployed technical writer, not a software heiress. I only have about two thousand dollars to my name."

"*What?*"

She shook her head. "It was all lies. Someone lied to the tabloids about me, and then I went along with it."

"Katy, *why?*" He looked like he'd just seen her step on a small animal.

"I wanted . . . to be a princess. Or at least to pretend, for a little while." Her nose was running and she sniffed it back loudly, then sobbed. "I wanted a castle, and towers, and four-poster beds, and an entrance hall with a suit of armor. I wanted to be Lady Katherine instead of plain old Katy from Seattle."

He looked at her with suspicion. "And how were you going to get all that?"

"I thought Prince Charming was going to give it all to me. But everything has gone so wrong! No one will want me now." Not even Will.

He was leaning away from her, repulsion on his face. "It was all about money?"

She took a gulping sob and wiped her nose on the back of her hand. "It was about the fairy tale."

He shook his head, backing away from her.

"Don't hate me," she pleaded. "You don't understand."

"I think I do."

"I wanted to be safe. I wanted to stop the wolf from snuffling at my door."

"You wanted money. That was what mattered to you more than anything else." He turned away from her.

"I wanted the fairy tale," she protested weakly.

He walked away.

Tears streamed down Katy's cheeks as loss bore down on her heart, crushing it beneath its weight.

Why had the money mattered? The country estate and the title? The roast duck, the fancy clothes, the Jaguar-driving aristocrat in tweeds—none of it meant a thing.

The fairy tale wasn't about the kingdom; it was about the love of a lifetime. Too late, she saw what had mattered all along: not Prince Charming, but a prince of a man. A man who might have loved her, and sheltered her, and made her happy to be Katy Orville whether she wore diamonds or a cubic zircon, whether they lived in a castle or in a cave.

A man like Will.

Chapter 18

"You have your own stubborn pride to blame," Harold said.

Will lifted his arm off of his face and blinked up at his uncle. "For *what?*"

"For putting you here, lying half dead on the ground like a pulled weed."

"It's a good place to think." He was in the small back garden of his aunt's Chelsea house. He had meant to go back to Marreton the night of George's party; he had meant to go back the morning after; and then the afternoon after. It was now five days later, and still he had been unable to leave London.

There wasn't much question as to why. Inexplicably, despite having discovered that she was a liar, a title hunter, and a gold digger, he could not force Katy from his mind and heart.

And so he lay in the grass, listening to the noise of the London streets beyond the walls of the garden, and went over again and again the words they'd exchanged in the drive at Carleton Hall.

"It's a good place to feel sorry for your proud self," Harold said, sitting on a wrought-iron chair. Sadie came and put her head in his lap and he patted her on the head. "I've never seen such an arrogant fool as yourself."

Will sat up. "*Arrogant?* Since when have I ever been arrogant?"

"You're too proud to ask for money that is rightfully yours. Too proud to ask for help. Too proud to explain or cajole, and too proud to do things any way but your own." Harold crossed an ankle over his knee and leaned back, making himself comfortable. "It is actually rather nice out here, isn't it? Lovely place for a pout."

"I'm not pouting. If I had so much pride, why would I still be thinking about Katy?"

"If you had some humility, you wouldn't be wasting your time in this garden. You'd go straighten things out with your aunt, then find this girl and sweep her into your arms, and never let her go."

Will narrowed his eyes at his uncle. "You see how well taking your advice turned out last time."

"*I* never said to undress her in a garden full of people. Your aunt still refuses to leave her bedroom, by the way. She's talking about renting a house in Provence for several months, until she can show her face again amongst her friends."

"Agatha is never going to forget this, or forgive me. And she'll never approve of Katy, not after those pictures appeared in the *Weekly Moon*." Will had called on the family lawyer to try to prevent the possible publication of the photos in any tabloid or on the internet, but there had been no way to stop it.

He'd seen the pictures when they came out a few days ago, and been grateful that Katy had mostly been a blur, no part of her clearly defined, her face unrecognizable. His own face was in sharp focus, but that didn't matter to anyone but his aunt.

"Your aunt loves you very much, William," Harold said gently. "She wants you to be happy."

"She wants me to find my happiness *her* way."

Harold shook his head. "You never have understood her. All she wants is to be a part of making it happen for you. She wants to feel like she helped."

"Then why didn't she ever release the trust monies?" Will asked angrily, the resentment of five years flying to the surface. "She knew how badly I wanted to restore Marreton House and get the farm going. Why didn't she release the money in the trust?" When Will was a baby, his parents had drawn up a trust in the event of their untimely death and named Agatha as the trustee. It was up to her to decide when and for what purpose to release monies to Will.

The only exceptions to Agatha's control were that Will's education must be paid for; he must receive the entirety of his inheritance by the age of thirty-five; and he must receive the monies upon his marriage, if the marriage received Agatha's blessing.

The strict conditions had been designed to protect his inheritance from being squandered in his youth, and to keep him from marrying solely to lay claim to the funds. His parents had seen too many of their own friends lose their fortunes that way.

"Why didn't she ever help me?" Will asked.

"Why did you never ask for help?" Harold countered. "All she wanted was to be asked."

Will shook his head. "I wasn't going to beg for my parents' money. I knew Agatha didn't approve of the farm."

"You never asked." Harold's face turned sad. "You've been as close as we could come to having a son. She wanted to be part of your life, and your decisions. When you didn't ask for help, she realized that you weren't a boy anymore and needed to do it on your own. And now she's afraid that she'll never see or hear from you if she doesn't have that money to draw you to her."

Will was stunned into speechlessness. "But . . . How could . . ."

"Love makes us do strange things. She's scared to death that she's going to lose you."

"But then why does she . . ."

"Make herself so difficult that you want to stay away? One of the depressing truths about human nature is that what we fear, we manage to create." He cocked a brow at Will. "I don't suppose you're afraid of anything?"

I'm afraid of being alone and unloved. The answer came to him without thought, a quiet voice that spoke from the deep silence of his soul. It was the same truth that had been sitting in his heart when he first saw Katy, and knew that she might be the answer to his heart's lonely call.

Yet he'd pushed Katy away when she was at her most vulnerable; when she had bared first her body to him, and then her soul. He'd abandoned her when she needed him most.

Why? Why had he done it? All she had wanted was the romance of a fairy tale, and someone to protect her from the wolves. It was no worse a wish than his own to have a beautiful wife who would think him her hero, and welcome him into her bed. But his pride had made him leave Katy alone in the cold. He'd been afraid that she could never love him for himself, that all she'd want was his title and his house.

She never *would* love him after this.

"Oh God, what have I done?"

"Made an ass of yourself, I'm afraid."

"I've got to find her." Will scrambled up off the ground, looking wildly about the garden as if the shrubberies could tell him where she was.

"Will you talk to your aunt?"

Suddenly it clicked. Agatha. Paddington Station. The momentary look of remembrance that had come over his aunt's face when he was talking to her about finding Katy. "She knows," Will said.

"Eh?"

"She knows where Katy is. When Katy was getting into your car by mistake outside Paddington Station, thinking it was a cab, she must have named her destination."

"You think Agatha will remember what she said?"

"I'm sure of it." Anger flushed through him and as quickly ebbed away again as he recalled all that Harold had revealed to him about his aunt's secret fears. "I did ask her for help on this, but she didn't give it. She didn't want me to find Katy."

"She's always had her heart set on you marrying that Helena chit—probably thinks Helena would keep you close by. The girl seems to me to have all the charm of a crocodile, though." Harold shuddered. "Wouldn't want her, myself."

Will was already marching toward the house.

"What are you going to to?" Harold asked.

"Find Katy. And find a way to make her believe I *am* her prince after all."

"I've got a great idea for that, if you're interested!" Harold called after him. "It's sure to work!"

Will grunted in response. It was past time he came up with his own idea on how to win the heart of his princess.

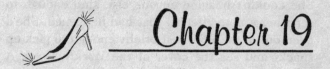 # Chapter 19

"A letter was delivered for you," Millicent said, poking her head into the TV room.

Katy peered over the edge of the old couch that had become her lair for the past week as she waited for the date of her departure from London. Half-eaten bags of candies and chips were strewn about her, and she hadn't taken a shower in at least three days. "For me?"

Her landlady walked over to her, holding out a creamy white envelope. Katy took it, turning it over in her hands. "There's no stamp. No return address," she said in puzzlement. And who except for Rebecca knew where she was staying? The script on the front of the envelope said simply *Katy Orville, Titania's Bower, Mayfair*, and appeared to have been written with a fountain pen.

"It was delivered by hand."

"By whom?" Katy asked, puzzled.

Millie shrugged. "He looked like a chauffeur."

Maybe it was from the Marquis of Palmerston. She couldn't imagine anyone else kind enough to send her a note after all that had happened. She'd been out of the B&B just briefly enough to pick up snacks and see the cover of the *Weekly Moon*. A split-second glance at the blur of flesh-toned photos on the front had been enough to tell her that her worst fears had come true.

She reluctantly eased open the envelope and pulled out a thick white card. As she scanned the words, her confusion deepened.

"It's an invitation to a 'Peter Pan Charity Ball,' for a children's hospital," Katy said. "It's for two nights from now."

"Midsummer's Eve!" Millie exclaimed, eyes wide. "It's a night of magic."

Katy ignored her landlady's comment because something more important on the invitation had caught her eye. "It's at Kensington Palace!"

Kensington Palace was the former home of the late Diana, Princess of Wales, and was once the home of Queen Victoria. It sat on the edge of Kensington Gardens.

The landlady's mouth made an O of awe, her eyes going round behind her glasses. "Blimey!"

"Blimey is right!" Katy turned the card over, but there was nothing to say who it was from.

"Someone paid a pretty penny for that," the landlady said, nodding at the invitation. "The Peter Pan is an annual event, and tickets are at least three thousand pounds."

"Three thousand pounds?" Katy said, jaw dropping.

"At least."

Who would pay £3,000 for her to go to a charity ball and then not even sign the invitation? It made no sense! "You have no idea who this could be from?" Katy asked. "The chauffeur said nothing?"

"Who do you want it to be from?"

Will, her heart whispered. It couldn't be, but how she wished it were so.

Katy shrugged. "I don't know."

Millie's expression said she knew different.

Katy tucked the invitation under the sofa cushion.

Millie's brows lowered. "Aren't you going to go?"

"How can I?" She'd told Millie about the tabloid— told her everything.

"Because you have your pride."

"Not anymore."

"You're not going to let other people tell you who you are," Millie insisted.

"But they got it right."

Millie shook her head. "You've got to show them you are no coward. Englishmen love a brave front, even more than they love a naughty photo."

"And Englishwomen?"

Millie tapped her fingertip on Katy's forehead. "It's up to *you* to say who you are. Now go have a bath. You don't smell much like flowers, and I need to clean this room."

*　　　*　　　*

Being clean cheered Katy's spirits somehow, and after her shower she found just enough courage to leave the B&B and go check her email.

The mysterious invitation was in her purse. She thought about the price she would have to pay Melanie if she were so foolish that she decided to go to the ball and needed a dress.

Not even a ball at Kensington Palace could make her go into partnership with that curly-headed devil again. No more spying, no more selling photos. She'd gotten a nasty taste of being on the receiving end of such treatment.

If she couldn't afford a new dress, she wouldn't wear one. She was Katy Orville of Seattle, and that would have to be enough.

Only she feared that it wasn't.

The pain of loss washed through her as she remembered Will walking away from her, disgusted with the lies she had been a part of, and with her obsession with riches. He'd been too angry to listen to her, or understand.

Maybe he had calmed down now and might listen to her?

Maybe they could at least part as friends?

She picked up her pace, new hopes tripping through her head. She could email him and ask him to meet her for lunch somewhere. Or if he wouldn't do that, then at least she could explain herself in email.

She got to the Internet place and installed herself in front of a computer. There was one new message, from Rebecca.

To: *Katy Orville*
From: *Rebecca Treinen*
Subject: *moving in the right direction*

Katy!

What's going on? I haven't heard from you in ages. I want to know what's happening—if anything—with Will. I keep thinking that he's the one for you, money or no money.

Here's good news: I got a job! It's with Alpine Internet, down in Oregon. I figure I need a change from Seattle, and the cost of living will be less (maybe I'll be able to do something about my credit card debt). The company is located near Mt. Bachelor, so at least I'll have someplace to ski. Maybe I'll find myself a ski bum to call my very own. :)

At any rate, this obviously means that I'll be moving soon. You're either going to have to find another roommate or find a different place to live. Sorry about that.

Keep me updated. I'm dying to hear about what happens between you and Will! If anyone could find a way to make ends meet with a poor organic farmer, it would be you. You've never cared about expensive stuff anyway.

Love,
Rebecca

Katy stared at the screen. Now she was homeless on top of all the rest. Her fingers were poised above the keyboard, ready to tell all to Rebecca, but it suddenly seemed too much to describe.

Instead she wrote an email to Will. After half an hour of writing, deleting, and rewriting, she managed to come up with:

To: William Eland
From: Katy Orville
Subject: ashamed

Dear Will,

I'm so sorry for how I've behaved. Will you give me a chance to explain? There is so much I want to tell you. Can we have lunch?

> *Yours,*
> *Katy*

Before she could second-guess herself yet again, she hit "Send."

She stared at the screen. How long until he got it? How long until he replied? Maybe he was online right now. Maybe he was reading it. Her stomach roiled with nervousness.

She let one minute go by, then another. No new mail came in. *Damn it!*

She spent fifteen minutes writing a letter congratulating Rebecca on the new job, avoiding any mention of Will or photos.

Still no mail.

Katy surfed over to Oprah's website and went to the "E-mail Us" page.

Your Question:
Please do not exceed 2000 characters

Dear Oprah,

Who is Katy Orville? I thought she was supposed to be the woman in my Life Map. But could it be that the Life Map, for some people, is just a picture of who they've always fantasized about being, not who they really should be? Could it just be a dream, a fantasy, a fairy tale they tell themselves to make life bearable?

We're told to strive for our dreams, but maybe dreams are more about who we wish we could be— a wish formed by all the weaknesses and vanities of the human heart—instead of about who we would be happiest being. I don't think my authentic self really wants to eat duck in cherry glaze. I'd be bored in a castle if I didn't have work to do. And I don't want big breasts—they'd be heavy and uncomfortable.

I know you'll never read this, and it's just one incomprehensible letter in a pile of thousands. Thanks anyway, though, for all the help you've given me. And

I'm sorry I tried to tackle you in my dream. You were right in everything you said.

> *A loyal, newly authentic viewer,*
> *Katherine Orville*
> *(SUBMIT)(CANCEL)*

There. It would make no sense to whichever staff member read it, but in some obscure way it made her feel better. It was a message to her goddess, even though that goddess might only be the still small voice inside her, which had been there all along.

She checked her inbox. *Will!*

Her fingers shook as she clicked to open the message.

Katy,

I could come into town on Tuesday. 10 a.m., in front of the Dorchester, unless I hear otherwise from you.

> *Take care,*
> *Will*

"Take care"? And he couldn't come until Tuesday? Her heart sank. He no longer cared about her—he wasn't eager to see her. Why didn't he say more? And why had he phrased it so that she didn't have to reply? He didn't want another email from her. He couldn't bear to see her name in his inbox.

She logged out before she could send a snotty, defensive mail back. Oh, God. Two minutes ago, she was thinking there was hope at least for a reconciliation. Now . . . nothing.

Damn it. Damn it. DAMN IT! Being in love sucked. Yes, she could finally admit it. She was in love. Sucky, sucky love.

Tuesday was the day after the charity ball. Obviously Will hadn't sent the invitation (well, obviously—£3,000 a ticket!) if he would be out of town until Tuesday. There was no hope that he would be at the ball.

Should she go?

Her stubborn, rebellious, contrary side reared up and snarled. *Yes*, she would go. *Yes*, she would show everyone that she was no coward. She'd show them that Katy Orville was made of sterner stuff than they had ever guessed. She would make one last glorious appearance, head held high, and then she would disappear forever from their world. She would leave on her own terms, thank you very much!

She left the internet café and headed for Oxford Street. She made her way to Selfridges and rode the escalators up to the designer department.

Katy found the devil returning dresses to a rack of Gaultier. She approached her from behind. "Melanie."

Melanie turned, her curls today pulled back at either side by small barrettes. She looked strangely frightening, like a blond demon. "Katy! Why haven't you left the phone on? I've been trying to reach you—"

"I'm returning the phone," Katy interrupted. Melanie had given it to her again in the car, on the way back to town from George's party. "I'm leaving in a few days, and I obviously am not going to take any more pictures. I never should have in the first place. It was wrong of me."

Melanie raised a brow. "Oh? You were willing enough when no one knew or cared who you were. You would be nowhere without *me,* darling."

"At least I wouldn't have ended up nude on the cover of a tabloid."

"That wasn't my fault."

Katy examined Melanie's face, noting the tightly controlled edge of a smile. "Wasn't it?" Katy asked.

"Don't make accusations you can't back up."

Katy opened her purse and dug around for the phone. Where had it hidden itself? It was right there a minute ago. "I don't want to discuss it any further. We're even, and it's past time to call it quits."

"You think you've moved above me, now?"

Katy stopped in her rooting to stare at Melanie. "*Above you,* after what's happened?"

"I've made you into a celebrity. I've gotten you the attention of the aristos. You even had a duke panting after you."

Was the girl insane? "I'm tired of pretending and tired of the lies."

Melanie reached into the opening of Katy's purse and snatched out the invitation. "What's this?"

"None of your business," Katy said, making a grab for it.

Melanie danced away from her and quickly took the card out of the envelope. Katy would have to wrestle her to get it.

But what harm could Melanie do now? None. Katy let her read it.

"Ha! What do you think you're going to wear to *this?*" Melanie asked, putting the card back in the envelope and handing it to her. "You can't wear a shiny piece of cheap satin from a teen shop. You *need* me."

"I'll find something on my own," Katy said, taking the envelope and tucking it safely back into her purse. She found the phone and charger and held them out to Melanie, who pretended not to see them.

"Have you seen our full-length gowns? There's a white Grecian one that would be stunning on you."

"I'll find something on my own, thanks."

"You owe me," Melanie said, her voice lowering.

Katy shook her head. "I've paid too much already."

"You *owe* me. Do you think you would have gotten that invitation if it hadn't been for me? Or that you would have had your picture taken with the queen?"

Katy set the phone and charger on the floor, and started toward the nearest doorway.

"Whatever your reputation is now, it would just

take a word from me, and you'd lose whatever shred of respect you might still have left. You'll be shut out of their world forever."

"I don't care about being in that world. I was better off being myself, with the farmer."

Melanie laughed. "Your farmer!" She shook her head. "Don't drop your end of our deal, Katy, or I'll make you regret it."

"We're even. And I could more easily make you to lose your job than you could hurt me any further."

"Didn't I tell you? The *Weekly Moon* is considering hiring me on. I won't be here much longer."

"Good-bye, Melanie."

Katy hurried from the store.

It was several hours later when she finally returned, footsore, to the B&B. She'd spent all day looking for a ball gown, but had seen nothing that appealed. Even the designer gowns were all wrong somehow—too modern, too sleek, too loud, too boring, too ugly. Nothing was right.

She rang the bell at the B&B and Millie let her in. Katy walked into a cloud of deliciously light floral scent, underlaid with a spiciness she couldn't quite recognize. "What is that?" she asked, sniffing the air.

Millie smiled and held out a small gold jar full of an opalescent ointment. "It's a perfume that my women's group made. Try it!"

Katy dipped in a fingertip and felt a pleasantly cool tingling. She rubbed the lotion onto her wrist, the delicate scent so light it was barely discernible on her skin. "Is there glitter in it?" Her skin was shimmering softly where she'd applied the perfume.

"The ingredients are secret."

Katy sniffed her wrist, losing herself for a moment in the beautiful smell, then tried to break free of the spell it held over her. "You wouldn't happen to know where some good vintage clothing or resale shops are, would you?" Katy asked.

Millie grinned. "You're going to the ball."

Katy shrugged helplessly and took one more sniff of her wrist. What *were* those scents? "If I'm going to go, I'll need a gown. I can't find anything I either like or can afford in the shops."

The landlady pursed her lips, cocking her head to the side. "Do you have a style in mind?"

"I don't know. Something . . . pretty. I don't care about sexy or stylish. I just . . . want to feel like a princess."

The landlady came up beside Katy, grabbed her T-shirt from behind, and pulled it, making the front plaster itself against her body.

"Hey!" Katy protested.

Millie tilted her head, examining Katy's figure. "Are you about five one?"

"Yes."

Millie nodded. "I was five one, before I started to hunch. Drink your milk, young lady. That's my advice to you, unless you want a back like mine." She released Katy's shirt.

"Er, okay."

"My waist was about your size when I was your age. Without a girdle, that is. We always wore girdles. We had to, the way the clothes were."

"Oh." What was she supposed to say? Maybe she should promise to lay off the chocolate.

"You wouldn't be interested in an old Christian Dior gown, from 1954, would you?"

"Dior?"

The landlady smiled, her gnomelike face transforming to one of sweet mischievousness. "Would you like to see it?"

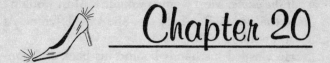

Chapter 20

$\mathscr{W}$ill paced alongside the yew hedge in the garden between Kensington Palace and its French-doored brick tearoom, The Orangery. Strings of glowing lanterns were draped all through the grounds, and a chamber orchestra sent soft classical strains through the gentle Midsummer's Eve air. A dance floor near the musicians awaited use.

Guests murmured and strolled, their numbers steadily increasing. Few stayed inside the palace or The Orangery, the warm evening and the romance of a night under the stars more appealing than the interiors.

Will scanned each new face that came through the doors at the back of the palace, his heart in his throat, feeling young and vulnerable. Katy had yet to arrive, and he'd promised himself he'd wait for her in the garden—not by the gate in front of the palace, as his impatience demanded. *Mystery! Romance!* he repeated to himself. *Make her wonder!* It would be more exciting for her this way.

If she came. Most women wouldn't. Most wouldn't have the nerve. But Katy . . . she was different. At least, he thought she was.

He clasped his hands behind his back and continued pacing, feeling like a character in a historical drama with his white tie and black tails, and his hair subverted by Harold into the same style Cary Grant used to wear.

Aunt Agatha *had* remembered the name of the place where Katy was staying: Titania's Bower. He had written up the invitation, then gone with the chauffeur to find the place. They'd had no luck until they stopped a short, strange-looking woman on the street outside the Embassy of Qatar.

"You must be looking for Katy," the woman had said as soon as they asked for the B&B. She wouldn't take them to it, but she swore to deliver the envelope. Inexplicably, Will had trusted her.

He checked the arriving guests again. Ah, Christ, what were *they* doing here? Helena and Trevor were walking down the pathway toward The Orangery, Helena clinging tightly to Trevor's arm, Trevor looking none too happy. Helena wore a smug, supercilious smile, and a dark green body-fitting dress that reminded Will of a snakeskin. He turned away until they'd passed.

He was beginning to sweat under his evening jacket. She *would* come, wouldn't she?

When he turned around again, Katy was there. She stood at the edge of the grounds, a look of wonder on her face as she took in the lights and the music. Will could only stand and stare, his breath stolen away at the sight of her.

She wore a strapless, pale gold gown, its bodice heart shaped, its waist tiny against the full skirt beneath. Tiny sparkles in the layers of filmy skirt caught the light of the lanterns, as did a circlet of crystals in her now curly short hair. Her very skin seemed to shimmer in the light.

He walked slowly toward her. Her gaze passed over him and then came back. She looked at his face for a long moment, confusion on her features, and then her eyes widened. A blush stained her cheeks, and her lips parted.

A shaft of uncertainty suddenly ran through him, a fear that she would reject him, a fear that she would be disappointed that he was here, her evening ruined by his presence. Her brief email to him may have been only a plea for friendship.

"Will?" she said quietly. "I thought . . . I thought you were at your farm."

He shook his head and stopped in front of her. A light, intoxicating scent drifted off her, enticing him yet closer despite his fears.

She looked up at him. "You . . . you weren't the one who sent the invitation, were you?"

Was she disappointed? "I was."

"Oh, Will," she said, shaking her head, her expression saddening, making the fear balloon in his chest. "You didn't spend all that money on me, did you? Tell me you didn't."

His heart sinking, he said, "No. My uncle gave me the tickets. He and my aunt had intended to go but changed their minds."

To his surprise, Katy smiled. "Really? I'm so relieved! Your house needs that money far more than I need to go to a charity ball." She looked at the grounds and the crowd of people, then said in a low voice, "I almost didn't come. Do you think they'll laugh at me?"

He barely restrained the urge to wrap her in his arms. "No one will laugh."

She met his gaze. "I'm glad that you were the one to send the invitation." A glaze of tears filled her eyes. "I've been so stupid. The things I thought mattered don't. Will, I—"

"Katy, I—" he said at the same time.

"Miss Orville, is that you?" someone said.

Damn!

Katy blinked in surprise at the Marquis of Palmerston. "Mr. Wilton?"

"You're looking even lovelier than before," he said, and then raised his brows. "I say, have I chosen a bad moment?"

"Not at all," Will said, holding out his hand. "Palmerston," he said, nodding in greeting. The marquis had been at school with Will's deceased uncle and had spoken movingly at the funeral.

"Marreton! It's good to see you," the marquis said, clasping his hand. "And it was good to see your battle with that puppy Stanley. It looked like you got a few good jabs in."

"I did my best, sir."

The marquis turned back to Katy. "This one is the far better choice, m'dear. But you know that."

She blushed scarlet.

The marquis's eyes twinkled. "I'll leave you two then. Take good care of her, Marreton. They're playing a waltz now—don't leave her standing in the shadows all night."

"Yes, sir. Good to see you, sir."

The marquis nodded and sauntered off.

"Would you like to dance?" Will asked.

She nodded, and took his arm. "Did he confuse you with someone else?" she asked.

"Hmm?"

"He called you 'Marreton.' Didn't you notice?"

"Oh, that's because—" he started, and then stopped, as a domino effect of understanding tumbled through his brain. *She still didn't know.* She didn't know about his title. How had she remained in ignorance? Had no one told her? And yet she was smiling at him, holding his arm.

Every conversation they had had replayed in his mind. Her concern over his buying her dinner. Her questions about whether he would have children if he couldn't afford them. The details of his house repairs. Even her concern tonight over his having purchased the invitations.

She thought he had nothing except a few green-houses full of vegetables, a tumbledown farm-house—she probably didn't know that it was a moated manor house—an ancient van, and a dog. She thought he had no prospects beyond a meager living from organic vegetables. She must think he had no means to support her or any children.

And she still wanted him.

"It's because what?" she asked, as he failed to complete his explanation.

"It's because I'm a crazy fool," Will said, and laughed. He pulled her onto the empty dance floor, his hand at her waist, and swirled her round and round. She laughed, her eyes crinkling, her head thrown back. The warm, spicy scent rose off her skin, and he wanted to lay his lips against the base of her neck.

Other dancers joined them, the dance floor becoming a dizzy whirl to the strains of Strauss's "Roses from the South." Dancing had never felt so right to him as it did at this moment, with this woman in his arms. It was as if there was magic in every note of the music, every step of their feet on the wooden floor. His world had finally come right, and he felt whole in a way he hadn't since his parents had died.

Katy felt the skirts of her gown sway and fly out as Will turned her around the dance floor. His strong hand on her waist was strangely intimate, as if guiding her to do more than float across the dance floor. She felt wrapped up in the magic of the moment, safe from all evil. Nothing could destroy the magic.

The music came to an end, and there was a screech of electronic feedback as someone turned on a microphone.

"Good evening, and welcome to the Peter Pan Ball to benefit the South London Children's Hospital," a male voice said.

The guests all turned toward the speaker on a small dais in front of the orchestra. Katy clutched Will's arm. "It's Ioan Gruffudd!" she whispered excitedly. She almost felt faint—although she could blame that on the tight control garment she had to wear to fit into the dress.

"To borrow from J. M. Barrie, the author of *Peter Pan*," Ioan went on, "It's after lock-up time in Kensington Gardens, and the fairies have come out to dance." For a moment he looked right at Katy. "On behalf of the organizers, I would like to thank . . ."

Katy tuned the words out and just stared at the actor, still stunned to see the messenger from her dreams.

"Hey, I'm still here," Will said, nudging her.

Katy smiled up at him. "I'm not starstruck. He's my lucky omen, you see," she whispered.

"Ioan Gruffudd?" he asked in surprise.

She nodded, and squeezed his hand.

"And now, there is someone who has asked to make a special announcement. Miss Dawby?" Ioan said, letting Helena take his place on the dais.

A tremor of cold foreboding went through Katy.

Helena adjusted the microphone, then looked out over the crowd. She found Katy, and her lips pressed into a narrow, evil little smile. "Before we all enjoy our evening," she said into the microphone, "I want to warn you all that there is a spy and a fraud in our midst."

Katy's skin went cold, a chill sweat of panic breaking out.

"An American by the name of Katy Orville has not only been plastered nude on the front of the *Weekly Moon,* but she's also been taking photos for that same tabloid and spying on people in such places as ladies' lavatories."

A gasp went through the crowd.

"That's a damn lie!" Will shouted.

Katy tugged at his hand. "Will, don't."

He looked down at her. "Why the hell not?"

She said nothing, her helplessness on her face.

Confusion came over his features, and he shook his head in denial. Katy dropped his hand.

"Miss Orville has also been pretending to be a wealthy woman," Helena went on, "but the South London Children's Hospital would do well to examine any checks she offers, because she is in fact an unemployed tech writer with no assets to her name."

A murmur of discontent went through the crowd, and someone shouted, "Boo!"

"Stop it!" Will shouted up at Helena. "Helena, stop this!" He moved toward the dais.

Katy began to shake, tears filling her eyes.

"And what's *more,*" Helena went on, her face glowing with malicious, defiant glee, "she came to London with the express purpose of finding a titled, wealthy gentleman to marry. I was told all this by a salesclerk in the designer department at Selfridges, where Miss Orville has been borrowing clothes to better pull off her fraud."

Will reached the dais as the crowd's murmurs of discontent turned into a chorus of "Boo!" He grabbed Helena's arm and pulled her off the little stage.

Katy sucked in a sob and pushed her way through the crowd, trying to escape. The booing grew louder, filling her head, and each body she bumped into seemed to rumble with the noise of disapproval. She shouldn't have come here; she should never, ever, have come!

She broke free and ran down an open, shaded path. It ended in a wrought-iron gate and she pushed through. A few steps later found her on the paved bank of a shallow pond.

"Katy!" she heard from behind her.

She was too ashamed to face Will. He had barely accepted that she had lied about her wealth. But to have taken pictures and traded them to the tabloids . . .

Broad moonlit walkways led off from the pond. She chose one at random and ran into the darkness of Kensington Gardens. No streetlamps lit the unpeopled, tree-shaded acres, and she ran deeper and deeper into the parkland. At a crossroad of paths, she turned right.

"Katy!" Again, from somewhere behind her.

The path she had chosen ended at a giant statue of a man on a horse, its silhouette a deeper blackness against the sky, moonlight picking out a swish of tail, a plane of horse's head. More paths radiated out from the statue.

Again she chose at random and ran. One of her shoes—the vintage shoes her landlady had lent her, crystal flowers encrusted across the vamp—fell off. She left it, and ran a few awkward steps before kicking off its mate and leaving it, too, on the pathway.

She didn't know where she was going, only that she had to get away.

Will caught glimpses of Katy as she flitted through the shadows of the gardens, and continued the chase. At the statue he turned around, looking down the many avenues. Down one path he caught a glimmer as of fairy dust, shimmering in the air as if lighting the way he should go. He blinked and it was gone.

Cautiously, he headed down that path. A minute later he came across a lady's evening slipper, and a few steps later, another. He picked them up. They were still warm.

"Katy!" he shouted, and again started to run.

Instinct led him to the bank of the Long Water. The path alongside it led into a secluded spot walled by high hedges, where a bronze Peter Pan blew his horn to the sky, fairies and rabbits swirling around the tall base on which he stood. Collapsed against that pedestal, gasping for breath like a deer at bay, was Katy.

"Katy," he said softly, moving slowly toward her. "You dropped these," he said, and set the shoes at the base of the statue. He was wary of startling her, and unsure what to say. "Do you like Peter Pan?"

"What?"

He nodded up at the statue. She glanced up in confusion.

"It's Peter. He flew away, just like you did."

"It's true, Will. Everything Helena said is true."

"The photos, that part was true?" he asked.

She nodded, her gaze on the ground.

"Why did you do it?" he asked, kneeling beside her.

"It was the only way I could dress to fit into that crowd," she said. "I couldn't afford the clothes on my own. Melanie, the clerk, said she'd lend me clothes from the store." She looked up at him, her gaze imploring. "But I'm sorry I did it! It wasn't worth it. Everyone hates me now, don't they? They were booing."

"It was Helena they were booing," Will said.

"*What?*"

"They may not like paparazzi, but even worse is a mean-spirited tattletale. By the time Helena was finished, they felt sorry for you and were ready to lob rocks at her. Palmerston stood up for you, too."

A tear slipped down her cheek. "I don't deserve his friendship."

He caught the tear on his fingertip and softened his voice even more. "You've more than paid for your sins, such as they were. But I haven't paid for mine."

She sniffled. "What sins?"

"I abandoned you when you needed me most. I didn't stay and listen. I judged."

"You did," she muttered grouchily.

"Ah, Katy," he sighed. "We're all of us flawed, aren't we? I'm going to make mistakes. I'm going to hurt you sometimes when I don't mean to."

She wiped another tear off her face, looking at him with a question in her eyes. "What are you saying?"

"Do you think you'll be able to forgive me, both for leaving you at Carleton and for all the mistakes I'm going to make in the future?"

Hope filled her voice. "The future?"

He tucked a wisp of hair behind her ear, his hand shaking. "Do you think there's a chance we might have one?"

In reply, she fell against his chest, nuzzling her face into his neck. His arms came around her and he held her close.

"A very good chance," she whispered against his ear.

He closed his eyes, and felt a tear of his own slip from between his lids.

*   *   *

"Wendy and Peter Pan always did have a weird thing going between them. Wendy was a sexually frustrated young lady, if you ask me," Will said.

"The B and B is down this alley," Katy said, pointing between the parking garage and the Embassy of Qatar.

This thing between her and Will was still fresh and new, still fragile. They had walked slowly back to Titania's Bower, saying little of import. She thought he might be as uncertain as she was, and as frightened of shattering what had been so carefully built anew.

He laughed softly. "I stood right here, and I never saw it."

"Prepare yourself for further delights once you see the inside." She led him down between the buildings to the door.

To her surprise, taped to the glass was a note and two keys. "What's this?" She peeled the note off the door. It was written in an elegant script on thick paper.

The renovation of one of the rooms is finally completed. I've moved your things to Room 101. Enjoy!

—Millie

"I'm almost disappointed you won't get to see the garret where I've been staying," Katy said—almost disappointed, but not quite. Had Millicent somehow known that Katy would be returning with company?

She handed Will the front door key and they went in. "It's terrible, isn't it?" Katy whispered as they entered the lobby, lit now only by low-wattage bulbs in dingy sconces.

He shrugged, looking around. "It's typical of a lot of English hotels."

"Well, *I* would never keep a B and B this way."

"You'll have your chance to find out."

She looked quickly at him, but he was looking away. He started to turn back toward her, but shyness suddenly overcame her, and she looked around the lobby. "I don't know where the door to the first floor rooms is."

"Why don't we go upstairs and find it?" he asked, pointing.

"The room is on the *first* floor."

"Yes."

It took her a moment, then she remembered the English method of counting storeys. "No *wonder* those stairs were such agony! My room wasn't on the fourth floor, it was on the fifth!"

They climbed the stairs and opened the swinging fire door onto a hallway with dark hardwood floors, an intricate oriental carpet running down its center. The walls were creamy white, real candles burning in crystal sconces down their length.

"This doesn't look so miserable," Will said.

Katy was speechless.

There was only one door, halfway down the hall: Room 101. Will fit the key into the brass lock and opened it.

A soft scent of flowers and spices drifted out. Katy stepped into a huge room that looked like it had been lifted straight from the eighteenth century. The walls were white panels edged in gold, with soft green trim. A crystal chandelier with burning candles threw golden light over the room. There was an enormous tester bed draped in a rich brocade of pale green and gold. And everywhere, in vases and in urns, were flowers.

"Most of these aren't even in season," Will said in awe, touching the petals of a flower.

"I don't believe it," Katy whispered.

"I'm not sure we can do *this* well in our B and B." She shook her head, still in wonder.

He took her hands, looking into her eyes. "It's beautiful, and a suitable setting for my princess. I'll build you a room like this if it is what you want."

"Ah, Will. I'd be happy with you in a barn, sleeping on the hay."

"I'd prefer a bed." He held her face gently between his hands and kissed her. Lightly. A soft pressure, and then with caresses of his lips.

She reached up and wrapped her arms around his neck, digging her hands into his hair. He deepened the kiss, his movements more forceful and in control. One hand slid down to her waist, pulling her up against him.

He kissed his way down her neck, and as he did so she pressed a kiss to his neck, then swirled a circle on his skin with the tip of her tongue. His arms tightened around her, and she captured his earlobe between her lips and sucked.

He tugged at the zipper at the back of her gown.

"Naughty boy," she whispered, and licked the bare space behind his ear as the zipper came down.

"Very naughty," he said.

Will lowered the bodice of her dress, revealing the sturdy, concealing undergarment beneath. "It's like unwrapping a Japanese package," he said. "Layers and layers and layers."

She helped him ease the gown down her hips. Her cream satin body shaper had suspenders holding up her cream silk stockings, but she had gone commando on the panties. She hadn't been able to figure out how she'd use the restroom with those suspenders in the way.

As the dress fell down around her feet his gaze went straight to her dark patch of curls, that and her upper thighs being the only bare bit of body below her neckline. "Good God," he growled deep in his throat.

"Am I going to be left frustrated, like Wendy?" she asked archly.

He reached in his pocket and pulled out a small silver packet. "Not tonight."

"That was bold of you, assuming you'd need it," she teased, feeling naked and nervous.

He growled again and pulled at his bow tie, ripping at the buttons of his vest, shrugging out of his coat.

Katy laughed, encouraged, stepped out of the

pool of her dress, then lifted her arms and pulled the pins out of the crystal circlet in her hair. She bent over, being sure to give him a good view of her backside, and set the circlet on top of the gown.

"I brought three," he said.

"Lucky me," she said wickedly, and reached down to undo the stocking suspender atop her thigh.

"Don't," he said.

She raised her brow.

"There's something . . . a little kinky about you dressed that way."

"You like it?" She grinned.

He shucked off his shirt, bare now from the waist up. Then he grasped her face between his hands and kissed her long and hard, and with a selfish hunger that birthed an answering greed in herself.

She fumbled at the fastening of his trousers as they kissed, then slid her hands inside his boxers, reaching around to squeeze his buttocks. He did the same, his palms shocking on her bare flesh when the rest of her was covered. His arousal pressed hard against her corseted belly, a thick ridge of promise.

With a couple of tugs, she had both his trousers and boxers falling down around his knees. She reached between them and took his manhood into her hand, finally getting to feel it.

"You're a *big* boy," she said, laughing softly. She couldn't quite get her fingers around him. The hard feel of him in her palm sent a thrill of anticipation through her body, and a contraction of desire pulsed through her.

She kissed her way down his chest, down his flat, hard belly, and sank to her knees in front of him.

She took him into her mouth, his head like a rosebud against her tongue. She played with him, tracing the small slit at the tip, tasting the salt of his arousal, then running over the contours and edges, dawdling in those places that made a moan rise from deep in his chest. Her hand lightly held his sac, fingertips playing against the skin in back.

He moaned again, his body shuddering. His hands came back to the sides of her head and he gently pulled her away, then sank down to his own knees and kissed her, his tongue plunging deep into her mouth. His fingers worked at the hooks and eyes running down the front of her bodice, releasing them with deft efficiency.

The snaps of her suspenders followed and the corset was gone, falling behind her, her breasts free against his chest. He lifted her and carried her to the bed, then set her gently down.

He kicked off the rest of his clothes and then was with her, his hand massaging her breast, his fingertips lightly pinching her nipple while he hungrily took her mouth, then kissed and sucked his way down her neck. She felt like she was being devoured and willingly gave herself over to it.

His hand moved down to her sex, gently delving between her legs, encouraging them to part. She obeyed as his mouth settled over a nipple, hot and pulling. She throbbed deep inside, her flesh swelling with arousal.

His fingertips used her moisture to caress her folds, taunting her with slowness, sliding up and down with such leisure that soon her hips were following every move of his hand, shadowing it like a dog its master, begging.

His fingertip circled her entrance, then dipped inside, thrusting gently. She arched her back, a mewling moan deep in the back of her throat. He slid his finger out and slowly traced back up to the nub of her desire, painting short strokes on its hood.

She put her hands over her head, writhing, wanting him back inside her, yet not wanting him to stop a moment of what he was doing.

He stopped both, and she heard the tear of a packet. A moment later he was back. He rose up, arms on either side of her, the tip of his manhood pressing against her.

She opened her eyes. "Yes." She reached down between them, guiding him into perfect place.

"Katy." He lifted one of her knees against his hip, and pushed into her.

A long, soft cry came from her as he stretched her, the pressure at once a pain and a pleasure. He withdrew the short distance he had won, then thrust again, deeper. She raised her other knee and grasped his back.

The third time he thrust, she raised her hips to

meet him, and he settled full inside her. It felt as if he had invaded every inch of her body, as if he were everywhere inside her.

He pulled back again, nearly but not quite out, then quickly plunged deep. Her nails dug into his back. Again and again he plunged, then he suddenly slowed his pace, his thrusts shallow. She whimpered, the sensation intensified by the focus at her entrance.

He reached between them and touched her as he now thrust slowly and deeply. She cried out, and he did it again. She felt her climax coming and met his eyes. "Now," she said.

Deep satisfaction filled his expression, a wicked smile on his lips. He stopped his hips while he was all but withdrawn from her, and let his fingers play against her.

"Will, now. Now!" she begged, as she felt the waves come, rolling out from where his body joined hers.

He finally obeyed, thrusting with a pure animal hunger that was all about his own need. She reveled in it, wrapping her legs around his hips, urging him onward as her own climax exploded and then melted into a blissful afterglow. She clenched her inner muscles as tight as she could.

"Katy . . ." he groaned, holding her hard against him as he came. "Katy," he whispered in her ear as he relaxed atop her, then rolled to the side, taking her with him.

Sated, she cuddled against his side, her fingertips playing over the planes of his chest. Glimmers of the perfume Millie had given her to wear had transferred from her skin to his, making him shimmer in the candlelight. She kissed his chest, and made a happy sound deep in her throat.

They dozed lightly, and then stirred, crawling beneath the covers and nestling up close to one another.

He put a fingertip against her lips, tracing their shape, and started to softly sing. She recognized it as "Can't Buy Me Love." " 'I'll give you all I've got to give if you say you love me too.' "

"Love you, *too?*" she asked hopefully.

"I love you, Katy. I've loved you since the moment I almost ran you over."

She sniffled. "No one's ever said that to me before."

He chuckled. "Glad to hear it." He lifted her chin with his fingertips. "What say you? Do you love me?"

"Of course I love you, you organic nut," she said, and started to cry. She had to do something about this weepy tendency that came out whenever she was near him.

"You don't sound very happy about it," he teased.

"No princess could be happier than I am at this moment," she said with a sniffle.

He played with her hair. "Do you think a duchess could be happier?"

"No. Nor a viscountess nor a . . . a . . . baroness, or whatever earls' and marquises' wives are."

"I think a duchess could be *as* happy," he said.

She lifted her head, looking confused. "Why?"

He tilted his head up to meet her gaze. "She'd be married to . . . er . . . me."

Katy wrinkled her nose. "What? Oh—the Duke of Lavender." She chuckled. "Silly boy!"

He shook his head. "Remember Palmerston calling me 'Marreton'?"

She suddenly felt wary. He couldn't be saying . . . No, he really couldn't mean . . . "Yes, I remember." A sense of unreality slowly separated her mind from her body.

No, it couldn't be. It *could not!*

"I'm the Duke of Marreton. And my house isn't a farmhouse. It's a moated manor house. I live on three thousand acres, and now that I finally swallowed my pride and asked my aunt to release the monies in the trust fund my parents left for me, I have about two and a half million pounds to my name. I thought you might want to know. Just in case you were worried about how we'd afford to have children."

She gaped at him.

"Katy?"

She managed a blink.

"Katy? Are you in there? Katy? I would have said something sooner, but I assumed you knew about the title. Everyone here just seems to know these things, as if by osmosis."

"If we marry, I'm going to be *duchess?*" she finally

said. "And I'm not going to have to eat rutabagas and cabbages every night?"

He laughed. "Yes and no, respectively."

"Can we still have a B and B in the house?"

"Whatever you want, my love. Whatever you want."

She stroked his lower lip with her fingertip and shook her head in disbelief. "I had my heart set on being a poor farmer's wife. I think you'd better make it up to me."

He rolled her onto her back, his weight on his arms as he looked down at her, his hips between her thighs. "I'll do my very best."

Katy smiled.

Fairy tales *could* come true.

Epilogue

Dear Oprah,

It's been a long time since I've written, but I wanted to let you know that I have married my soulmate and started a B&B in his home, Marreton House. Running a B&B has been a lot more work than I expected, but I have loved every minute of it.

Next spring I will begin giving themed countryside tours to our guests, and I hope they survive the terrors of my driving better than my husband does. I have yet to master the roundabout, and several white hairs have appeared on his head recently.

Strangely, the B&B where I stayed while in

London has disappeared. We went back there to find Millicent, the landlady, and offer her a job at Marreton House. But Titania's Bower was gone, the doors and windows boarded over, and no one knew where she had gone, or even who she had been. Odd, isn't it?

In another bit of strangeness, a cable company has offered me 150,000 pounds for the right to dramatize my adventure in London. I'm thinking about it. Old manor houses eat money by the bucketful.

If you ever find youself in Kent (that's in the south-east of England), know that we have a bed for you. Two past queens of England have stayed here, and I would be proud to put your name alongside theirs in the history of Marreton House.

Yours faithfully,
Katherine Orville Eland,
Duchess of Marreton

P.S. I had a picture of an iguana in my Life Map. Do you have any idea what it meant? I never could figure it out.

(SUBMIT)(CANCEL)